JAMES HADLEY CHA

As the author of no less than eighty-eight thrillers, among them such famous titles as NO ORCHIDS FOR MISS BLANDISH and AN ACE UP MY SLEEVE, James Hadley Chase received some remarkable reviews in his lifetime.

'Master of the art of deception'
New Statesman

'Chase is a born novelist. Under his pen, adventures unfold without a hitch, characters begin to live. Graham Greene apart, Chase is the only one to have succeeded in expressing romanticism, purity through violence, hardness and wilful realism of the American tough school'
Le Monde

Also by James Hadley Chase

BELIEVE THIS, YOU'LL BELIEVE ANYTHING
CADE
THE DEAD STAY DUMB
I HOLD THE FOUR ACES
TRY THIS ONE FOR SIZE
WE'LL SHARE A DOUBLE FUNERAL
YOU HAVE YOURSELF A DEAL
YOU MUST BE KIDDING

and published by Corgi Books

GET A LOAD OF THIS

James Hadley Chase

GET A LOAD OF THIS

A CORGI BOOK 0 552 13428 7

Originally published in Great Britain by Robert Hale Limited

PRINTING HISTORY
Robert Hale edition published 1988
Corgi edition published 1989

This book is set in 10/10 Plantin

Corgi Books are published by Transworld Publishers Ltd., 61-63 Uxbridge Road, Ealing, London W5 5SA, in Australia by Transworld Publishers (Australia) Pty. Ltd., 15-23 Helles Avenue, Moorebank, NSW 2170, and in New Zealand by Transworld Publishers (N.Z.) Ltd., Cnr. Moselle and Waipareira Avenues, Henderson, Auckland.

Printed and bound in Great Britain by
Cox & Wyman Ltd, Reading

CONTENTS

GET A LOAD OF THIS

It sometimes happens that you meet a dame who's such a hot number that you want a second look. Maybe you're driving a car at the time of seeing her. Most likely you'll run up on the kerb or have a collision. Then, again, you may be walking along the street, and, turning your head as she passes, you bang into someone who starts bawling you out. Well, Fanquist was one of those take-a-second-look-dames. You know what I mean, don't you? An all-metal blonde with a build-up that does things to you, and a figure that weakens your resistance.

I saw her for the first time when she was working for a guy called Rabener. This guy ran a smart restaurant-floor show on Broadway. I'd known Rabener off and on for several months. He was smart; maybe he was too smart. Anyway, I didn't like him. He was a cold, hard-faced guy, and I guess he had a mean streak somewhere. It always knocked me how the hell he ever made a success of his restaurant; but he did.

Fanquist acted as his secretary. Odd name that, but it came out after that it was just a glamour build-up. I've forgotten her real name, but it was something pretty terrible. Anyway, we don't have to bother with that.

As I was saying, I used to see quite a lot of her when I went to the restaurant. My work as a society columnist took me there most nights. It was as good a joint as any for meeting the sophisticated mob I wrote about. She didn't mix with the customers. I'd see her pass through from time to time on her way up to Rabener's office. Her appearance generally made the men splash soup on their shirt-fronts. She was that kind of a dame.

I played around with the idea of getting to know her, and I guess I wasn't the only one. Rabener wasn't having any. When I suggested that I'd like to meet her, he just looked at me as if I were something that'd crawled out of an exhaust pipe. So I actually never spoke to the broad. And what's more, after what happened, I don't suppose I ever shall.

You see, one evening she killed Rabener. It was quite a spectacular killing. It happened when Rabener was in the restaurant – slam bang in front of everyone.

Rabener had been hunting around for a publicity stunt

for some time. He wasn't satisfied with the entertainment he was giving. He thought all the other night-spots were doing the same sort of thing, and of course he was right. He even asked me for a suggestion, but I didn't see why I should help to fill his pockets, so I played dumb. Well, he did hit on an idea. He staged one of those crazy thriller nights on us unexpectedly. You know the kind of thing. We were given a horrific ballet – a faked gun-fight, a guy pretending to be stabbed, someone punching his pal in the eye and other such harmless stuff which went down big with the moronic mob. The evening was nearly over when it happened, and the crowd was well oiled. There had been a great deal of shooting, and believe me it sold a lot of liquor.

Rabener came in and walked around the tables, having a word here and there with the customers. He could never unbend, but we were used to him by now, and we gave him a big hand for the fun and games he'd arranged for us.

I was sitting with a party near the stairs leading to the office. As Rabener was going round, Fanquist suddenly appeared at the head of the stairs. I forgot about Rabener and concentrated on her. Believe me, she certainly was the tops. There was just one little thing that kept me from insisting on an introduction. She looked tough. When I say tough I mean she didn't look the type who'd give in without a fight. My time's so tied up that unless they give in quick I have to pass them up. It's too bad, but that's the way I live. Anyway, I should worry. There are still a lot of broads even today who do it for the joy of it.

Fanquist came slowly down the stairs. Her large eyes were like ice-blue chunks of sky. She passed close to me. I saw she had a small automatic in her hand, which she held by her side. For a moment I thought she had joined in the fun and games, but something about her made me think otherwise. I suppose I ought to have grabbed the gun, but I didn't. I was curious; I wondered what the hell she was going to do. I thought I was going to get a front-row seat at a first-rate news scoop. I was so sure that I grabbed the telephone that was plugged in at the table. I rang the night editor.

Rabener became aware of her when she was about twenty paces from him. He looked up and met her eye. He reacted like he had trodden on a rattlesnake. I guess that guy saw death staring him right in the face and did he sweat! His face went loose and yellow. His eyes stood out like toadstools.

Everyone sat watching. I don't suppose anyone in the room realized that this wasn't play-acting – but me!

She didn't take her eyes off Rabener. The gun came up slowly, and the little black muzzle stared Rabener right in the face. Just before she shot him, the night editor came through. I gave him a running commentary on the whole set-up. Boy! Was that guy shaken!

The gun made a vicious little crack. It startled us into a half-foot leap. A spot of blood appeared in the middle of Rabener's forehead. He swayed over with his hands pushed out, as if imploring her not to do it. Then he went down on his face.

She turned and walked back to the office without haste and without looking at anyone. It was the coolest killing of the century.

The uproar didn't start until she had disappeared. Then holy hell started popping.

I just sat there, feeding the night editor with the stuff while he slammed it down on paper. It was on the streets within half an hour.

Handling a murder like that gave me a reputation that I've been trying to live down ever since.

There was no bother about arresting the broad. She just sat in the office until the cops came. They didn't like to bust in on her at first. They were scared she'd start some more shooting. One of the braver ones went in at last. He found her smoking a cigarette as calm as a chink in a hop-dream.

When I got home I was as jumpy as a flea; even a couple of double ryes didn't do me any good. I just could not imagine what had made her do it. It wasn't as if it was in a jealous rage. It was all so utterly cold-blooded.

The stink the newspapers raised in the morning would have suffocated a skunk. They played it all over the front page. There were photos of Rabener; there were photos of Fanquist behind the bars. She looked as calm in jail as she did when she shot him. I guess nothing this side of hell would rattle that baby. But she wouldn't talk; she wouldn't say why she had shot Rabener. They worried her for hours in a nice way. That's one thing she had in her favour. She was such a dizzy-looking number that there was no cop strong enough to get tough. A week or so before the trial came on I ran into the local police captain. He was having a snack at Sammy's Bar. I spotted him through the window. I walked right in and parked on the next stool.

He looked at me with a cold eye that the cops reserve for newspaper guys and started bolting his food like he was in a hurry.

'Don't strangle yourself, Cap,' I said, 'I've got plenty of time and I won't run away.'

'I know,' he said, sticking a sandwich way down his throat. 'But I ain't got nothing for you.'

'Tell me one thing,' I returned, 'has she talked?'

'Not a word; not one goddam word.'

'O.K., Cap. I won't worry you again.' I slid off the stool. 'That was a nice little red-head you were leading into temptation last night; I admire your taste. Well, Cap, I'll beat it.'

The Captain looked like he was going to have a stroke. His neck expanded and his eyes looked like poached eggs. 'Hey!' he said in a strangled voice. 'Where do you get that stuff?'

I paused. 'I didn't get any stuff, Cap,' I said, 'it was you who were doing the trafficking.'

'Now, listen,' he said feverishly, 'you've got to keep your trap shut about that. It was business – you understand?'

'You're of interest to the public,' I pointed out; 'it's got to go in the column. If your wife gets mad, what the hell do I care?'

He sat like an exploded balloon. 'O.K.,' he said bitterly. 'What do you want to know?'

I resumed my stool and ordered a club sandwich. 'Give me the dope, Cap. You're not telling me that you haven't unearthed a lot of stuff that would interest me. I won't print it until you say so. I've been in on this from the start, and I may as well finish it.'

It took me a little time to handle him, but the red-head threat worked like a charm.

Rabener, he told me, was the brain behind one of the biggest dope-rings in the country. He used the night-club as a front. He had to have some place where pedlars could come with safety each month to collect the dope. What better place than a well-established, busy night-club? Rabener was a killer too. Years ago he'd been a small-time heist man. His ruthlessness as a killer took him slowly to the top of the ladder of gangdom. He was smart. He always kept in the background. Whereas other big-shots were rounded up by the F.B.I., Rabener managed to keep clear. When repeal came in, he decided to go in for dope. So thorough were his preparations that no one had ever suspected the night-club to be the distributing centre of the dope-ring.

Somehow or other Fanquist fitted into this picture. The Captain wasn't quite sure where she did fit in. But they couldn't tie her up with the dope traffic. They could get nothing out of her. The smaller members of the ring had vanished. Fanquist was the only one who could enlighten the police, and she wouldn't talk.

'Maybe she thinks someone will knock her off if she squeals,' I suggested.

'Yeah, it might be that; but why did she kill Rabener?'

'I'd like to know too,' I returned. 'Think she'll get off?'

The Captain shrugged. 'I don't mind if she does,' he said. 'Nice-lookin' dish, ain't she?'

I agreed very heartily.

The trial was fixed at last, and the court-room was packed to the ceiling. Strong men trampled on weak women to get in; strong women gave up in despair. It was a real picnic for the men all right. They'd come to see Fanquist, and nothing on two legs would stop them.

The Judge was a dopey-looking old hound. The D.A. seemed nervous, but the defending counsel was as cocky as hell. There was not one woman on the jury. I thought that it was almost inevitable the Fanquist woman was going to get acquitted.

I had a front seat, a packet of sandwiches, and a flask of rye. No one was going to stampede me. Jackson, the night editor, was with me. We both felt that we had an interest in the case.

Fanquist looked good. She sat by her counsel, quiet, still and restful. Boy; how she could dress! Any young dope wanting to know what the female form looked like had only to step up and get an eyeful of Fanquist. He'd learn more in that glance than all the text-books on anatomy could teach him in a year.

'If I have to watch that dame all day,' the night editor grumbled, 'I shall go nuts.'

I understood how he felt even though he was a coarse-minded slob. I knew the court-room was steamed up to hell.

The D.A. got to his feet for his opening speech. It lacked the ginger and hate he usually worked into his openers.

'That guy,' the night editor grumbled, 'ain't got his mind on his job. If you ask me, he's worried by his lower nature.'

It didn't matter how much the D.A. played the killing down, the facts were undeniable. Fanquist had shot Rabener in front of a hundred witnesses. Even if the D.A. didn't want to be responsible for burning her nice little tail, he couldn't very well help himself.

The counsel for the defence rose to his feet. 'Your honour,' he said with a bland look on his face, 'before going further with this trial, I would like to ask the District Attorney a question.'

The Judge told him to go ahead.

The defence turned to where the D.A. was sitting. 'Can you assure me,' he asked, 'that the bullet found in Rabener's skull could have been fired from my client's automatic?'

You could have hung your hat on the silence that followed.

The D.A. went all colours of the rainbow. He got to his feet with a feeble, 'Your honour – I object!'

The Judge, who had been giving himself an eyeful of Fanquist, looked at him coldly. 'I think that is perfectly in order. In fact, I will go further and say it is a very proper question.'

The defence smiled. 'I take it that you are unable to do so,' he said blandly. 'In which case, I must ask for an adjournment while this point is verified.'

The Judge looked at him intently. 'Why have you raised this point?' he asked.

'Your honour,' the defence returned, 'my client did not kill Rabener. It will be found that the bullet in Rabener's skull could not possibly have been fired from a small automatic. The bullet, I should imagine, came from a Smith-Wesson revolver. Perhaps at this point I should wait until the bullet has been checked.'

So the Judge adjourned the Court for two hours.

It caused a sensation. There wasn't one person who left

the building during those two hours' wait; the atmosphere was electric.

When the Court sat again, I think the only person in the room who wasn't worked up was Fanquist.

The Judge looked at the D.A. 'Well,' he said, 'what are your findings?'

The D.A. looked a sick man. 'Your honour,' he returned, 'the defence is right. The bullet that killed Rabener was fired from an Army service revolver.'

When the uproar died down, the Judge scowled at the defence. 'Why was this case ever brought to trial?' he demanded.

The defence rose to his feet. 'I can explain, your honour, and will do so, immediately. You will recall that on the night of the killing, Rabener had put on a special form of entertainment. The idea being that his usual floor-show was continually interrupted by faked shootings, thrills and so on. Rabener had arranged with Fanquist that she should participate in this publicity stunt. He thought it would be amusing if she pretended to murder him. She was given a gun loaded with blanks, and she carried out her instructions. She had no more idea that Rabener was killed when she fired than she had that someone, using a gun fitted with a silencer, had fired at the same time as she had at Rabener. She returned to the office. And when she was arrested she instantly thought that by some accident the gun had been loaded with live ammunition instead of blanks. The realization that she had killed a man was such a shock to her that her reactions were slightly abnormal, which was only to be expected. Rabener was killed by a person unknown who used a silencer and an Army service revolver. This is pure supposition on my part, but I did take the trouble to examine the wound, and thought it very unlikely that so small a bullet could have made such a big hole in Rabener's head. The prosecution, having so many witnesses who actually saw my client apparently kill Rabener, did not think of checking the matter, or even of checking Fanquist's gun, which was only loaded with one blank round.'

There was a great deal of talk, but of course she got off. Who killed Rabener was never discovered. After all, he was an enemy of society, and the State didn't want to spend too much money tracking his killer down.

I've thought a lot about this since. It did strike me that if Fanquist had a lover who wanted, for some reason or other, to kill Rabener, this method was an exceedingly good one. Suppose this lover had suggested to Rabener to stage the crazy thriller night? Rabener never had those kind of ideas himself. Suppose this lover and Fanquist arranged that she should pretend to kill Rabener, whilst the lover, hidden somewhere, actually did the shooting, using a much heavier type of gun. While she was waiting the two months for her trial, the lover could have plenty of time to leave the country and set up somewhere, so that when it was over she could join him. It was obvious to me from the expression on Rabener's face that he certainly had not arranged for Fanquist to join in the fun. He knew all right when she shot him that he was going to die.

Of course, this is just my theory. I'm probably wrong; but you know how newspaper guys get when there's a story around. But I did hear that she had sailed for South America, and that spot is as good as the next if you're hiding from the cops. What do you think?

(The story of the London Hippodrome Musical, presented by George Black and produced by Robert Nesbitt.)

TWO THUMB A RIDE

Denny Merlin hit the north end of Daytona Beach in the late afternoon. He drove the Lincoln Zephyr V-12 slowly past the stadium and the ornamental coquina-rock bandstand. He looked enviously at the crowded beach and wondered if he had time for a swim, but decided that he had better get on and kept the car rolling. At the farther corner of Ocean Avenue he spotted the red triangular sign of a Conoco Service Station. He pulled over and ran up the half circular drive.

Three attendants in smart white uniforms, with red triangular badges on their breast pockets, came out of the office and began servicing the car. Denny pushed open the door and climbed out stiffly.

'Fill her up,' he said, 'and look her over. I'm going over to get somethin' to eat.'

A short thick-set guy, wearing a foreman's armlet, came out of the office and said 'Good evening.' He looked at the Lincoln with approval and then ran his eye thoughtfully over Denny. This guy was trained to recognize a good client from a bad one. He considered that Denny had a lot of money, was going on vacation, and didn't care a great deal how much he spent. He was right on every point.

Denny took a cigarette from a heavy gold case and lit it. 'Where can I get a decent meal?' he asked.

The foreman pointed across the road. 'There you are, sir,' he said. 'Chesney's will give you good food and quick service; you don't have to look further than that.'

Denny said: 'O.K., that'll do. Have the bus ready for me in half an hour. I've still got some way to go.'

'Yes, sir, it'll be ready. Goin' to Miami, sir?'

Denny nodded. 'Yeah, I guess so. How did you know?'

The foreman grinned. 'Oh, I guess they all go to Miami on vacation,' he said. 'The traffic's mighty heavy this time of year. You'll have to keep going. There's a hurricane blowing up, and it wouldn't do to run into that.'

Denny shrugged. 'No hurricane's goin' to stop me,' he said. 'What do I care about a hurricane?'

The foreman grinned again. 'Thought I'd tell you, sir,' he said. And thought to himself: 'O.K., sucker, if that's the way you feel. Maybe you'll change the record when it starts to blow.'

Denny said: 'Well, I guess I'll go on over and have somethin' to eat. I'll be right back.'

The foreman watched him cross the road and disappear behind the discreetly curtained doors of Chesney's, then he wandered over to the Lincoln and glanced inside. 'Nice wagon,' he said to one of the attendants who was cleaning the windscreen. 'I guess that guy's got a heap of jack.'

The attendant spat on the sidewalk. 'I bet he tips in dimes,' he said bitterly. 'The bigger the car the smaller the tip. I know these guys.'

The foreman agreed. He was watching two girls who had been standing under a shop canopy for some time, just opposite the station. They had stood in the shade for over half an hour watching the cars come in a pull out. He had noticed that they had been intently interested in Denny

Merlin when he went into Chesney's and now they were talking to each other very seriously. They were an odd couple. The little one was a honey, the foreman thought. She was beautifully curved and blonde. She wore a thin red sweater which revealed her figure, and a short, pleated yellow skirt. Her well-shaped legs were bare and her feet were shod in yellow sandals. She was bare-headed and her face was tanned by the sun and wind. Her companion was a good six inches taller. She also was fair, but she had no feminine charms. In fact, she was almost mannish in her dress and appearance. She wore a pair of shabby yellow-white trousers and a black polo sweater. Her hair was cut short, like a man's, and her complexion was almost mahogany.

As he watched them, they suddenly made up their minds and crossed the road, coming towards him. He moved away from the Lincoln, looking at the smaller of the two with an appreciative eye.

The tall girl walked right up to him and said, 'Like to do something for two deserving girls?'

The foreman eyed her thoughtfully. She puzzled him. He couldn't place her at all. She had very hard green eyes, and her mouth was thin and cruel. Now that she was close to him, he was a little startled to see how broad and muscular she was. It irritated him that he had to look up at her. So, he said rather abruptly, 'What do you want?'

She smiled. Her teeth were big, white and beautiful. He noticed that her smile didn't reach her eyes. 'The Lincoln over there,' she said, 'where's it goin'?'

The foreman looked at the smaller of the two and gave her a wink. She flushed and looked away quickly.

The tall girl said: 'Never mind that stuff for the moment. Where's the guy goin'?'

'Miami – lookin' for a lift?' The foreman continued to ogle the small girl.

'Yeah. Can you fix it for us?'

The foreman shook his head. 'Why should I?' he asked, shifting his feet a little. 'We don't do that sort of thing on a station like this.'

The tall girl turned to her companion. 'Let me talk to him, Stella,' she said. 'Move out of the way.'

The girl called Stella hesitated, then walked away a few

paces and stood watching the other two with fixed intentness.

The tall girl moved a little closer to the foreman. 'Nice, isn't she?' she said. 'She's shy, but she could go for a guy like you in a big way.'

The foreman took a step back. 'Yeah?' he said. 'What of it?'

'We want that ride, playboy. I guess Stella would do her stuff if you fixed it for us.' The tall girl smiled with her mouth again. 'How about it?'

The foreman shook his head. 'Once you're in the car, I'm left holding the can – nothin' doin'.'

The tall girl shifted a little impatiently. 'Got anywhere where you can take her?' she said softly. 'You can't give her the works, there ain't time for that. But you can play around. Will that satisfy you?'

The foreman began to sweat. 'Nice sortta bitch, ain't you?' he said, looking over at Stella and licking his dry lips. 'She wouldn't stand for it.'

'Of course she would,' the other said sharply. 'Come on, for God's sake. Haven't you got anywhere where you can take her?'

He looked uneasily over his shoulder. 'Why, yes, I guess so. She could come into the office.'

'Well, go on then. I'll send her to you. Work fast and fix that ride, playboy, or I'll start somethin' for you.'

The foreman hesitated, then turned on his heel and walked over to the office. He glanced back at the two girls. The tall one was talking very fast. Every now and then she would emphasize a point with her hand, cleaving the air. Stella suddenly left her and walked rapidly towards the office, and the foreman stepped inside and waited for her.

The tall girl sat down on the low wall that surrounded the station and lit a cigarette. She smoked slowly, her eyes intent on the restaurant across the road. She didn't once look towards the station office.

About ten minutes later she saw Denny signal the waiter for his bill and she got to her feet. She walked over to the office and pushed open the door. The attendants were watching this little scene with puzzled grins, but she took no notice of them. She stepped into the office, but couldn't see anyone there. She called, 'Come on, you two, he's on his way.'

She waited a minute, her eyes searching the room impatiently, then called again. The foreman came through a door at the rear of the office. He was breathing heavily, and she could see the blood-congested veins on his neck. She smiled at him very contemptuously. 'Go out an' fix that ride, Mr. Sheik,' she said. 'An' fix it good.'

He went past her without a word, and she went to look into the room beyond. 'Never mind about those,' she said impatiently. 'Take them off and leave them here. We're about to pull out. For God's sake, don't cry or you'll spoil everything.' She turned back to the office again, her face angry and her eyes viciously cold.

Denny Merlin walked over to his car and nodded his satisfaction. The boys had certainly made a good job of it. He felt satisfied and good after his meal. He tossed a big leather and silver flask full of Scotch on to the front seat. He looked at the foreman and winked. 'Got to have a little help on the way,' he said. 'What do I owe you?'

The foreman told him and Denny paid, giving him a five-dollar bill. 'Split the change amongst the boys. I guess they've done a nice job.'

The foreman licked his lips and said awkwardly: 'There are a couple of dames in my office looking for a lift as far as Miami. Nice kids. Do you feel like giving them a hand?'

Denny looked at him, startled. 'I guess not,' he said abruptly; 'no riders in this car. I don't want a couple of dames hanging around. What should I do with two of them?'

'Sure, I just asked, sir,' the foreman said. 'If they hadn't been something special I wouldn't have mentioned it. Maybe you'd like to see 'em first?'

Denny got into the car. He thought the foreman had got a hell of a crust. 'No, I'm sorry, but I don't take riders,' he said firmly.

Stella came out of the office as he slammed the car door shut. She came down the concrete path into the sunshine.

The foreman said very quickly: 'That's one of them. Nice little thing, ain't she?'

Denny looked over casually and then leant forward. He wasn't expecting anything as good as Stella. He hesitated, and the foreman, seeing him wavering, said: 'Tough on those girls. They seem pretty anxious to get to Miami. It'd be a long walk for them.'

Stella came timidly towards the Lincoln. Her eyes looked appealingly into Denny's. He put his hand to his tie and then opened the door. 'You the little girl who's looking for a ride?' he asked, sliding out of the car again.

Stella looked up at him. 'We want to get to Miami,' she said. 'We won't be a nuisance, honest.'

The foreman noticed that the tall girl had kept out of sight. He grinned evilly. She was fly, that one, he thought.

Denny nodded. 'Sure, I shall be glad to give you a lift.' He looked round. 'Where's the other one?' he asked the foreman.

The tall girl had been waiting her cue. She came out of the office and walked with long strides to the car.

Denny stared at her, his face falling a trifle. He didn't quite like the look of her. 'You the other one?' he asked, raising his hat awkwardly.

The tall girl smiled with her mouth. 'Thank you,' she said. 'May I introduce my friend here and myself. This is Stella Fabian and I'm Gerda Tamavich.'

Denny would have preferred to have left her behind, but he had committed himself, so he just smiled and said: 'Well, that's fine. I'm Denny Merlin from New York. If you're all set, let's go.'

Gerda glanced at Stella and opened the front door of the car. 'You sit with Mr Merlin. I'll sit at the back.' She revealed her teeth as she turned to Denny. 'I like plenty of room. My legs are a little long.'

This arrangement suited Denny all right. He helped Stella into the car and climbed in beside her. Gerda got in the back.

The foreman touched his peaked cap, but none of them looked at him. Denny felt that he had been impertinent, and the other two hated him. Denny rolled the Lincoln slowly out of the station drive into Ocean Avenue and headed down Broadwalk.

At the cross-roads a traffic cop signalled him to stop. 'What the hell does he want?' Denny asked, as the cop moved over to him.

The two girls sat very stiffly in the car, watching the cop. Gerda took out a handkerchief and held it near her face.

The cop saluted Denny with a friendly smirk. 'Goin' to

Miami, sir?' he asked, putting a large foot on the running-board.

Denny nodded. 'Yeah,' he said. 'Can't I?'

'At your risk,' the cop returned. 'Sorry to stop you, but we're warning all traffic. Hurricane's on the way an' it's likely to catch you up around Fort Pierce.'

Denny nodded. 'I know,' he said, 'the Conoco people told me. I'm going to get as far as I can. I'll stop at Fort Pierce if it looks tough.'

The cop saluted. 'O.K., sir, just as long as you know.' He took his foot off the running-board and waved them on.

Denny scowled into the small driving mirror. 'They're making a hell of a fuss about a storm,' he said. 'It's got to be mighty bad to stop me.'

Gerda leant forward. 'You're a stranger to Florida, ain't you?' she asked.

'Yeah, what makes you ask?'

'It sticks out a yard. Folks who live around this district take these hurricanes seriously.'

Denny was bored with this talk about hurricanes. The sun was still very hot and strong and there was only a mild breeze coming from the coast. There was not a sign of a rain cloud anywhere. He glanced down at Stella, who sat away from him in the corner of the seat. From that angle he could see her firm beautiful curves and he wished that Gerda wasn't with them. He said, 'You don't worry about hurricanes, do you?'

Stella glanced at him and shook her head. 'I guess not,' she said. 'I've seen a good few, and they don't really amount to anything.'

Denny liked her voice. 'What are you two girls, anyway?' he asked. 'What's the idea of hitch-hiking?'

Gerda took charge of the conversation. 'We're looking for a job,' she said, almost in his ear. Her voice was low and flat. 'Daytona Beach bored us, so we thought we'd go on to Miami. I guess we'll find something there.'

Denny turned into the old Dixey Highway that led to Port Orange. He trod on the gas, sending the Lincoln forward with a sudden rush. 'Well, what do you do?' he wanted to know, looking with interest at Stella's nicely rounded knees.

'Who we can,' Gerda said, with a harsh little laugh. 'Don't we Stella?'

Stella didn't say anything.

'I see. That sounds sort of bad,' Denny said, wondering what she meant. 'I'm in real estate myself. I was wondering if either of you could shorthand or something. I might be able to get you fixed up.'

Gerda laughed again. Denny frowned. He didn't like her hissing little laugh so close to his ear. 'Don't do that,' he said sharply. 'What's so funny about it?'

'Nothin',' she said quickly, 'we think you're swell to offer, don't we Stella?'

Stella said after a pause: 'You see, we do a song an' dance act. I guess office routine is way up the wrong street.'

Denny grunted. 'Sure,' he said, 'I understand that. If you're an act, you don't want any sort of job. What makes you think Miami'll take to you?'

'Oh, we don't know,' Gerda said, 'we just hopin'. When you've pushed around as we have, hope is about the one thing that gets you anywhere, and nice-looking Stella.' She laughed again.

Denny watched her in the driving mirror. 'So Stella helps too, does she?' he said for something to say.

'Sure, it's her capital to look nice,' Gerda said with a tiny sneer in her voice.

'And what do you do?' Denny said curiously.

'Me? I guess I run the outfit. We've got along all right so far, haven't we, Stella?'

Stella didn't say anything. She shifted uncomfortably and her short skirt rode up a few inches. Denny could see a long expanse of bare thigh and he pursed his lips. If it wasn't for Gerda in the back, he could go for this honey in a big way he told himself.

They swept through Port Orange and on to the U.S. Highway 1. They were now in the heart of the East Coast citrus country and the road curved across lowland meadows, pink with rose mallow. The mandarin trees were heavy with fruit. Denny thought it was all very beautiful.

'This part of the country does things to me,' he said. 'Don't you think it's swell?'

Stella said: 'You don't think of the ugly things in life after this, do you?' She spoke very tensely, as if she meant every word.

Denny glanced at her curiously. He wondered what sort

of a life she had been leading. She didn't look like a little tramp. He shook his head, giving up.

They stopped at New Smyrna for petrol. Evening was drawing on rapidly and the sun, wrapped in a yellowish haze, was sinking behind the skyline. Denny got out of the car to stretch his legs and the two girls followed his example. Up the road they could see a long line of trucks moving slowly towards them, crowded with farm hands and bedding.

Denny asked the mechanic who was operating the gasoline pump what it was all about.

The man shrugged. 'Oh, I guess they're coming in because of the hurricane,' he said indifferently. 'The radio says it'll hit us before long.'

Denny felt a sudden wave of apprehension. 'Listen, I'm goin' through to Miami tonight. This hurricane won't stop me, will it?'

The man screwed the cap on the gas tank and hung up his pump hose. 'That depends on you, mister,' he said. 'Two bucks, please.'

Denny paid him and walked over to the edge of the road, where the two girls were watching the trucks pass. 'Think we ought to go on?' he asked. 'These people are coming in from outlying farms because of the hurricane.'

Gerda said very decisively: 'A little rain and wind wouldn't stop me. It's your car, you can please yourself what you do.'

'Well, let's get on then,' Denny said, turning to the car.

'You wouldn't like to stake us a meal, would you, Mr Merlin?' Gerda asked, smiling with her mouth.

Denny looked at her. 'Say, what is this?' he asked. 'Are you two flat broke, or something?'

Gerda moved over to the car. 'Think no more about it, Mr Merlin. Forget I ever spoke.'

Denny turned to Stella. 'You tell me. I can talk to you.'

Stella hesitated and then nodded. 'I guess we're tight for money just now,' she said awkwardly. 'But we ain't really hungry. Please don't—'

Denny said, 'Wait for me,' and walked over to a coffee-shop. He came back with two paper bags and dumped them down on the seat. 'There you are,' he said, 'that ought to hold you until we get to Fort Pierce. We'll have a decent meal then. Let's get on before we waste any more time.'

He drove out of New Smyrna in silence. The two girls ate the chicken sandwiches silently and ferociously. Gerda said, 'Is that Scotch you've got there?'

Denny handed the flask over his shoulder without a word. He was beginning to understand why Gerda looked after the outfit, as she called it. She wasn't slow in getting what she wanted.

They drove along the Indian River. It was just dusk enough to see the luminous water, ruffled by an increasing wind. Every now and then faint flames seemed to be flickering along the top of the water. The scene so enchanted Denny that he forgot to be annoyed any more, and slowed down so that he could concentrate. Overhead a flight of herons passed, looking dark against the evening sky. Woodpeckers still continued to plunge from the telephone wires like rockets after minnows.

'This is a grand country,' Denny said to Stella. 'I'm glad I decided to come here for my vacation.'

'Why are you alone?' she asked. 'Haven't you got a wife or a girl-friend?'

Denny shook his head. 'I guess not,' he said. 'I've been too busy making money. Believe it or not, this is the first real holiday I've had in ten years.'

Gerda said softly in his ear, 'Have you made a lot of money?'

Denny grinned. 'Oh, I guess so. Enough to get by.'

'What do you call big money?' she persisted. 'Ten grand, twenty grand, fifty grand – how much?'

'Five hundred thousand,' Denny said, half to himself. 'Believe me, it's nice to feel you've made that little lot just by yourself.'

Gerda drew a deep breath. The amount left her speechless. They drove in silence for some minutes, then she said: 'I guess you can do what you like with all that money.'

Denny nodded. 'It certainly helps,' he said lightly.

They were running through a road bordered by Australian pine windbreaks which swayed in the increasing wind.

Stella said suddenly: 'Look, the wind is rising. Do you see the trees? It is getting rough.'

'Well, we'll be all right in this bus,' Denny said confidently. 'This old hearse doesn't leak; it can blow and rain as much as it likes.'

The sun had given place to a big moon. It was almost dark now and Denny switched on his head-lamps. 'I like driving in the dark,' he said, 'especially in this country. Look at the river now. It looks as if it were on fire.'

The wind had whippped the water into large waves which flickered like tongues of flame. Overhead small clouds began to race across the moonlit sky, joining up with each other rapidly. They were dark clouds that fled before the wind, gradually building up a barrier between the earth and the moon.

'This looks like it,' Denny said as the landscape began to fade into darkness. 'I guess if it gets too bad we'll have to put up at Fort Pierce.' A thought suddenly struck him. 'Haven't you girls got any luggage?'

Gerda said, 'No.'

There was a long silence and then Denny said, 'You two seem to be having a bad time.' He began to feel uncomfortable, as most very wealthy people do when they run into real poverty. He began to wish he hadn't given them a ride. He supposed that they were going to be a damn' nuisance before he'd seen the last of them.

Gerda said, casually: 'Oh, we've been in the same sort of spot before. We'll get by.'

Fine rain appeared on the windscreen and the darkness came down like a shutter. The two brilliant pools of light from the head-lamps lit the road, making the grapefruit trees and the lemon trees look grotesque as they flashed by them.

Above the soft note of the Lincoln engine they could hear the moan of the wind, and out to sea came the thundery roar of the rollers smashing themselves to foam on the beach.

A vivid and jagged flash of lightning lit the sky and the first clap of thunder startled them. The rain began to fall in earnest and Denny switched on the rain-wipers. He drove slowly, as he found it difficult to see through the windscreen.

'I hope it's not going to get worse than this,' he said suddenly.

'Oh, it will,' Stella told him. 'This is just the beginning. The wind hasn't reached its height yet.'

As she spoke the wind suddenly increased, making a shrill, whistling noise. Denny felt the car shudder against it, nearly coming to a halt. He fed the engine more gas and the speedometer needle crawled up to twenty miles an hour.

'I guess we'd better get under cover,' he said. 'I wish now that we had stayed at New Smyrna for the night. Keep a look-out for a house, will you? I don't care to drive much further in this.'

'Oh, let's go on,' Gerda said quickly. 'Fort Pierce is only about twenty miles from here.'

Denny grunted. The lightning was beginning to worry him. It leapt about the dark sky, lighting the trees which swayed almost to the ground from the blast of the wind. The Lincoln was crawling now, although he kept his foot hard on the accelerator. He reckoned the wind must be blowing at well over a hundred miles an hour.

The rain drummed on the top of the car, blotting out the noise of the thunder, and the wind had risen to a shrieking howl.

Over to the left he thought he saw a building in the flash of brilliant lightning and his head-lights picked out a narrow road that turned abruptly from the highway. He didn't hesitate, but swung the car into it. The wind caught them broadside and he felt the off wheels lift a little.

'There's a house here,' he said. 'We'll take shelter. This is beyond a joke.'

He drove as close to the building as possible, and then stopped the car.

'Be careful how you get out,' Stella said anxiously, 'or you'll get blown away!'

Denny thought that was most likely, and opened the car door gingerly. He slid out, keeping his body hunched. The wind and rain struck him solidly, and if he hadn't been holding on to the car door he would have gone over. He steadied himself, feeling the rain driving through his clothes as if they were paper, then, keeping low, he began a desperate struggle to the house. He had only to walk a few yards, but by the time he had reached the shelter of the house he was nearly exhausted.

He could see that all the windows were boarded up, and he hammered on the front door. Fortunately, he was on the lee side and he could remain there without being battered. No one answered his knocking. Finally he lost patience and taking a step back, aimed a violent kick at the lock. The door creaked, and a second kick sent it flying open. He stepped inside, peering into the darkness. He called loudly once or twice, but his voice hardly sounded in his own ears above the roar of the rain and wind.

Taking his cigarette-lighter from his pocket, he made a tiny flame and finding an electric-light switch near his hand, he turned on the light. He found himself in a well-furnished lounge with three rooms leading off. A quick examination of the house proved that it was empty. The owners had most likely, he thought, gone to Fort Pierce, away from the hurricane. Anyway, the place was well furnished and comfortable. The next step was to get the two girls inside.

He again stepped into the hurricane and fought his way back to the car. He tried to shout to them that it was all right, but the wind blew his words down his throat, leaving his gasping. He pointed to the house and took hold of Stella's arm. She hesitated for a moment, then slid out of the car. It took quite a time to get her into the shelter of the lounge. Twice they lost their balance and sprawled into a big pool of rain water, and by the time they got inside both of them were soaked and plastered with mud.

Even at that moment Denny felt his blood quicken a trifle when he saw Stella in the light. Her jersey and skirt clung to her figure, revealing every line. The superb sweep of her hips down to her feet and the curve of her firm full breasts enchanted him. He said, 'You look cute like that.'

She turned her head. 'Oh, don't look at me,' she said. 'Please go and help Gerda.'

He laughed a little nervously and turned away from her. Gerda stood in the doorway watching them. The wet jersey on her big figure made her look even more mannish than she actually was.

She said: 'I've locked the car. The rain isn't getting in. I think it will be all right to leave.'

Denny shrugged. 'It'll have to be,' he said. 'I've had enough of that wind for tonight. My God! I'm wet through. Maybe I'd better get a suit-case in.'

Gerda went to the door. 'You'll need some help,' she said, and together they battled their way once more to the car. Denny was a little piqued to see that Gerda managed the wind much better than he did. In fact, once she came to his aid and shoved him forward. He was equally astonished at her strength. Together they brought the suit-case back and closed the door on the storm.

'You're hellish strong,' Denny gasped, wrenching off his sodden collar. 'Quite a Samson.'

Gerda didn't say anything. She disappeared into the kitchen. Denny wandered into the lounge, where Stella was standing shivering before an empty grate. She held her wet skirt away from her body as he came in.

'Have a nip of this,' Denny said, producing his flask, 'otherwise you'll catch a cold.' He was feeling shivery himself.

They both had a long pull from the flask and immediately felt better for it.

'You ought to get out of those things,' Denny then said with a grin, 'although they suit you like that.'

Stella flushed hotly. 'You're making me feel awfully uncomfortable, Mr Merlin,' she said. 'I wish you wouldn't.'

Denny took another pull from his flask. 'Well I guess I don't want to do that,' he said. 'But you shouldn't have such a nice little figure.'

Gerda came in with some paper and wood. 'Get those things off, Stella,' she said, 'the bathroom's down the passage. There's an electric geyser and I've turned it on. I've found a wrap for you. Hurry up.'

Stella went away and Gerda knelt down before the fire. In a few minutes she had a roaring fire going.

Denny looked at her admiringly. 'I can see why you're the boss of the outfit now,' he said. 'Are you always as efficient as this?'

Gerda looked over her shoulder at him with her hard green eyes. 'I have to be,' she said. 'You aren't a great help, are you?'

Denny scowled. 'You didn't give me much time,' he retorted.

She got to her feet. 'Don't let's fight,' she said. 'Suppose you change too. I've had a look in the pantry. There's some food there. I guess we can make ourselves quite at home.'

Denny scratched his head. 'Bit rough on the owners,' he observed.

'I see you haven't my philosophy,' Gerda returned, moving across the room to the door. 'Still you have plenty of money, haven't you? Leave them something. That's what money is for, isn't it?'

Denny undressed quickly after she had gone, and gave himself a brisk rub down with a towel. He couldn't help thinking how much more pleasant it would have been to be in this house with Stella alone. He dressed in a pair of flannel trousers and heavy sweater over a white silk shirt and took his wet clothes into the kitchen.

Gerda, dressed in a dark red dressing-gown, her long slender feet in a pair of Turkish slippers, was preparing a meal. On the table close at hand stood a large cocktail-shaker and three glasses.

Denny picked the shaker up and sniffed at it. 'Gin and du Bonnet,' he said. 'Hell! This is going to be quite a party.'

Gerda said, 'You like Stella, don't you?' She said it very casually, without looking at him.

Denny paused, his hand hovering over one of the glasses he was about to pick up. 'What do you mean?' he asked sharply.

'What I say,' Gerda went on, turning a thick slice of ham on the grill. 'I know what you've been thinking. You'd like to sleep with her, wouldn't you?'

Denny controlled himself with an effort. He poured out the cocktails and then came over and put one of them close beside her. 'I'm not used to that sort of talk,' he said quietly. 'I suppose it is pretty general where you come from?'

Gerda sipped her drink. 'That still doesn't answer my question,' she said, suddenly looking at him. 'You would like her in bed, wouldn't you, Mr Merlin?'

Denny finished his drink and poured out another one. 'I'm certainly not going to discuss a subject like that with you,' he said abruptly. 'After all, you're the third party, and as such you have no business at all to suggest such a thing.'

Gerda put her drink down and went to fetch eggs from the pantry. When she came back she said: 'In a way, I suppose I'm unfortunate. I think along the same lines as a man. I noticed your eyes when Stella was showing off her body. It rather gave you away. Not that I blame you in the slightest. I'm sure I'd feel exactly the same in your place.'

Denny said acidly, 'Don't you?'

'You mean am I one of those?' She shook her head. 'Oh no. I might have been if I let myself go, of course, but I saw what an awful mess it would get me in. Stella is very much in love with me, but I don't do anything about it.'

Denny lit a cigarette. 'You know, you're rather an unpleasant person,' he said. 'I'm damn' sorry I ever had anything to do with you.'

Gerda smiled. 'Suppose we stop fooling around like this. You want Stella. I know you do. You are wishing I wasn't here so that you could be alone with her. You have a lot of money. I haven't any. I want money. I don't make any bones about it. I must have it. Tell me, Mr Merlin, how much would you pay to have Stella alone for tonight?'

Denny took a step towards her. His face had gone suddenly white. 'Shut your beastly mouth, you bitch!' he said. 'I've taken all I'm going to from you. So shut up, do you understand?'

She stood very still, looking at him, then her mouth smiled. 'Does that mean you'll think it over?' she asked, putting two eggs and the ham on a plate and putting it into his hand. 'But eat this. I'll go and hurry Stella. I should like a bath too.'

She left him standing staring after her with an angry, puzzled expression on his face.

Stella was still in the bath when Gerda came in. She looked up and smiled. 'Am I keeping you waiting, darling?' she asked, cupping her breasts in her hands and lying back on her elbows.

Gerda looked at her beautiful white figure and sat on the edge of the bath. 'No,' she said, 'take your time. I want to talk to you.'

Stella's face clouded. 'What do you want now?' She laid stress on the word now.

'What do you think I want?' Gerda said, her hard eyes suddenly brightening. 'There's five hundred thousand dollars outside wolfing ham and eggs. I want a little of him.'

Stella swirled the water with her legs. She didn't say anything.

'Go out and start on him. He's really soft on you so he'll treat you right. Leave it to me to get the dough out of him.'

Stella shook her head. 'No,' she said, biting her lip. 'No – no – no!'

'You can do it. It would be easy. I'll go to bed and then you go to him. Tell him you're frightened by the wind. Play up to him. Give him the works. He's only waiting for you to start. Then I'll come in and you can go to bed. You don't have to go far with him – just enough to get him going.'

Stella said 'No' again.

'Think what it will mean. I could knock him down for a grand. Think what that would mean. You and I could go to the best hotel in Miami. We could buy clothes and we could eat what we wanted.'

Stella put her hands to her face. 'And when the money was finished you would find someone else to sell me to. Like you did in Daytona beach, like you did in Brooklyn, in New Jersey. No – no – no!'

Gerda got slowly to her feet. 'You are the only capital we have,' she said. 'You wanted to come with me, didn't you? I didn't ask you to, did I? Do you think I should have any difficulty in getting along by myself? How do you think I've managed before? I'm not afraid of work. I'm strong, not like you. You wanted to be with me – how do you think we can live unless you help? Do you think I'd mind what I did to make you happy? If men wanted me and would pay for me, do you think I should care? Can't you get outside your body and forget that it is you? Use it to get us somewhere, use it as a singer uses his voice.'

Stella climbed out of the bath and wrapped a towel round her. She shivered a little. 'How long have I got to do this?' she asked. 'Don't you love me any more? Doesn't it mean anything to you that I'm used like this?'

Gerda went to her, her eyes half closed, knowing that she had got her way, and therefore willing to be kind.

Denny had finished his meal when Stella came out in a light blue wrap, which suited her. He was mixing some more cocktails, having drunk six in a row, and he felt a lot better tempered. In fact, he greeted Stella with a grin as she came in.

'How are you feeling now?' he asked. 'You're looking grand. Have a gin and du Bonnet. Can you cook yourself a meal? I wish I could, but I've never learnt how.'

Stella took a cocktail and began preparing supper. 'Don't you want a bath, Mr Merlin?' she asked.

Denny shook his head. 'No, I'm fine. I guess I've been having a few drinks instead.'

She turned on the grill and stood waiting for it to heat up.

With her back turned to him, she loosened her wrap, then pulled it closely round her as if to avoid spotting the material from the hissing fat.

Denny could see the slim outline of her figure, the soft curve of her buttocks, and he suddenly wanted her very badly. He turned away and took another drink. 'Where's your unpleasant friend?' he asked abruptly.

Stella stiffened. 'Gerda?' she said, looking over her shoulder at him. 'What do you mean – unpleasant?'

Denny shrugged. 'Forget it,' he said; 'I was forgetting she was a friend of yours.'

'Gerda's in the bath. She won't be out for ages. She loves to soak. She told me that she'd get her own supper. Odd way we're eating. We ought to have all sat down together.'

'How old are you?' Denny asked, leaning against the stove, so that he could watch her face. 'Right now, you look like a lovely little girl.'

Stella blushed. 'Oh, I'm nineteen,' she said. 'I'll be twenty at the end of the month.'

'Isn't it a pity that you're living this sort of life? I mean, haven't you any parents to look after you?'

Stella broke an egg into the pan. 'No,' she said, 'I guess not. I get along, really, Mr Merlin, only just now we're in a jam. We had some bad luck and the landlady took our bags in payment – you know.' She broke off and gave a little sniff.

Denny came a little closer. 'This girl, Gerda. I don't think she's a suitable companion for you. Tell me, don't you get into trouble sometimes because of her?'

Stella looked at him, trying hard to force anger out of her eyes. 'Gerda has been very wonderful to me,' she said.

Denny shrugged and turned away. He couldn't make this business out. Stella didn't look like a tramp, he kept telling himself. She wasn't that type at all, he could swear to it, yet why did Gerda make that suggestion? Why was she so sure that Stella would agree? Could it be that Stella liked him? By now the cocktails had made him a little drunk and he was very sure of himself. It would be rather a joke if Stella went for him in a big way and Gerda was left holding the can.

He followed Stella into the dining-room and sat opposite her while she ate her supper. Outside, the wind and rain lashed the walls of the house, making it shudder and forcing them to shout a little when they talked. He insisted on taking her plate away when she had finished, and came back with the cocktail-shaker full again. Stella was sitting on a big settee near the fire. Her wrap had fallen open, showing her neat bare legs. As soon as he came in, she hastily adjusted the wrap, but he had seen all right.

He felt the blood mounting to his head and he came over and sat beside her.

She said, 'Do you like being rich?'

He was a little startled. 'Why sure,' he said. 'Why do you ask?'

'You know, money means so much to some people. To me, it doesn't mean anything at all. Once I saw a man with a hundred-dollar bill. I had never seen a bill like that before. He was awfully pleased with himself.'

Denny laughed. He put his hand behind him and pulled out a big wallet from his hip pocket. 'Ever seen a thousand-dollar bill?' he asked, opening his case. 'And I don't look so pleased with myself, do I?'

He opened the wallet and took out a fat packet of currency. He had eight one thousand-dollar bills and a number of hundred-dollar bills. Stella went very white. 'Oh,' she said, 'put it away. Don't let—'

Gerda said softly from behind them: 'It's there. Enough money to live on for months. To go down Lincoln Road and buy what you want. To go to Dache's or Miller's. To eat at Allen's. Miami would kneel to us.'

Denny spun round, snapping the wallet shut. 'Where the hell did you come from?' he asked.

Gerda stood looking at him, her green eyes like bits of glass, without expression, shiny and hard. 'You are a very fortunate man, Mr Merlin,' she said. 'I am going to bed now. Perhaps by tomorrow the storm will be over. We shall go our different ways soon afterwards. I don't think I shall ever forget you.' She went to the door and then turned. 'I should come too, Stella,' she said. 'Mr Merlin will want to sleep. Good night,' and she went out, shutting the door behind her.

Denny looked at Stella. 'What did she mean – never forget me?'

Stella was still looking very pale. 'I don't know,' she said: 'I wish I did.'

There was silence but for the howl of the wind, then Denny forced a laugh. 'She's gone to bed, anyway. Will you have another drink?'

Stella shook her head, and made as if to rise to her feet, but Denny stopped her. 'Don't go,' he said. 'You know, I was hoping that we should be left alone. I want to talk to you. I want to hear your voice. Look, let's be comfortable.' He got up and switched out the light. The room was lit only by the fire. He came and sat down close to her. 'Isn't that rather nice?' he asked, putting a glass into her hand. 'Come on, drink up. After all, the evening is still very young and we might be here for days. We ought to get to know each other.'

Stella put the glass down on the table beside her. 'I must go,' she said. 'Really, Mr Merlin, I can't stay with you. It's – it's not right.'

'Can't you call me Denny? Isn't this rather thrilling to meet as we have and to be sheltering from a hurricane in someone else's house before a fire, like this? Listen, Stella, it is like a fairy tale. It can't be treated like any other day.'

'Oh, I know, Denny, but I shouldn't really be here. Gerda will be wondering—'

He slid his arm along the back of the settee behind her head and leant over her. 'Do you mind what Gerda's thinking?' he asked. 'Can't you let time stand still for an hour? Let me tell you that I love you. That you are the most lovely thing in this ugly world. You make this hurricane seem thin and pale beside your beauty. Look at me, Stella, can't we go into fairyland together just for an hour? Can't we forget that you are you and I am I? Won't you leave this world and come with me?' He drew her towards him, and pale, almost fainting with fear, Stella relaxed against him.

Denny touched her lips with his and then, as he felt them yield to him, he caught her to him urgently. He was deaf to the storm raging outside and blind to reason. Stella affected him like no other woman had ever affected him. He slid his hand into her open wrap and eased it off her shoulders.

In the firelight he could see her whiteness and he drew her down on the settee, pushing her back so that he was leaning right over her. He lowered his face against the coolness of her breasts and he groaned softly with the ecstasy of the moment.

Gerda, coming into the room like a dark shadow, stole up behind them. The firelight reflected in her fixed staring eyes, and Stella, looking over Denny's shoulder, bit back a scream of fear as she saw Gerda's hand suddenly sweep up, holding something that glittered.

Stella tried to push Denny away, but already the glittering thing was coming down swiftly and Denny relaxed limply on her with a choking cough. With a wild scream, Stella pushed him on to the floor and scrambled up.

'What have you done?' she screamed at Gerda. 'What have you done?' She stumbled over to the lamp and turned it on.

Gerda was standing over Denny, her face white and hard. She said, without looking at Stella, 'Shut up! Don't make a sound.'

Denny rolled over on his side and struggled up on his elbow. A long, thin-bladed table-knife was driven deeply into his neck. Stella could see the silver handle protruding, and she pressed her hands against her mouth in horror.

Blood began to flow over Denny's white shirt and run on to the carpet. He touched the handle with his hand as if he couldn't believe that this had happened to him. He said in a very low, choked voice, 'Did you do it?' to Gerda.

Gerda didn't say anything. She was watching the red ribbon running on to the cream carpet.

'Couldn't you have left me alone?' Denny said. 'My God, I was a fool to have had anything to do with you two. It was the money, I suppose. I didn't think you were as bad as that. Do you think it will do you any good? Don't stand there looking at me. Get me a doctor. Do you want me to bleed to death?'

'Yes,' Stella said wildly, 'get him a doctor, for God's sake!'

Gerda just said, 'Shut up!' and drew away from Denny with a little grimace of disgust.

'Do you want me to die?' Denny said, panic coming into his eyes. 'Help me! Don't stand staring. Help me, you bitch! Can't you see I'm bleeding to death?'

Stella threw herself on to the settee and began to scream wildly. Outside, the wind continued to roar and the rain drummed on the roof.

Gerda took a quick step forward and struck Stella across her face. Stella fell back, her mouth open, but silent. 'I said shut up,' Gerda said harshly. 'Do you understand?'

Making a terrific effort, Denny crawled on to his knees and then levered himself upright. He stood holding on to the back of a chair, making a sobbing noise in this throat. 'Help me, Stella,' he gasped. 'Don't let me die, Stella – help me.'

He put his hand on the knife and tried to pull it out, but the sudden wave of pain was too much, and he fell on to his knees.

Stella scrambled off the settee and ran out of the room. She came back a moment later with a towel. 'Here,' she said frantically to Gerda, 'stop him bleeding.'

Gerda snatched the towel from her savagely and went over to Denny. She took hold of the hilt of the knife and jerked it out of the wound. Denny gave a high-pitched cry like the whinnying of a horse. Blood welled out of him in a scarlet stream. He fell forward on his face and clawed at the stained carpet. He writhed for a moment, then relaxed limply. Blood continued to gush from the wound until eventually it ceased.

The two girls stood watching him. Stella in horror, unable to move or to take her eyes from him, and Gerda hard, inscrutable and cold.

She said: 'He's dead now. You'd better go into the kitchen.'

Stella ran to her. 'You mustn't. I know what you're going to do. You're going to take that money. You killed him for it, didn't you?'

'It's no use to him now,' Gerda said. 'Go into the other room, or I shall be angry with you.'

Stella hid her face in her hands and stumbled out of the room. The noise of the hurricane rose to a terrific crescendo as she slammed the door behind her.

Gerda didn't hesitate. She stepped round Denny very carefully, avoiding the blood on the carpet, and pulled the wallet from his hip pocket. She took the eight thousand bills and the rest of the small notes and put the wallet back in his pocket. She stood for moment looking at the notes, then she closed her fingers over them tightly and heaved a great sigh. At last, she thought, I am free. Nothing matters now. I can live as I want to live. She didn't think of the dead man for one moment.

She found Stella in the kitchen, sobbing quietly and shivering with shock. She took no notice of her but began to dress in her half-dried clothes. She put the roll of notes in her trouser pocket, pulled on her damp black sweater with a little grimace and then turned her attention to Stella.

'Get dressed at once,' she said. 'Stop that snivelling; it won't get you anywhere.'

Stella took no notice of her, and Gerda, losing patience, jerked her out of her chair and shook her.

'Get dressed, you fool!' she shouted. 'Do you hear?'

Stella looked at her blankly and began to wring her hands.

Gerda pulled off her wrap and began pushing her into her clothes. Stella stood quite still, sobbing the whole time like an hysterical child, and let Gerda dress her. When at last she was ready, Gerda shook her again, but she could see that Stella was going to be utterly useless to help her in the work she had to do.

She pushed Stella into the chair again. 'Stay here,' she said. 'And don't move until I come for you.'

She went out and opened the front door. The rain still came down heavily, but the wind had dropped somewhat. She ventured out and found that she could walk without much difficulty.

She went back to the house and collected Denny's clothes. She took them and the suit-case to the car. Then, picking up a large rug from the back seat, she went back to the lounge. She dropped the rug over Denny, rolled him into it and then dragged him out of the house into the pouring rain. She opened the back door of the Lincoln and dragged him into the car. It took her a long time, but eventually she did it.

She was wet through and her clothes stuck to her body as if they were painted on her. She was feeling completely exhausted after the struggle to get Denny into the car, and she poured herself out a stiff shot of whisky. She felt better for that.

So far so good, she told herself, looking round the disordered room. She dare not leave it like that. There was only one quick way to destroy that sort of evidence. She remembered seeing a spare can of gasoline on the running-board of the Lincoln and she went out and got it. She left the can in the lounge and walked into the kitchen.

Stella was still sitting where she had left her. She had stopped crying, but her limbs continued to shiver and tremble.

'We're getting out of here,' Gerda said. 'Come on, pull yourself together for God's sake.'

Stella gave a little shudder at the sound of her voice. 'Go away,' she said, 'I don't ever want to see you again. Oh, God, whatever shall I do? Look what you've got me into.'

Gerda stood very still. 'What do you mean?' she said softly. 'You're to blame as much as I.'

Stella sprang to her feet. She looked a little insane. 'I knew you'd say that,' she screamed. 'But I didn't kill him. I never wanted to kill him. I didn't want him to make love to me – you made me! Do you hear? You made me!'

Gerda said: 'Pull yourself together. If you want to get away with this you've got to use your head and help me.'

'Leave me – go away! He said you were bad, and I didn't believe him. He warned me against you. Oh, how could you do such a thing?' She buried her head in her arms and began sobbing again wildly.

A sudden expression crossed Gerda's face, making her look old and ugly. She said: 'Don't you see it was as much for you as for me? We can be rich now, Stella. We won't have to pinch and scrape any more. You won't have to lie with any more men. We've got all that behind us. Isn't that worth something?'

'How can you talk like that?' Stella demanded, confronting her. 'Does his death mean nothing to you? Are you so hard and callous that you're not frightened by the awful thing you've done?'

Gerda shrugged. 'Oh, very well,' she said. 'What shall we do? Call the cops?'

Stella beat on the table with her fists. 'There's nothing we can do,' she cried. 'We can't bring him back. You've finished us both!'

'I've got him in the car,' Gerda said. 'We can dump him and the car in the river. It is very deep. He may never be found. Then we can get another ride into Miami. With the money, we'll be safe and happy.'

Stella stopped crying and stared at her. 'Is that what you're going to do?' she said. 'What about the house and the bloodstains? Do you think we can get rid of them?'

'I'm going to set fire to the house. They'll think it's the lightning.'

Stella went very white. 'Then he was right. You are utterly bad. You have no feelings for anything but yourself. Go on, do what you've planned. I can't stop you. But I'm not going with you. I'd rather go on the streets than go with you. I don't ever want to see you again.'

Gerda looked at her thoughtfully. 'But I couldn't let you do that,' she said reasonably, 'you might talk. I'm very fond of you, Stella, but you mustn't try my patience too much.' Her voice was toneless and her eyes shone strangely.

Stella shook her head. 'I shan't talk,' she said; 'you needn't be afraid of that. I'm going right out of this house and I hope I shall never see you again.'

She had recovered from her hysteria now that she had a fixed purpose, and her one thought was to get as far away from Gerda as possible.

Gerda held out her hand. 'Because we have been happy, won't you shake hands? I know I've done wrong, but . . .' She shook her head. 'Oh, what's the good? Come, Stella, say good-bye and I wish you good luck.'

Stella hesitated and then came back to her. 'God help you, Gerda,' she said. 'There is no one else who can.'

Two hands reached out and fastened themselves like steel hooks on her throat. 'You stupid mouthing little fool,' Gerda said, forcing Stella's head back. 'Do you think I'd trust you? Do you think I'd have a moment's rest knowing that you were at large to tell the first man who made love to you? What do I care if you aren't with me any more? There are a hundred girls like you to share my eight thousand dollars. You can go with Denny. Do you hear? You can go with him.'

She had forced Stella on the floor and was kneeling over her. Stella struggled wildly, but she had no strength to get free. Gerda held her vice-like grip, one of her knees pressing against Stella's chest, holding her flat.

Because she hadn't got a proper hold, it took her a long time to kill Stella, but at last Gerda got to her feet, flexing her aching fingers. She felt a little wave of pity surge up in her when she looked down at Stella, but only for a moment. The wind had ceased to howl and every moment was precious.

She picked the dead girl up in her arms and almost ran out to the car. She dumped her in on top of Denny and slammed the door shut, then she ran back to the house. A few minutes were enough to splash the rooms with the gasoline, and when she came out smoke began drifting through the window-shutters. She drove the car to the end of the road and then looked back. The house was burning fiercely. Long flames were licking through the roof and a column of black smoke drifted in the wind towards her. She was satisfied that the place would be completely gutted in a very short time, and she drove on to the highway.

The rain still fell, but the wind had died down. Far away she could see the lights of Fort Pierce. She thought even if the worst came to the worst, she could walk there.

The Indian River glowed in the darkness as she drove the car, and finally selecting the most favourable spot she turned the car so that it faced the river. She got out and looked up and down the long straight highway, but she could see no signs of an approaching car. She didn't once look in the back of the Lincoln and, as she adjusted the hand throttle, she felt herself shivering. She stood on the running-board and adjusted the gear, then, as the car began to bump forward, she dropped off and stood watching.

The car seemed to hesitate just as it reached the steep bank, then went crashing over into the leaping, flaming river. She ran forward and could see it plunging down, leaving behind it a great sheet of flame. It looked to her that it had gone into a furious furnace rather than the river, and she took two steps back with a feeling that it had gone for ever.

It was almost an hour later when she heard a truck coming along the road. She had been walking steadily for that time and she was feeling cold and nervy. The rain had stopped, but her clothes were still wet, clinging to her as she moved. She stood in the middle of the road and waved as the truck rattled towards her. It pulled up with a squeal of brakes and she ran up to it.

A dim outline of a man leant down from the cab and peered at her.

'Fort Pierce?' she asked, trying to see what he looked like. 'Can you give me a lift?'

He pushed open the off door of the cab. 'Sure,' he said, 'come on up.'

She climbed in beside him and he started the cab rolling. He was very big and the shadowy outline of his face gave him the appearance of an ape. He, too, was regarding her under the broken peak of his cap.

'Where you come from, baby?' he asked in a hoarse, snuffling voice.

'Daytona Beach,' Gerda returned, rubbing her arms and shivering. 'Got caught in the hurricane, sheltered for some time and then decided to walk on.'

'Huh,' the man said, spitting out of the cab. 'Saw a house on fire way back. I guess it must have been the lightning.'

Gerda didn't say anything. She was feeling tired and would have liked to have gone to sleep.

'Ain't you scared being around in a spot like this on your own?' he asked her.

Gerda stiffened. 'I don't scare easily,' she said coldly. 'The last guy who tried to get fresh with me is still wondering what hit him.'

'Sortta tough, huh?' the driver said with a hoarse laugh. 'Well, I like a dame to be tough.'

'That's nice for me, isn't it?' Gerda rejoined sarcastically.

The driver laughed again. 'I guess before we go any further I'll collect your fare,' he said, stopping the truck with a jerk. 'Let's get in the back for a while.'

Gerda shook her head. 'Get goin',' she said sharply. 'I don't wear that sort of thing. I'll give you a fin when we reach Fort Pierce. That's all you'll get.'

The driver screwed round in his seat. 'Yeah?' he said, his voice suddenly menacing. 'I ain't used to that sort of yappin' from a dame. Get into the back of the truck quick, before I get rough. You're taking what I'm goin' to give you, an' you goin' to like it.'

Gerda opened the door. 'If that's the way you feel about it,' she said, her eyes hard and calculating. She slid into the road. The moment her feet touched the wet tarmac she made a dart towards the thick citrus groves. Before she reached them a terrific jar struck her just above her knees and she went down in a heap. Her breath was knocked out of her body, and for several minutes she was powerless to move. She felt herself being picked up, carried a few steps and then banged down again.

'How do you like that?' the driver asked, kneeling over her.

She realized that she was in the back of the truck and she lay very still, waiting to recover her breath.

'Now, baby, do you play or must I rough you around until you do?' the driver asked.

Gerda said breathlessly: 'O.K., you big caveman, let me get up an' fix myself.'

The driver moved away from her with his back to the entrance of the truck, so that she couldn't pass him. 'Not so tough, huh?' he said. 'I tell you, baby, I've gotta way with dames.'

Gerda got slowly to her feet. Her body ached from her fall. She poised herself, and then with all her strength she swung over a punch aimed at the driver's jaw.

The driver had been expecting it and shifted his head a trifle. Gerda's fist scraped his ear and he countered with a heavy slap across her face with his open hand. The blow stunned her and she fell on her knees, suddenly frightened. She knew that this guy was too strong and smart for her.

The driver knelt down beside her and smacked her face several times. The pain made tears run down her face and she tried to protect herself with upraised arms. All he did was to poke her with his forefinger very hard in her belly which brought her hands down very quickly, and then he went on slapping her.

'Had enough?' he asked after a while.

Gerda was too dazed to speak. She lay limply waiting, shudderingly, for him to take her. She felt his hands on her clothes, but she hadn't the strength to resist him. A red haze hung before her eyes and her face and head seemed to be on fire.

She was suddenly conscious that something awful for her had happened. She heard the driver suck in his breath sharply and she heard him mutter, 'For Pete's sake,' and she realized with a dreadful sinking feeling that he had found the roll of money.

She struggled up and tried to snatch it away from him, but he was too quick for her. He shoved her away roughly and stood up.

'Where did you get this?' he shouted, holding the roll in a trembling hand.

'Give it to me – it's mine.'

'Yeah? Well, prove it's yours.'

'I tell you it's mine,' Gerda said, nearly sobbing with fury. 'Give it to me!'

The roll disappeared into the driver's pocket. 'You pinched it,' he said. 'Maybe you got it from the house that was on fire way back. A tramp like you wouldn't have so much dough.'

Gerda threw herself on him, her fingers clawing for his eyes. He hit her between her eyes as she came in, sending her in a heap on the floor-boards, then he stepped over her and booted her out of the truck. She landed in the wet mud of the road with a thud that shook the breath out of her.

He said, as he dropped to the road beside her: 'If you want the dough, come along to Fort Pierce an' ask the cops for it. Maybe they'll have it for you.' He gave a little snigger. 'Somehow I don't think they'll know much about it,' and he ran back to the truck and drove away.

MORNING VISIT

The Lieutenant stopped and held up his hand. Over to his right he had seen the farm, half hidden by a clump of coconut palms.

The four negro soldiers shuffled to a standstill, grounding their rifles and leaning on them.

Overhead the sun beat down on the little group. The Lieutenant, the sweat oozing out of his fat hide, wriggled his body inside his uniform which stuck to him uncomfortably. He was acutely aware of the great patches of damp that stained his white uniform; and he cursed the heat, the President and, above all, the A.B.C terrorists.

Contemptuously he regarded the four negroes, who stood staring with vacant eyes on the ground, like emasculated cattle. 'This is the place,' he said, thrusting forward his bullet head. 'Two of you to the right; two to the left. No noise. No shooting – use your bayonets if there's trouble.'

He drew his sword. The steel blade flashed in the sunlight.

The soldiers opened out and advanced towards the farm at a trot. They held their heads down, and their rifles hung loosely in their hands. As they shambled over the uneven ground they looked like bloodhounds picking up a scent.

The Lieutenant moved forward at a slower pace. He walked gingerly, as if he were treading on egg-shells. Inside his once beautiful uniform, his fat body cringed at the thought of a bullet smashing into him. He took the precaution of keeping the coconut palms between him and the farm. When he could no longer shelter himself behind the slender trunks he broke into a run. The heat waves coiled round him like a rope as he lumbered over the rough ground.

The four soldiers had already reached the farm, and they stood in an uneven circle, waiting for the Lieutenant to come up. They were more animated now. They knew that very soon they would be back in the barracks out of the heat of the afternoon sun.

The farm was a squat dwelling, with a palm-thatched roof and whitewashed walls. As the Lieutenant approached cautiously, the door of the place opened and a tall, poorly dressed Cuban stepped into the sunshine.

The soldiers jerked up their rifles, threatening him with the glittering bayonets. The Cuban stood very still, his hands folded under his armpits, and his face wooden.

The Lieutenant said, 'Lopez?'

The Cuban's eyes flickered round at the soldiers, seeing only the ring of steel before him. He looked at the Lieutenant. 'Yes,' he said, a dry rustle in his voice.

The Lieutenant swung his sword. 'You may have heard of me,' he said, a wolfish smile pulling at his mouth. 'Ricardo de Crespedes.

Lopez shuffled his feet in the sand. His eyes flinched, but his face remained wooden. 'You do me much honour, señor,' he said.

The Lieutenant said, 'We'll go inside,' and he stepped past Lopez, holding his sword at the alert. He walked into the dwelling.

Lopez followed him with two of the soldiers. The other two stood just outside the door.

The room was very poor, shabby, and dirty. De Crespedes moved to the rough table standing in the middle of the room and rested his haunches on it. He unbuttoned the flap on his revolver-holster and eased the revolver so that he could draw it easily. He said to one of the soldiers, 'Search the place.'

Lopez moved uneasily. 'Excellency, there is no one here – only my wife.'

The negro went into the other room. De Crespedes said, 'See if he's armed.'

The other soldier ran his big hands over Lopez, shook his head, and stepped back. De Crespedes hesitated, then reluctantly put up his sword. There was a long, uneasy pause.

The negro came back from the other room pushing a Cuban woman before him.

De Crespedes looked at her and his small eyes gleamed. The woman ran to Lopez and clung to him, her face blank with fear. She wore a white blouse and skirt; her feet were bare. De Crespedes thought she was extraordinarily nice. He touched his wax moustache and smiled. The movement was not lost on Lopez, who tightened his hold on his wife.

De Crepedes said: 'You're hiding guns here. Where are they?'

Lopez shook his head. 'I have no guns, Excellency. I am a poor farmer – I do not trade in guns.'

De Crespedes looked at the woman. He thought her breasts were superb. The sight of her drew his mind away from his duty and this faintly irritated him, because he was quite a good soldier. He said a little impatiently: 'It will be better for you to say so now than later.'

The woman began to weep. Lopez touched her shoulder gently. 'Quiet, he said, 'it's Ricardo de Crespedes.'

The Lieutenant drew himself to his full height and bowed. 'He is right,' he said, rolling his bloodshot eyes a little. The woman could feel his rising lust for her.

Lopez said desperately: 'Excellency, there has been some mistake—'

De Crespedes lost patience. He told the soldiers to search the place for guns. As the negroes began hunting, he pulled the woman away from Lopez. 'Come here,' he said, 'I want to look at you.'

Lopez opened his mouth, but no sound came from him, his eyes half closed and his hands clenched. He knew he could do nothing.

The woman stood close to de Crespedes, her hands clasped over her breasts. Her fear stirred his blood.

'Do you understand why I'm here?' he said, putting his

hand on her bare arm. 'Traitors are arming the people against the President. Guns have been hidden here. We know that. Where are they?'

She stood quivering like a nervous horse, not daring to draw away from him. She said: 'Excellency, my man is a good man. He knows nothing about guns.'

'No?' De Crespedes pulled her closer to him. 'You know nothing about these terrorists? Nothing about plots to overthrow Machado?'

Lopez stepped forward, pushing his wife roughly away, so that de Crespedes' hold was broken. 'We know nothing, Excellency.'

De Crespedes shoved himself away from the table. His face hardened. 'Seize this man,' he barked.

One of the soldiers twisted Lopez's arms behind him and held him.

The woman ran her fingers through her thick hair. Her eyes grew very wide. 'Oh no . . . no . . .' she said.

De Crespedes himself supervised the search, but they found nothing. He went out into the sunlight again and shouted to the remaining soldiers to look round the outside of the farm. Then he came back. He stood in the doorway, looking at Lopez. 'Where are the guns?' he said. 'Quick – where are they?'

Lopez shook his head. 'We know nothing about guns, Excellency.'

De Crespedes turned to the soldier. 'Hold him very tightly.' The he began to walk towards the woman. She turned to run into the other room, but the other soldier was standing against the door. He was smiling, and his teeth looked like piano keys. As she hesitated, de Crespedes caught up with her and his hand fell on the back of her blouse. He ripped it from her. She crouched against the wall, hiding her breasts with her hands, weeping softly.

De Crespedes looked over his shoulder at Lopez. 'When you are dead,' he said, 'I will have your woman – she is good.'

Lopez controlled himself with a great effort. He was completely powerless in the grip of the soldier.

De Crespedes said to the soldiers who came in at this moment, 'Cut off his fingers until he's ready to talk.'

The woman screamed. She fell on her knees in front of de

Crespedes, wringing her hands. 'We know nothing, Excellency,' she said wildly. 'Don't touch my man.'

De Crespedes looked down at her with a smile. Then he put a dusty boot on her bare breasts and shoved her away. She fell on her side and lay there, her head hidden under her arms.

The soldiers forced Lopez to sit at the table, and they spread his hands flat on the rough wood. Then, using his bayonet like a hatchet, one of the negroes lopped off a finger.

De Crespedes sat looking at the blood that ran across the table and dripped on to the floor. He stood up with a little grimace of disgust.

A thin wailing sound came from Lopez, although he didn't open his lips. The two soldiers who held him shifted as they strained to keep his hands in position.

'Until he talks,' de Crespedes said, unhooking his jacket and removing his sword-belt.

The negro raised his bayonet and brought it down with a swish. There was a little clicking sound as it went through bone, and he had difficulty in getting the blade out of the hard wood.

De Crespedes threw his jacket and sword-belt on the bench and walked over to the woman. With a grunt, he bent over her. Taking her under her arms, he dragged her into the other room. He threw her on the bed. Then he went back and kicked the door shut. He noticed that it was very hot in the room, although the shutters kept out the sun.

The woman lay on her side, her knees drawn up to her chin. She kept her eyes shut, and her lips moved as she prayed. De Crespedes lowered his bulk on to the bed. He took her knees in his hands and turned her on her back. Then he forced her knees down and ripped the rest of her clothes from her. He did not hurry, and once, when she resisted, pushing at him with her small hands, he thumped her on her chest with his fist, like he was driving in a nail with a hammer.

Then, because he knew this rigid body could give him no pleasure, and because he had much experience, he set about breaking her down. His two hands settled on her arms and his fingers dug into her soft muscles. Her eyes opened and she screamed. He leant on her, crushing her with his bulk, and dug further with his fat, thick fingers. It was not long before the violence of the pain turned the woman into a weeping, gibbering thing of clay on the bed. And when he took her, she lay placid, her tears falling on his shoulder.

Later on, one of the soldiers had to go out and get a bucket of water to throw over Lopez, and although they did many things to him they could not get him to speak, so they lost patience with him and they killed him.

When de Crespedes came out of the room he found his soldiers standing uneasily waiting for him. He looked down at Lopez and stirred him with his boot. He wiped his face with the back of his hand and yawned. 'Did he talk?' he asked indifferently. He was thinking of the long tramp back to the barracks. When they shook their heads, he shrugged and put on his jacket. He was feeling devilishly tired. Listlessly he tightened the sword-belt round his thick middle and put on his cap. Then he went back and looked at Lopez again. 'It is possible he knew nothing about guns,' he said half aloud, 'they've made a lot of mistakes before.' He shrugged and turned to the door.

The soldiers picked up their rifles and moved after him. Outside, he paused. 'The woman,' he said irritably, 'I was forgetting the woman.' He looked at one of the soldiers. 'Attend to her. Use your bayonet.'

While they waited in the blinding heat, he thought regretfully how much better it would have been if she had loved him. There was little satisfaction to be had from a weeping woman. Still, he felt better for it. Women were necessary to him.

When the soldier came out, they gave him time to clean his bayonet and then they all tramped across the uneven ground towards the barracks.

TWIST IN THE TALE

The first time I met George Hemingway was when I was after marlin off Key West. I ran into him in a casual sort of way in the Plaza Hotel. He was with a large crowd and I was on my own. It was my first experience of deep-sea fishing, and I rather wanted to experiment by myself. I had had a year of worry and hard work steering my firm through the depression, and now that things were looking pretty good again, I considered that I had earned a few weeks off. So down I went to Key West. I had heard a lot about the fishing there, and I thought it sounded just the right sport for my frame of mind.

I put myself in the hands of Joppy, one of the finest fishermen on the coast. He and I went out in a fast motor-boat nearly every day. He was a soft-spoken, patient sort of a guy, and I guess he wanted all his patience by the time I got through. We fished those waters for over a week without seeing anything remotely resembling marlin. I guess they thought I was too mean a guy to bother about, and even Joppy began looking at me thoughtfully towards the end of the week.

I remember sitting in the lounge bar of the 'Plaza' after a completely uneventful day, wondering what the hell deep-sea fisherman could see in such a slow sport, when about a dozen people drifted in, making enough row to scare all the marlin right out of the Mexican Bay. They crowded up to the bar, and because I was at a complete loose end I watched them with, what must have amounted to, almost rude curiosity.

The girls were the usual type of brittle beauty that infest the luxury hotels during the season. There were five of them, and they all were wearing beach trousers, sandals, and gay-coloured handkerchiefs that hid their firm, curved breasts. They were chattering and laughing as they always do, and as soon as they had settled their neat little bottoms on stools they began drinking pink gins at an astonishing rate.

With the exception of George Hemingway, the men were also true to type. They wore white trousers, a handkerchief of various hues round their necks and, of course, the inevitable doe-skin shoes.

My eyes swept over the group and came to rest on George. He immediately attracted my attention, and I wondered who he was. His personality was so strong that he made the others seem mere paintings on the wall. He was tall with big powerful shoulders, tapering away to a small waist and very long legs. You could see at a glance how much he enjoyed the good things in life, and his enormous vitality for absorbing them.

I noticed that he paid for all the drinks out of a well-worn wallet. It amused me to watch these people and to see the clever way the women out-manoeuvred one another to be the centre of attraction.

After a while they all got through with their drinks and decided to go out for a bathe. George told them to go on as he'd left his costume in his room. He stood with a big humorous grin on his bronzed face watching them troop out, and then turned to the elevator. As he turned he caught my eye, and realizing that I had been watching him for sometime he came over.

'I'm Hemingway,' he said. 'Are you all by yourself?'

I explained that it was of my own choosing, and went on to tell him about the deep-sea fishing. His eyes lit up at the mention of marlin. 'What sort of sport have you had?' he asked.

I shrugged. 'I find it mighty slow,' I said ruefully. 'I haven't seen anything that looks like a big fish since I've been here.'

Hemingway looked rather guiltily out of the big window at the group running down to the bathing-pool. 'Listen buddy,' he said, 'how about you and me having a go tomorrow morning early? Believe it or not, there's no one interested in fishing in my party, and I've been itching to get my hands on a rod. What do you say?'

I readily agreed. By now I had seen the error in not having a companion on this trip. I had imagined that I should have been so busy fishing that another person would have only been in the way.

Well, to cut a long story short, we had a day's fishing which will remain long in my memory. George seemed to know where to find the fish, and Joppy, who came with us, was almost as excited as I.

During that day, cruising in the dark blue waters of the Mexican Bay, we formed a friendship which was altogether remarkable, because neither of us had anything in common. My real interest was in my work. I was unmarried, and had little or no use for a gay life. I was fortunate in having a number of good friends, most of them connected with my business, and as a hobby I wrote light novels which had a moderate success.

On the other hand, George lived recklessly, drank heavily, and, in his own words, 'chased dames'. His absorbing passion was speed. He owned a number of cars, but his favourite was a big racing Bugatti, which he would drive, whenever he could, at an almost fantastic speed.

I often wondered why it was that he so obviously liked me and sought my company. During the three weeks I remained at Key West he was my constant companion. The little regiment of lovelies who followed him around regarded me with suspicion. I could quite understand my unpopularity. In my company, George seemed to find them boring, and that meant they had to look elsewhere for someone to buy them their drinks and the hundreds of other little luxuries they could not afford for themselves.

On the last night of my stay at the 'Plaza' I remember George coming into my room and sitting on my bed. I was just putting a finishing touch to my toilet, and I recollect having difficulty in fixing my tie to my satisfaction.

George sat there watching me. Then he said: 'I'm going to miss you a hell of a lot. I wish you were staying.'

'Yes, I'm sorry to go. I've had a grand time. Maybe we'll see something of each other later on.'

George said seriously: 'When I come to New York I'd like to see a lot more of you.'

I was pleased that he felt that way, and we exchanged cards. I hoped I would see him soon, as I found his company very exhilarating.

Well, you know how it is. I got back to New York and was immediately caught up in arrears of business. For several weeks I forgot all about him. Then one morning I saw his photograph in the *Times* and an account of a motor-race he had taken part in. The racing correspondent considered that he was going to be a leading star in the racing world. I was surprised that he had entered this field, but I sent him a note of congratulation, as I thought it would please him. Whether he received the note or not I don't know, but I didn't have any reply. I had to go to Washington for a couple of months as we were operating a new branch there, so any hope of meeting George in New York had to be postponed.

His rise to fame in the speed world was remarkable. Soon no motor-race was considered anything at all unless he was a competitor. In fact, he began to win so consistently that his name rapidly became a household word. He apparently had no nerves. It was not that he was more skilful than the other drivers, but that he attained a maximum speed and kept to it. Cornering rough roads and dangerous hills meant nothing to him. He sent the machine he was driving forward like a bullet, and by some miracle finished in one piece. So great was the enthusiasm and talk about his daring that one Saturday afternoon I made an effort and attended one of the races in which he was competing.

I shall never forget that afternoon. And when his car hurtled past the flag a good quarter of a mile ahead of the next man, I found that my legs were almost too weak to support me to the Club bar, and that my shirt was sticking to my back in a most unpleasant manner as I sweated with fear for him and morbid excitement.

I knew it was quiet hopeless to get near George until the admiring crowd had moved away, so I fortified myself in the meantime with some very excellent bourbon.

About half an hour after the race George came into the bar, followed by a large crowd of people. One glance was sufficient to tell me that his company was the usual hard-drinking, empty-headed lot. As I hadn't seen him for over six months, I regarded him with interest. I thought he looked a lot thinner and a lot older. I was rather astonished to see that he was drinking ginger ale, whilst the crowd was belting neat Scotch.

I hesitated to approach him, surrounded by so many obviously ardent admirers; and while I was making up my mind what to do, he happened to glance up and see me. For a moment he looked puzzled, then his face lit up, and with an abrupt excuse he left his party and hurried over to me.

He shook my hand almost feverishly. 'This is marvellous,' he said; 'for God's sake where have you been all this time?'

I told him about my business engagements, but I could see he was only giving me half his attention. In fact, he broke in to say: 'I must talk to you. I've got to get rid of this crowd first. Will you meet me outside and have dinner with me?'

I readily agreed, and he returned to his party, who had been watching us with curious attention, no doubt wondering who I was.

He didn't keep me waiting long. It was really quite

astonishing how quickly he got rid of so many people, but in less than fifteen minutes he joined me outside the Club. Grabbing my arm, he hurried me across the road to where his Bugatti was standing.

'Still got the old bus, I see,' I said, climbing in rather gingerly.

'Yes, she's been overhauled from time to time, but I wouldn't part with her.' He settled himself in the driving-seat. 'It's grand to see you again. Where shall we go? How about Max's? They give you a good dinner there.'

'Sure, any place. Only take it easy,' I pleaded. 'I'm not used to high speeds.'

George laughed and engaged the gears. He drove at quite a reasonable speed. He wanted to know the fullest details about my trip to Washington, and so insistent was he that I suspected he was anxious not to talk about himself until we had settled down from our sudden meeting.

We got a quiet table at Max's, which was not overcrowded, and ordered a light meal. I asked him what he would drink, but he shook his head. 'I've given it up,' he said. 'It wanted a lot of doing, but in my game it just doesn't pay.'

I ordered a bottle of light wine for myself. 'You certainly have jumped into fame, George,' I said. 'What on earth made you take up racing so seriously?'

He looked at me in an odd way. 'Why shouldn't I? You know how keen I am on speed.'

'I know, but I didn't think you were as keen as all that. After all, if you do want a burst of speed now and then you have the Bugatti. Frankly, I think you are taking the most damnable risks. You scared the life out of me this afternoon.'

George nodded. 'You're a wise old guy. There is a reason, and a very good reason too.'

'It must be,' I said. 'I've never seen, nor do I hope ever to see again, such mad driving in all my life. Do you honestly mean to tell me that you have been doing this for the last six months?'

'It is very difficult for me. I have nothing on these professionals in the way of tricks – and believe me, there are plenty of tricks in this game. In order to win I just keep going as fast as I can and that's my one ace.'

I couldn't understand this at all. 'Surely it isn't so important to win as all that,' I said, frowning. 'I mean, you don't strike me as a person who must win at everything, and it is not as if you can't afford to lose sometimes.'

The waiter interrupted us just then with our first course, and for a few minutes there was silence. Then George said, 'You see, Myra expects me to win.'

I said, 'Oh,' rather blankly, and then: 'I'm sorry, George, but I'm rather out of touch. Who is Myra?'

George said with an effort: 'Myra is the girl I'm going to marry.'

Automatically I murmured my congratulations, but I was extremely puzzled, as he didn't seem at all happy. In fact, my congratulations fell rather flat.

There was rather a long, strained silence after that, then I said, 'Well, tell me all about it.'

George sat back with a little shrug. 'Oh, I don't know,' he said, 'I don't want to bother you with details. You see, Myra likes celebrities. At first she wouldn't look at me. Then some of the crowd began to talk about my driving and she took a little interest. I sort of took up the racing to please her, and now we are going to get married.'

All the time he was talking he avoided looking at me, and I thought it was a most extraordinary story. 'But surely, George, she must realize what risks you are taking. I mean, she wouldn't want anything to happen to you.'

I found that I was floundering, and stopped talking, annoyed at myself. I am old-fashioned enough to believe that marriage should be founded on a quarter of love and three-quarters companionship. It seemed too much like a Hollywood wedding to please me.

George shook his head. 'Why, I guess she's got a lot of confidence in my driving.'

I said, rather dryly, 'I see.'

'No, you don't,' George said miserably. 'You think it is most odd, and so it is. What is more, this racket is getting too much for me. I can't keep it up much longer.'

As he spoke his face relaxed, and I saw a horror in his eyes that startled me. It is not often that one sees naked fear in a man's face, but I saw it that night and it wasn't a pleasant experience.

'I don't think there is a man alive who could,' I said. 'Why don't you drop it right away? After all, you have enough fame now. You've done quite enough.'

'No, I can't do that. I can't expect you to understand. I've got to go until I'm married – then perhaps—'

I said: 'Let's go to the bar and have a brandy. It'll do you good.'

'I daren't touch it,' George said. 'If I once start again, I'm sunk.' He ran his fingers through his thick hair. 'My God! I had a close shave once. It was when Myra came to see me race for the first time. I wanted to put on a good show, but I felt edgy and nervous. So I hit the bottle. That cured me. I took a bend at over a hundred miles an hour. Everyone thought it was marvellous driving, and Myra got a tremendous kick out of it, but I knew how close I had been to a smash-up. I found I was losing my sense of judgement, so I gave up the booze. I tell you, sometimes I get pretty scared.'

I began to get seriously worried. It was quite obvious to me that he was making a tremendous effort to seem casual, but every now and then I would get a glimpse of an expression in his eyes that told me he was in very bad shape. There was no doubt that he was terrified, almost as pathetically as a child awakening from some evil nightmare.

I asked him when he was getting married.

'Early next month. I have two more races, and then I'm going to Key West for my honeymoon. That's really what I want to speak to you about. I want you to come along for some fishing.'

I stared at him. 'My dear fellow. Not on your honeymoon. Why, damn it—'

He laughed. 'For God's sake don't be so old-fashioned. Of course you can. Myra likes plenty of company. Quite a lot of the crowd will be there.'

I shook my head. 'No, I'm sorry, George, it's quite impossible. I've got my work to think about, and I'm just finishing a novel. No, I'm sorry.'

When I said that, I realized that there was a lot more behind this peculiar wedding than George had told me. He suddenly seemed to lose control of himself, and I thought he was going to break down. He seized my arm in a grip that made me wince. 'Don't let me down,' he said, 'I've been relying on you. I don't think I could stand it if you weren't there.'

I said, rather sharply, 'What the devil is this business?'

He shook his head. 'Don't ask me. You'll know in time. Don't say you won't come. You must come.'

I finally gave him my promise. Almost immediately he braced up and seemed anxious to get away. 'I'm sorry about all this,' he said, signalling to the waiter, 'but I am frightfully nervy after a race. A good night's sleep will put me right, I expect. I can't say how glad I am that you're coming. It'll be like old times, won't it?'

He drove me back to my apartment, but refused to come in. 'I'll write and give you the details as soon as I get everything fixed up. Myra will be tickled when she hears you are an author. She gets a big kick out of that sort of thing.'

I looked at him sharply because I was almost certain that there had been a sneer in his voice, but I could detect nothing from his expression. We shook hands and parted. I went up to my apartment in a very thoughtful mood. It had been an evening full of strange and uncomfortable incidents.

The following day I obtained a clue to the whole thing. It came about in the course of a casual conversation with Drayton, my senior director. He and I had just finished an excellent lunch, and I was on the point of leaving to buy a harness for the fishing trip with George.

Drayton asked me where I was going to fish. I told him how I had met George, and I could see an immediate interest at the mention of his name.

'Hemingway? He's the fellow in oil, isn't he?'

'I really don't know. I have never asked. This Hemingway is the motor-racing fellow.'

'Yes. I didn't know you knew him. Between you and me, I'm afraid he's going to run into a packet of trouble before long.'

Sensing that I was on the very clue that might explain all this business I sat down again. 'What sort of trouble?'

Drayton lowered his voice. 'I understand that the particular oil-fields he's invested in have dried up without warning. His firm are facing one of the biggest crashes in the history of Wall Street. No one knows about it yet. Engineers are out there making a report. It has never happened before. Everyone thought oil had been struck in a big way. It lasted until all the necessary machinery was set up and then – finish. It is incredible.'

I stared at him. 'He's getting married next month,' I said. 'Poor devil. I suppose he's aware what has happened?'

Drayton coughed. 'His future wife is Myra Luckton. She is an heiress in her own right to over six million dollars. I should imagine the marriage comes at a very opportune moment.'

Well, there it was. The cat was out of the bag, and I didn't have to wonder any more. I knew. It was now perfectly obvious that George was marrying this girl in order to save his financial position, and he fell very considerably in my estimation. I didn't say anything to Drayton, but went out to make my purchases. Now that I had seen the beginning of this thing I was determined to see the finish.

Time passed fairly quickly, as I was working hard to finish the book before going to Key West. I noticed that George had been in another race. This time the newspapers carried two-inch type about his sensational escape from death. It appears that he rounded a corner with the utmost recklessness, and got into a skid while travelling well over a hundred miles an hour. The car overturned several times, throwing him clear. He escaped unhurt, but the car was utterly destroyed by fire.

Reading the description made me think of the day I saw him race, and I tossed the paper away with a grimace of disgust. I could see the look of terror in his face and wondered doubtfully how his nerves were reacting to this last escape.

A week after this I received a note from George asking me down to Key West on the following Saturday. He said in his letter that he would not ask me to the wedding as he knew I should be bored with the hundreds of people who were turning up.

They are not your fun [he wrote], *nor are they mine, but Myra wants them to come. It will be better at Key West. I received a bad shaking the other day when my bus overturned. I feel now that that was my last race. Myra doesn't know yet.*

His handwriting revealed that he was in a very bad state of nerves, and the allusion to his last race struck me as significant. I hoped the change by the Mexican Bay would do him good, but I must confess the trip had lost a lot of its savour for me now that I knew why he was marrying the girl.

However, Saturday came round after a busy week clearing up and, to save time, I did the journey by air.

I went immediately to the very beautiful house near the beach that George had rented. As my car swung into the short circular drive I was conscious of a considerable amount of noise and laughter drifting through the large open windows. It seemed that George and noise were inevitably linked together.

George came running out. He was wearing white trousers, a dark red shirt and sandals. I had to admit that he looked extraordinarily handsome as he stood on the steps with a smile on his face. 'What a grand sight,' he said, shaking my hand. 'How are you? They are all longing to meet a real live author. Come on in.'

He had been drinking heavily and was slightly unsteady on his feet. The reek of whisky on his breath was so strong that I turned my head with a slight grimace of disgust. He said with a grin: 'Sorry, ol' man, but we've been cel-cel – you know. Come on in, an' get tight. I warn you, you've got to get tight an' stay tight if you're staying in this dump.'

He took me into a large lounge. At the far end, through open double doors, I could see a number of people sitting or standing with glasses in their hands. They all looked in our direction. One of the girls came to the door, then moved towards us.

George said, 'This is Myra,' and introduced me.

Myra Luckton's name was familiar to me as frequent references to her parties appeared in the Press, but I don't remember ever seeing a photograph of her, and, consequently, it came as a considerable shock meeting her for the first time. It was entirely due to a habit of wearing a poker face that I did not openly reveal my dismay.

It is exceedingly difficult to describe Myra. She was above the average height, small-featured, silky platinum hair, and, of course, she was perfectly groomed. So much for what God and money had given her, but her expression took away everything that could have counted in her favour. To be brutally frank, she looked like a very expensive street-walker. Her eyes were cold, calculating and vicious, and her mouth was hard. She gave me the impression that she was utterly brazen, and there was nothing she would hesitate to do to satisfy a lust for sensation.

I'm afraid I must have betrayed a little of my dismay, or else she was very shrewd, because, as she took my hand, she gave me a little jeering laugh and said: 'What a lovely man. I do believe I've shocked him already.'

George was watching me too. 'Take no notice of her,' he said, 'she's as tight as a tick.'

She laughed as he said that and put one slim white arm round his neck. 'Do come in and meet the others,' she said. 'They've all read your books and they think they're too marvellous.'

Later, when I escaped to my room, I was very thankful to sit by the window and look across at the beautiful bay. I had quite made up my mind that I could not stay in this house long.

I proceeded to change for dinner. As I wandered around the large airy room, shedding my clothes about the floor, I turned over in my mind the tragedy of George's wedding.

It was quite obvious to me that he detested Myra. She was obviously thrilled to have married someone so famous, but there was no question of her having any true affection for him. It was a thoroughly unpleasant marriage.

A tap sounded on the door, and George came in. He sat on the bed. I saw that he was still rather high, but his face was very serious and lined as he stared at me. 'What do you think of her?' he asked abruptly.

That was the one question I never thought he would ask me. It annoyed me to think that he was forcing me into a lie, as I could not tell him the truth.

He saw my hesitation. 'Say it. Speak your mind. You're the one guy I've met who has been on the level with me. So tell me.'

'I'm afraid you are not very happy,' I said. 'I'm sorry, George.'

'My God! You don't want to be sorry for me. I've brought it on myself, haven't I? I knew what I was doing. No, I'm a heel. I've sold myself to that woman for the stacks of dollars she's got. You know that, don't you?'

I lit a cigarette and wandered over to the window. 'I must tell you that there is a rumour that your firm, Hemingway, Sawyer & Curtis, are in a bad way.'

George stared at me. 'You know that?' he asked, his face going very white. 'Who else knows?'

'It's not common talk yet, but I'm afraid it will be very soon.'

'You think I'm a heel, don't you?' he said. 'You think I'm marrying this girl to save my own skin. Well, you're wrong. I'm trying to save all those little guys who put their money into the oil-fields because I told them they couldn't go wrong. I thought it was a good thing. We all did. We let the little man in and kept the big speculator out. It was to be the small man's dream. It was my idea; it is my responsibility. I was the fool who thought the idea up. My partners didn't care a damn so long as they got the backing. I said: "We'll give the little guy a chance," and then the wells went dry.'

I went over and sat by his side. 'What's Myra going to do about this?'

'She wants her pound of flesh. She'll give me enough capital to pay out the shareholders if—' He got up and began to wander round the room.

'Well, go on. If – what?'

'There's a big race at Miami next week. The trophy is for the fastest speed on land. You don't just have to beat the other guy, you've got to beat your own previous best record. She says if I get that, I can have the dough.'

'Why are you drinking again?' I asked.

'Because I'm so scared that I've got to drink. I hate this house and everyone in it; I hate the sound of her voice and her laugh. If I don't drink I shall crack up.'

'I'm sorry about this, George,' I said. 'Is there anything I can do?'

He made a little grimace. 'Yes, you can. I'm afraid it isn't a pleasant job. You see, I don't trust Myra. I want to get it down on paper. I want you to witness it and see that, in the event of an accident, she carries out her bargain.'

'Don't talk like that. There mustn't be an accident. Besides, the whole thing falls down if you don't win the race.'

He shook his head. 'No, as a matter of fact she would be more thrilled if I was killed. You see, it would give her a lot more fun being a widow of a racing-ace, and she is quite prepared to pay for that.'

What could I say? The whole business was, from the very start, fantastic, but now it was rapidly developing into a nightmare.

He was quite right about the week being grim. Myra seemed to find me amusing, and took special pains in keeping me away from George. We did not get one day's fishing during the whole week. In fact, I took refuge in my room as much as possible with the excuse that I was polishing the last chapter of my book.

The topic of conversation was entirely about the coming race. George was seldom sober, and joined in with the crowd as if he had nothing on his mind. Myra and he were never alone together, and the rest of the party seemed to find nothing odd in this. Myra came in for an enormous amount of admiration as George's wife, and I could see how she revelled in being the centre of attraction.

During the week I had the opportunity of studying her, and I came to the conclusion that she was an exceedingly dangerous woman. Sometimes, I would catch her watching George, and I could see a smouldering suppressed hatred in her eyes which made me extremely uneasy.

On the Sunday before the race, George asked me to come into the library. 'I've got a draft drawn up. I want you to look it over, and then witness her signature.'

We went into the library. Myra was sitting in an easy chair. She smiled at me as I came in. 'So George has let you into our little secret,' she said. There was a tigerish look in her eyes as she spoke. 'What do you think of him? Do you think it is awfully nice to marry a girl for her money?'

'Surely, Mrs. Hemingway,' I said quietly, 'it is not so one-sided as that. I believe you have struck a bargain as well.'

She laughed. 'Why, of course, and I always get the best of a bargain. I'm not so stupid as you think.'

George said abruptly: 'Shall we get this over, and join the others?'

She shrugged. 'Poor little George. He is so anxious to save his silly investors.'

George gave me a sheet of paper. It contained very few words:

I promise to pay the sum of one million dollars to my husband if he wins the Morgan Golden Road Trophy. In the event of an accident resulting in his death during the race, I will pay that sum to Hemingway, Sawyer & Curtis. My cheque to be given immediately the race has been won.

I looked at her. 'Have you seen this?' I asked her.

She laughed. 'My dear man,' she said, 'I drew it up myself. Are you satisfied? Here, give it to me. I will sign it.'

I re-read it and, finding no fault with it, I passed it over to her and she signed it. I witnessed her signature and handed the paper to George.

He shook his head. 'You keep it,' he said, 'it will be safer with you.'

She looked at him with her jeering smile. 'Run away, George. I want to talk to Mr. Arden for a few minutes.'

When he had left us she lit a cigarette and stood up. There was no doubt she was very beautiful. 'You must think my behaviour is very odd,' she said.

'The whole thing is so utterly preposterous that I would rather not discuss it,' I said tartly.

'George is afraid, isn't he?' she said. 'No one but you and I know that. He's horribly scared. I've been watching him for several weeks now. The last time he raced he was nearly killed because he lost his nerve. I don't think he'll win this race, do you?'

I faced her. 'Are you telling me that you think he will be killed?'

She shrugged. 'I didn't say that. I said I didn't think he would win.'

'Does he mean anything to you?'

Her eyes flashed. 'Why do you ask that? Has he been talking?'

'If he does mean anything to you, why don't you let him have the money and tell him you don't want him to race?'

'Are you mad?' She burst out laughing. 'Think of the thrill I'm going to have. I'm gambling with a million dollars. I shall watch every yard of the race. Think of George, scared stiff, knowing that if he doesn't win, hundreds of his little suckers will be ruined. Suppose others get ahead of him. Think how he will feel then. Suppose he finds he just can't win, then his only chance is to kill himself. By God! What a sensation! Will he value his little suckers more than his life?' Her eyes looked a little mad. 'I don't care what it costs me, I wouldn't miss this race for anything in the world.'

I went to the door. 'Your attitude is incredible,' I said. 'I don't think we have anything further to say to each other. Good night.'

She ran over to me. 'Wait,' she said. 'You write novels, don't you? What a wonderful story this will make for you. It only wants that little twist that all good stories have. Just wait for that.' She laughed in my face. 'Oh, it's such a lovely little twist. You'll be so very thrilled when you know about it.'

I went out of the room and left her there. I was sure that she was a little insane, and the thought of George getting himself involved with such a woman made me sick at heart.

The race was due to start at eleven o'clock. George and I went off early together. We left the house quietly without saying good-bye to Myra.

George said that he didn't want to see her until the race was over. He looked very ill as he sat at the wheel of the Bugatti, and he drove at a steady twenty-five miles an hour the whole way to the aerodrome. It took us a very short while to reach the Florida course, where the race was being held. He asked me to come to the pits just before the race was to start. 'I'd like to have your good wishes,' he said.

I hung about watching the bustle and activity that inevitably precedes a big race. I watched the vast crowd slowly arriving. I thought I saw Myra and her party arrive and take seats in the grandstand, but I wasn't sure. I had made up my mind to watch the race from the pits.

Finally, a mechanic came running towards me and I went to meet him. 'Mr. Hemingway is about ready now, sir,' he said.

I saw he was looking worried. And as we walked towards the pits, where I could see about two dozen cars lining up, I asked him what he thought of George's chances.

'He's got a load on, sir,' the mechanic said, shaking his head. 'No guy can drive if he's plastered.'

I quickened my pace. George was already sitting in his car. His reputation had brought him a stiff handicap, and he was going to be the last off the starting post.

I ran up to him. 'All right George?' I asked.

He nodded. 'Sure, I'm all right. There's nothing on four wheels that's going to catch me today.'

His face was very white and his eyes were glassy. He had certainly been drinking, and he looked completely reckless.

'Don't take chances,' I said, shaking his hand, 'I'll look after things for you. Good luck, old man.'

The noise of the engine made it difficult for us to hear each other. 'Good-bye,' George shouted, 'look after my little investors, won't you?' and at that moment the flag fell and he roared away.

I hurried to the pits and stood near a group of mechanics. They were talking in low voices, but I overheard what they were saying. They all seemed worried about George. 'Nearly a whole bottle of Scotch went down his throat,' one of them said; 'he must be crazy.'

'Yeah, well, look at him now. Look at the speed he's going.'

All eyes were on the small red car as it flashed round the course. George had already overtaken three of his competitors, and as he came into the straight he opened up and with a snarling roar the car shot forward. All the other cars had opened up, but the leading cars were slowing down for the bend. George came on, took the bend at full speed, tore up the bank, and for a moment we thought his wheels had left the track, but with a few feet to spare he was down into the straight again.

There was a terrific burst of cheering as he nosed his way into the first three.

'What do you call that?' a mechanic demanded. 'Do you call that driving?'

'Do you think he'll last?' Myra asked.

I turned abruptly and found her at my elbow. Her eyes were fixed on the red car, and I could see she was quivering with excitement.

I said rather bitterly: 'Don't you think you'll see better if you go to the stand?'

'I want to be with you. I want to see his face if he wins,' she said. 'Look, he's coming round again. He's getting in front. Really, isn't he marvellous? Oh, God! Look, they're trying to squeeze him. They've cornered him! Look, look, if he loses his head . . . he's finished.'

The three cars flashed past us. George was in the middle. The other two were trying to crowd him, but as he didn't fall back they were beginning to lose their nerve. There couldn't have been more than a foot between each car.

I shouted suddenly: 'He'll beat them on the bend. You see, they'll slow down for the bend. Come on, George, come on, for the love of Mike!'

I was right. Suddenly the red car shot clear and whizzed round the bend at a sickening speed. The others fell back and George was in the lead.

I heard Myra scream suddenly: 'Blast him! He's going to win after all.'

George was coming up for the last lap. The noise of the cars and the shouting was deafening. Round he came into the straight. It was like watching a red smudge. I don't know how it happened; no one knew. It was not as if he were taking a corner. It looked as if he knew he had won and then suddenly thrown in his hand. The car swerved right across the track, turned over, bounced in the air like a huge ball and then burst into flames.

Myra screamed and I ran forward. It was no use. Other cars were still thundering past and no one could get across the track. When at last we did get there, it was too late. George had been strapped in, and one look at the blackened, twisted car told me it was useless to stay.

I walked away, feeling sick and too stunned to really realize what had happened.

As I climbed into my car, Myra came up to me. Her eyes were very dark, and her mouth worked rather horribly.

'Give me that paper,' she said.

Because I wanted to get away I took the paper from my wallet and looked at her. 'This isn't the time now to talk about this. I'll come and see you later.'

'Oh no, you won't,' she said. She seemed to be speaking through locked teeth. 'I fooled George and I fooled you. Read what is says. Didn't I promise to pay my husband one million dollars? Well, he wasn't my husband, I can contest that. By the time the court has made a ruling, it will be too late. George's little suckers will be down the drain.'

I said: 'What do you mean? George married you, didn't he?'

'Yes, he married me, but that was all. He didn't lie with me. Oh no! My money was good enough for him, but I wasn't. He thought it was sufficient just to marry me – the fool.'

I stared at her. 'You can't prove that,' I said slowly. 'Surely you are keeping to your agreement?'

'Prove it? It will take years not to prove it. By that time the money will not be needed. Tear up the paper, Mr. Arden.

You know as well as I do that it's useless now. The poor fool killed himself, although he won the race . . . Do you know why? Because he despised himself for marrying me. No man can treat me like that. I warned you, didn't I, about the twist in the tale.' She laughed hysterically. 'Don't you think it's lovely?'

I engaged the gears and drove away, leaving her still laughing.

CONVERSATION PIECE

He was very tall, thin and distinguished-looking. He had a close-clipped moustache, a square jaw and the hair on each side of his head was white.

He sat on a high stool at the 'Roney Plaza' bar, a cigarette between his thin lips and a glass of Scotch-and-soda at his elbow. Every now and then he would glance up and catch his reflection in the bright mirror behind the bar. He would look at himself and adjust the wings of his evening dress-tie with his well-shaped fingers, and once he adjusted the set of his coat.

People kept coming up to the bar, but he ignored them. Sometimes they glanced at him curiously, especially the women, but no one spoke to him. He had been in the bar several times during the week, and the habitués began to wonder who he was.

Manuel, the barman, had tried to discover who he was without success. Not that he wasn't talkative, but that he steered the conversation away from any personal topic.

During a lull, Manuel came down the long bar towards him. He began polishing glasses. 'Not much about tonight,' he said casually.

The tall, thin man agreed. 'Why do you think that is?' he asked.

Manuel shrugged. 'You can't tell these days,' he said; 'there is too much entertainment going on. People get too much amusement. They don't know where to go next.'

'Personally, I find things very dull.'

Manuel looked at him sharply. 'It depends,' he said. 'It depends on what you want. Now, there's a fine show at the "Hot-Spot". You ought to see that. I went last night. Mind you, I've seen a lot of that kind of stuff, but this is the tops. You can have my word for it, you didn't ought to miss it.'

The tall, thin man tapped the ash of his cigarette. 'I've seen it,' he said briefly. 'It's not bad. No, I'd say it's not bad at all.'

Manuel selected another glass. 'That dame with the chest,' he said, rolling his eyes a little. 'You know the one I mean.'

'Did you find her amusing?'

'Amusing?' Manuel paused. 'That ain't quite the word, is it? Amusing? No, I wouldn't call it that. That's the kind of a dame that spoils married life. Comes a trifle flat to get home after seeing a dame like that.'

The tall, thin man winced. He finished up his whisky and ordered another.

Manuel went on: 'When you see a hot number like her, it makes you wonder what sort of a life she leads off the stage. Maybe she's married. She might have a flock of kids. She might sleep with anyone. You don't know, do you?'

'It's a great mistake to enquire into that kind of a person's life. They're making money because the people who pay to see them regard them as something totally unlike themselves. They are the escape valve of the public.'

Manuel nodded. 'Yeah, that's right, but I don't kid myself.' He had to go away to serve two elderly women, and when he got back again he said: 'There's a good fight on tonight. I can let you have a ticket if you fancied it.'

The tall, thin man shook his head. 'Not tonight. I'm waiting for someone. Maybe some other night. I like a good fight.'

'Yeah?' Manuel's face brightened. 'So do I. I like a good fight too. There has been some pretty bum shows recently. Did you see McCoy give up in the sixth?'

'Yes.'

'Why did he do that, do you think?'

'They say he was scared, but it wasn't that. He had something on his mind. It must be tough going into the ring with something bad on your mind. The public don't care. All they want to see is a fight. It doesn't matter how much trouble you've got, you've got to leave it outside. Well, I guess McCoy took it in with him.'

Manuel regarded the tall, thin man thoughtfully. 'You

reckon that's what the trouble was, do you?' he said.

'Of course. It couldn't have been anything else. McCoy isn't yellow. He wasn't getting the breaks.'

Manuel, who didn't miss anything, said: 'You'll pardon me, but are you waiting for a lady?'

The tall, thin man played with his glass, his eyes went frosty. 'Curiosity?' he said.

Manuel put down the glass he was polishing. He jerked his head. 'Some lady's lookin' for someone,' he said. 'I thought maybe it was you.'

The tall, thin man looked over his shoulder. 'You're quite remarkable,' he said, and beckoned to the girl who stood just inside the doorway.

She came across slowly. Manuel watched her, without appearing to. During his stay at the 'Roney Plaza' he had seen so many women that his standard of what was good had become exceedingly high. This girl was interesting. She was interesting in a ripe sort of way. She had a lazy, sensuous walk, and her big blue eyes looked sleepy. Her mouth was wide and very red. She wore a black dress that emphasized her breasts and hips without being tight on her body. Manuel thought she looked like a very beautiful genteel whore.

She said to the tall, thin man, 'Hello, Harry.'

He got off the stool and touched her fingers. There was a tense eager tightening of his face muscles.

'Come and have a drink,' he said. 'Do you like these stools, or would you rather sit at a table?'

She gave her answer by climbing up and perching herself on the stool.

He said, 'You're looking very, very beautiful.'

'Every time we meet you tell me that. Is it for something to say, or do you feel so strongly about it?'

He climbed up on the stool beside her. 'I want to talk to you.'

'Can't I have something to drink? Is it so urgent that I can't be asked what I should like?'

He looked at her, his eyes angry. 'I'm sorry.' He nodded to Manuel, who came down to them, then he said, 'What are you drinking?'

She turned her attention to Manuel. First, she gave him a very bright smile. It was a smile that unsettled Manuel's calm. He felt an urge to reach forward and pull her across the bar towards him. This urge so startled him that he became very confused. He stood looking at her uneasily.

'What shall I drink?' she asked him. 'Something that will set fire to my blood. Suggest something.'

Manuel turned to his bottles. 'I have something for you,' he said. 'You will not be disappointed.'

The tall, thin man she had called Harry said, 'I wish you wouldn't, it doesn't suit you.'

'That's only your opinion,' the girl said. She had very fine hands, slim and white and very beautiful. 'We are starting well tonight. Soon we shall be quarrelling, and then we shall go away from each other. I think I shall like that.'

Harry offered her a cigarette. 'You mustn't talk like that. I don't know what's come over you lately. Have a cigarette. Look, Manuel is bringing you your drink.'

She took the cigarette and smiled very brightly again at Manuel as he put the glass down.

Manuel said, 'You will like it. I have every confidence.'

She said: 'I am sure I will. Look, I'll taste it before I smoke.' She raised her hand to stop Harry from striking a match. When she had tasted the drink, she put it down with a little shudder. 'God!' she said.

Manuel looked at her closely and then looked at Harry. 'You like it?' he asked anxiously.

She said: 'It's like nothing I've ever tasted before. I wouldn't say I liked it, but it's what I want.'

Manuel went away, his face a little sullen. He wasn't sure what she meant.

Harry said softly, 'You've hurt him.'

'Why not? Why shouldn't I hurt someone for a change? You don't mind when I am hurt, why should you bother about a barman?'

He moved uneasily. 'I wish you wouldn't go on like this,' he said. 'Really, it doesn't do any good.'

'Very well, I won't. Let us change the subject. Let us talk about something else. I'll be very good. I promise I won't be difficult any more. There, now I've promised.'

There was a pause, then she went on: 'This morning I was very extravagant. I went out and bought a hat. It cost a lot of money, but I felt that I had to have something new. It made me feel very happy for a few minutes.'

'I'm glad. I wish you'd buy yourself what you want. You know you can have what you want.'

She shook her head. 'No, no, I can't. You think that your money will give me everything I want, but it can't.'

He bit his lips, annoyed at giving her the obvious opening. She went on before he could say anything. 'Your money can't make me Mrs. Harry Garner, can it? By the way, how is Mrs. Harry Garner, and how is your daughter?'

Harry finished up his whisky. 'Didn't we agree not to talk about that side of my life?'. he said, trying to speak gently.

'Oh yes, I know. We agreed not to talk about them, but sometimes I get very curious. You can't blame me, can you? I mean they are so important in your life, aren't they? They are much more important to you than I am, aren't they?'

'You know they're not. Look, we're getting on the wrong topics tonight. Let's go somewhere and have dinner. Perhaps you'd like to see the show at the "Hot-Spot".'

She laughed. 'I'll tell you something. I saw you take the Mrs. Harry Garner there the night before last. I couldn't go after that. It wouldn't be right.'

He clenched his fist. 'You can be very hateful sometimes,' he said, and she could see that for the first time he was really angry.

'No, not hateful. I wouldn't like you to call me that. Not after the nights I've given up to you. You can't say that. It's because it's the truth and it annoys you. Be honest, isn't that right?'

He drew a deep breath. 'All right, it does more that annoy me, it hurts. For God's sake, can't we stop this awful bickering?'

'I'm sorry.' She finished the drink Manuel had given her. 'Tell him to give me another. It's terribly, terribly dangerous stuff, but I don't care.'

Harry signed to Manuel, who smiled. If she wanted another, it must be all right.

They didn't say anything to each other until Manuel had brought the drinks, and then, when he had gone away, Harry said: 'He's a genius for finding new drinks. Will you thank him very nicely when we go?'

She sipped the drink, pulling a little face. 'Yes, I will thank him. I'll be very, very nice to everyone you like, including your wife and your daughter. There, I can't do more than that, can I?'

He felt the evening couldn't go on any longer like this. It was absurd that she should dominate him. He was determined to get things back to normal.

'Listen,' he said, 'are you going to say bitchy things all the evening?'

Her eyes opened a trifle. 'Am I?'

'It's no use going on like this. Tell me. Get if off your mind, then perhaps we can forget about it.'

'Forget about what? Mrs. Harry Garner and Miss Garner? They'd be very difficult to forget.'

'Four months ago you said they didn't matter,' Harry said, determined to keep his temper. 'You said you understood my position and you didn't mind. You didn't mind; I know you didn't. Why this sudden change?'

She didn't like this direct approach. 'Harry, do you think if I fell in love with a woman I should be any happier?'

'No, you can't side-track like that. You don't mean anything by that. You're just gaining time.'

'No, honestly. I've wondered. Women can be so much more understanding.'

Three people came up to the bar and ordered drinks. They stood close to Harry and the girl. One of them was a tall, flat-chested girl with a serious expression on her face. She wore heavy, horn-rim glasses. The other two were middle-aged men.

One of the men said, 'Manuel, you're looking pretty good tonight.'

Manuel pushed a bottle of Canadian Rye across the polished wood. He said: 'Yes , sir, I'm feeling pretty good. You don't look so bad yourself.'

The man turned to the serious-looking girl. 'I like this place. They give you the bottle and let you get tight, fast or slow, just as you feel. There's no waiting to be served.'

The serious-looking girl said: 'That's fine, because I want to get tight very fast tonight.'

Harry said: 'Let's go. I can't talk to you here. Let's go back to the apartment.'

She shook her head. 'No, not tonight. I'm feeling nervy. We should only quarrel. Not tonight.'

He hid his disappointment. 'Well, let's go, anyway. I'll see you home.'

He gave Manuel some money and she smiled at him. 'Your drink's been a big success. Mr. Garner says you're a genius.'

Manuel showed his surprise. He said good night rather stiffly. He felt somehow that she had insulted him.

The two of them walked out into the bustle of the street. He noticed that she was just a little drunk; it gave him hope.

'Let me come back with you,' he said, 'I have a lot to say to you.'

She shook her head. 'Not tonight.' She sounded very final.

He raised his hand to signal a cab.

'No,' she said, 'I'm much too tired. We'll walk.'

THE GENERAL DIES IN BED

It all happened so quickly he hadn't any chance of making plans. They had come to him and offered him three hundred dollars to give Pedro de Babar the heat. Three hundred dollars! They were crazy! Well, he'd got them up to five hundred and there they stuck. When he found they wouldn't give any more, he agreed. He knew once he had given it to de Babar he'd have to get out of Cuba. That didn't worry him. He was sick of Cuba, anyway.

In the afternoon he went up to de Babar's bungalow with the intention of having a look round. It was a nice place, fitting for a General of the Cuban War Department to live in.

The big garden that surrounded the one-storied building flamed with colours. Palm trees bent graceful heads against the blue of the sky. The place was so nice that the boy was violently envious. He would have liked to have been a devastating god with powers to destroy by a wave of his hand.

The heat of the afternoon sun had driven the guards to shelter. The boy could see no one as he made his way cautiously towards the bungalow. So he went on, until he came to a little path leading to the back of the building.

He moved soundlessly, beads of sweat running down his yellow-white skin. He was not frightened for himself, only that he might make some mistake that would prevent him from killing the General. He reached the bungalow and began walking slowly along the wall, glancing into the windows.

That was how it happened. He looked through the window and saw the woman and de Babar on the bed. He couldn't see very much of the woman. She stared up at the dirty white ceiling her eyes very wide. He could see she was chewing her bottom lip, and every now and then she would toss her head from side to side on the pillow. As he stood watching, she suddenly shut her eyes and began to drum on the bed with her heels.

He could only see the back of the General's head and his bull neck, creasing into three great rolls of fat. He could see the sweat running down behind the big fleshy ears, and the slow movement of the gross body.

Without thinking, the boy pulled the blunt-nosed automatic from inside his coat. He did not hesitate. Perhaps such an opportunity would never come his way again. The General was helpless. There was no one to protect him, and he would have to take his chance of getting away.

He hooked his fingers under the window and pushed it up. As it went up, it made a little grating noise. The General heard it. He moved his head languidly and looked over his shoulder.

The boy smiled at him. He thought it was very, very funny to kill the General like this. He wondered if any other man had ever been killed doing what the General was doing. He leant a little way into the room and brought the automatic up.

The General looked at the automatic. He remained very still. The blood congestion of his face gradually faded, leaving the pock-marked flesh a greenish white.

The woman said urgently. 'Go on – go on – why do you stop?'

The General didn't say anything. He couldn't do anything. He just stared with hot intent eyes at the gun. He was in a hell of a jam.

The woman opened her eyes. 'What is it?' she said. Her voice was unsteady, as if she were out of breath. 'What is it?' She looked across at the window.

The boy smiled at her too. The shock of seeing him there with the gun was so great that the blood even went away from her lips. She looked as if she were going to die.

The boy squeezed the trigger gently. He would have liked to delay the shooting longer, because these two did really look very ridiculous, but any moment the guards might come. The gun went off with a sharp crack just as the General began to move away from the woman. The heavy bullet smashed the side of his skull. He flopped on the woman, pinning her flat.

The boy leant further into the room. She had seen him. It wouldn't be safe to leave her. She made no attempt to move. She lay still, the blood from the General's wound running on to her cheek and neck. It was all so horrible for her that she wanted to die. There wasn't much to aim at, but the boy didn't have to fire a third time.

It was a great pity that he had to wait to kill the woman, because the guard, turning out on the first shot, saw him; and although the boy managed to get away, they knew who to look for and it made it very difficult for the boy to get down to the harbour where a boat waited to take him across the Straits.

By nightfall the search had intensified. They had no intentions of letting him get away. He had spent the evening hidden in a back room of an outlying farmhouse. The farmer asked no questions because revolution was constantly rearing its head, and General de Babar had deserved to die.

Under cover of darkness, the boy made his way down to the waterfront. He had still three hours before the boat that was coming for him would get in. The journey was very trying because of the heat and the soldiers who were looking for him. He was fortunate to see the soldiers first, but it meant crouching in dark shadows for a long time, and then running very hard when they went away.

So he was glad to sit down in a little café overlooking the waterfront, near the harbour. He sat at the table, very tense, and tried to control his laboured breathing. Such was his outward calmness, that no one, looking at him now, would believe that not five hours ago he had killed one of Cuba's most important generals and politicians. He looked tired, certainly, and he looked hot and untidy but he managed to control the shivering fear that possessed him, and the furtive feeling that at any moment the soldiers would burst in and shoot him.

A waiter came over to him and asked him what he wanted. The boy, fearing that the waiter might read the hunted look in his eyes, did not look up. He ordered beer.

While he waited for the waiter to bring it, he looked round the dim room. There were only two other people, besides the waiter and the barman, in the room – a sailor and his woman companion.

The sailor was terribly drunk. He was so drunk that he had to hold on to the table very firmly to prevent himself falling to the floor. The woman was talking to him softly and rapidly with a fixed smile on her face. Her big black eyes were hard and suspicious. It was obvious that she was trying to persuade the sailor to spend the night with her.

Watching these two, the boy forgot for a moment that he was a fugitive. He felt a sudden nausea as he watched the woman's desperate attempts to arouse the sailor's interest.

About a year or so ago the boy had gone with a woman. It was curiosity that made him go with her. It was not that he wanted her, but because he wanted to know. He went with her because he was tired of the sniggers and the whispers of the other boys. He was tired of listening and not knowing what it all meant.

The house was dirty, and the room seemed soiled, as if the things that had happened there had seeped into the walls, leaving dark stains. Even the woman wasn't very clean, but he learnt the reason for the sniggers and the whispers, and when it was over and he had got outside, he had been very sick in the street.

The boy was, and would be, fanatically virginal. He loathed the stirring of lust, which he couldn't understand, and over which he had no power of control. He hated any contact with anyone. He wanted to live entirely on his own, his pure, horrible little life. Nothing else mattered to him but money. It was for money that he had killed de Babar. It was for money that he had done so many mean things in his young life. And yet, he never had money. It slid through his fingers like grains of sand, urging him again and again to make more by further mean little deeds.

The waiter brought the beer and put it in front of him. He stood waiting until the boy paid him, then he went back to the bar. The boy drank the beer; he didn't stop drinking until the glass was empty. Then he set the glass down with a little shudder. His face twisted and he hurriedly wiped his mouth with the back of his hand.

A telephone rang sharply, startling the boy, so that he nearly jerked the glass to the floor. The barman reached under the counter and lifted the instrument. He listened for a few seconds, then grunted and hung up.

He leant over the bar and said to the sailor: 'You'd better get outta here. The soldiers are coming this way; they're searching all the bars.'

The boy heard him. He put his hands on the table so that they should not tremble.

The sailor sneered. 'What the hell do I care?' he said. 'I ain't movin'.'

The woman said quickly: 'Come on, honey. Come home with me where the soldiers won't worry you.'

The boy looked at the woman. 'Where the soldiers wouldn't worry him,' he thought. If he went with her, he'd be safe. He shuddered at the thought of being alone with her, but he was more frightened of the soldiers.

The sailor put his head on his arms. 'You go to hell,' he said, and began to snore drunkenly.

The boy pushed back his chair hurriedly and went across to the woman. 'Take me to your place,' he whispered urgently. 'Now – at once.'

The woman stared at him. What she saw didn't give her any confidence. This was just a down-at-heal bum. A kid without any dough. 'Go climb an alp,' she said, 'I'm busy.' And she shook the sailor roughly.

Shivering, the boy pulled out some money. He opened his fist under her eyes and showed her several crumpled bills. 'Don't wait for him – take me.'

The woman looked down at the notes. She forgot the sailor. A fixed smile came to her lips and she got up. 'Sure,' she said, 'you come along with me. For that amount of dough I'll give you a good time. I'm Thérèse. It's a nice name, ain't it?'

The boy was so anxious to get out of the bar that he didn't hear what she said. He said urgently: 'Is it far? Come on, let's get outta here.'

She went with him into the dark, hot night. 'It's behind the Custom shed,' she said. 'Hey, not so fast! Where's the fire?'

The boy went on, moving through the narrow back

streets fast. He didn't look back, although he wanted to, because he was scared that Thérèse would suspect something was wrong and would not give him shelter.

She almost had to run to keep up with him. 'You're a hot one,' she panted, with a giggle. 'I ain't goin' to run away – we'll get there soon enough.'

The boy shuddered, but kept on.

'Look over there,' Thérèse said, as they stepped into a dark square, 'that's my joint – where the stairs go up the side of the house.'

The boy said, 'Lead the way.' His whole body was tense with listening, but he could hear nothing that alarmed him.

They went up the stairs, and Thérèse groped her way into her room and fumbled for some matches. 'Just wait a second, honey,' she said, 'I'll get the lamp goin'. You'll be fallin' over somethin' an' hurtin' yourself.'

The boy felt the bile in his stomach rise. He stood in the darkness with his back to the room, looking down on to the dark square.

The lamp flamed up suddenly and Thérèse adjusted the wick. She walked over to the window and pulled the faded cotton curtain. 'Come on in, handsome,' she said, 'an' shut the door.'

With the light behind him, the boy no longer felt safe. He moved further into the room, and shut the door. He stood looking round uneasily. The unfinished wooden walls were decorated with cheap lithographs, and immediately over the bed was a photogravure sheet of a nude, taken from some magazine. A faded, rather ghastly Chinese screen partially concealed the small bed, and the inevitable Singer sewing-machine stood against the wall.

The boy said, 'Put the lamp out.'

Thérèse threw back her head and laughed at him. 'Don't you wantta see what you're buyin',' she said, 'or are you coy?'

The boy hated her with all his vicious little soul. He said, 'Put out that lamp.'

Thérèse took the hem of her skirt and raised it over her hips. She was naked under the dress. The boy felt the blood surge into his face. He shifted his eyes, feeling revolted and frightened. Thérèse had quite a nice little body, but the proximity of any woman nauseated him.

Thérèse stared at him. 'What's the matter with you,' she

said sharply, letting her skirt fall, 'don't you like me anymore?'

The boy wanted to scream that she was the filthiest thing he'd ever seen, but he stopped himself in time. Outside, the soldiers were looking for him. With Thérèse he was safe for a little while. He must not risk anything.

He said: 'I'm all right. The lamp worries me – that's all.'

Thérèse held out her hand. 'It's cash, honey. That's the way I run my business.'

The boy hated parting with the money. He hated parting with his money almost as much as he hated being shut in with this whore. The money was buying him safety and he pushed the crumpled bills across the table. Thérèse scooped them up and shoved them down the top of her stocking.

'There,' she said, 'now you can have the lamp out.' She leant forward and blew sharply down the glass funnel. As she leant forward, her breasts swung against the thin cotton of her dress. The boy stepped back. He thought, 'In another minute she will be coming to me.' He blundered across the room to the window and drew the curtain aside.

Thérèse said: 'What's up with you, honey? Don't you feel well?'

The boy didn't hear her. He was looking on to the dark square. Three soldiers were standing in the shadows. Now and then one of them moved, and the moonlight glinted on a naked bayonet. He hastily dropped the curtain and stepped back. His hot hands touched Thérèse's bare arm, and he jerked away.

'Come on, honey,' Thérèse said, 'let's get it over. I got to get out again tonight.'

The boy stepped away from her voice, collided with the screen and abruptly sat on the bed. Before he could rise, Thérèse put her arms round him and drew him down. His hand touched the soft inner part of her thigh, and he stiffened with the horror of it.

She said, 'I bet you ain't had a woman before.' She said it quite kindly.

'Don't touch me,' the boy almost whimpered; 'get away from me.'

Thérèse put her hand down on him. 'Don't be screwy. You got nothin' to be scared of.'

Under her touch, a long-forgotten lust stirred in

him. The quickening of his blood terrified him, and he threw her away from him so violently that she rolled on to the floor. He sat up in the dark. His shirt was plastered against his thin chest, and his eyes glared into the suffocating darkness.

For a moment there was a thick silence in the room, then she said, 'All right, John, if that's the way you want it.'

He swung his legs to the floor. 'That's not my name,' he said unevenly.

He heard her get to her feet and grope over to the table. 'I don't care a – what your name is, John. You're gettin' out of here quick.'

She struck a match and relit the lamp. She was quite naked, except for her shoes and stockings. The crumpled bills he had given her made a disfiguring lump in her leg. She adjusted the wick carefully and then turned. The boy saw she was furiously angry and he suddenly felt frightened of her. She mustn't turn him out now. He would run into those soldiers, waiting outside for him.

He said hurriedly: 'Don't get mad. I don't want it that way, see?'

She came and put her arms on the top of the bed rail. Her heavy breasts swung away from her olive-skinned body. 'What way do you want it, John?' she said. She looked like the great grandmother of all the whores in Cuba.

'Can't a guy feel lonely and talk to a dame?' he said, not looking at her. If she knew he was scared she would play hell with him.

Thérèse said, 'You came here to talk?'

'Sure, can't a guy pay you to talk to him?'

This got Thérèse. She ran her fingers through her thick, black hair. 'I guess you're screwy,' she said at last. 'We ain't got anythin' to talk to each other about. You better get outta here.'

The boy slid off the bed and wandered to the window again. Maybe the soldiers had gone. He lifted the curtain a trifle and peered into the street. The shadowy silhouettes were still there. He straightened and backed away from the window. Thérèse watched him curiously. 'What's wrong?' she said. 'Why do you keep lookin' out of the window?'

The boy stood by the table. The ray of the lamp lit his

white, pinched face. Thérèse could see a faint tick in his cheek.

'Aw, come on,' she said, 'you're just a kid. I'll show you a good time.'

The boy shook his head.

Her patience snapped. 'Listen, John,' she said, 'if you don't want it – get out. I've got a livin' to make. You can't come in here usin' up my time like this.'

'My dough's all right, ain't it?' the boy said, squeezing up a little spark of vicious anger. 'It pays for me to stay here, don't it?'

Thérèse pulled on her dress and smoothed it over her big soft hips. 'That dough's about used up. What do you expect – an all night run?'

Someone rapped on the door. The boy slid across to Thérèse. He put one slender hand on her arm and his grip nearly made her cry out. His dead black eyes frightened her. 'I'm not to be found here,' he said in her ear. 'Look, I've got a gun.' He showed her the heavy Luger. 'You'll go with me.'

Thérèse was scared. She knew she had got herself mixed up in politics, and her mouth went suddenly dry. She said, 'Get under the bed.'

The boy dropped on his hands and knees. He slid out of her sight. The knock sounded again on the door. She walked over and jerked it open.

The soldier looked at her with interest.

She flashed him a smile. 'Why, honey, you just caught me. I was on my way.'

The soldier shifted uneasily. He was a family man and whores scared him. 'You got a man in here?'

Thérèse shook her head. 'Come on in. You got a little present for me?'

The soldier spat on the floor. 'I ain't wastin' dough on a whore like you,' he snarled. 'What were you doin' foolin' with the curtain?'

She laughed. 'Don't get sore, honey. I saw you boys out there an' I thought you wanted some fun. Come on in.'

The soldier pushed past her and walked into the room. Thérèse felt her heart fluttering against her ribs. She knew that if the boy was found she'd have a bad time. She closed the door and went over to the soldier, who was looking round suspiciously. She put her arms round him. 'Put your big gun down,' she said; 'gimme a little somethin'. I'll give you a good time.'

The soldier shoved her away angrily. 'You better stay in tonight,' he said gruffly. 'We're lookin' for the guy who killed General de Babar. The streets ain't goin' to be too healthy.'

The boy, lying flat under the bed, could see the soldier's thick boots as he stepped to the door. He saw them hesitate, turn and come back. He saw them stand before Thérèse's shoddy mules. Then he heard Thérèse catch her breath. She said: 'No, you don't. You gotta give me somethin' first. Stop it, damn you! No, you can't get away with this. You gotta give me somethin'.'

The thick boots pushed the shoddy mules across the room until they stopped against the wall. 'You lousy, rotten bastard!' he heard her say.

The boy didn't watch any more. He wanted to be sick.

Later, the soldier said: 'If I catch anything after this, I'll come back with a bullet for you.'

The boy heard him go out and slam the door. He crawled out from under the bed. Thérèse had gone into the little bathroom and had shut the door. He heard her running water.

When she came back, her face was wooden, but her eyes smouldered. The boy stood silently watching her. She was suddenly conscious of the heavy gun in his hand. She took one look at his set face, and she knew he was trying to make up his mind if he should kill her.

She said sharply: 'Don't look like that. It won't get you anywhere.'

The boy had decided she was right, and he put the Luger in his hip pocket. He sat on the edge of the bed and rubbed his eyes. Terror had exhausted him.

Thérèse sat down beside him. 'De Babar killed my husband,' she said. 'I hate the whole goddam bunch of them. I'm glad you killed him. That lousy sonofabitch wanted killing.'

'I didn't kill him,' the boy said tonelessly.

Thérèse went on, as if he hadn't spoken. 'If they get you, it's going' to be tough. What are you goin' to do?'

'I didn't kill him, I tell you,' the boy said savagely.

'You don't have to be scared of me,' Thérèse said,

patiently. 'I'm glad you killed him. I'll get you out of here.'

The boy looked at her suspiciously. Her big eyes were quite tender. He wanted very much to smash his fist in her face. He got to his feet and walked away from her. His fury at being trapped like this made him physically sick. Her sudden sentiment sickened him.

She saw his uncertain look, and she misread it. 'Aw, hell, you're only a kid,' she said. 'Don't you worry. I'll fix it for you.'

It took a great effort to control his voice. He said, 'How?'

She got off the bed. 'I'll show you. Stand in front of the lamp; I want to look into the street.'

Unwillingly, because she had told him to do something, and he felt that no woman should tell him to do anything, he moved so that his back completely shadowed the lamp.

He watched her cautiously pull aside the curtain and glance into the dark square. Then she turned her head and nodded. 'They've gone,' she said; 'now I'll show you.'

She went over to a battered chest of drawers and pulled out a black, cotton dress. She threw it on the bed. A brassière and a pair of knickers followed. She went on her hands and knees and hunted in the chest of drawers. The boy, standing watching, could only see her broad hips as her head disappeared out of sight. He shifted his eyes uneasily.

At last she found what she was looking for and she climbed to her feet, in her hand she held a pair of shoes.

She nodded at the clothes. 'Get into them,' she said, 'you're about my size. Then we'll go out together. It'll be easy.'

The boy couldn't believe his ears. He stood glaring at her. The rage boiled up in his guts.

'Do hurry,' she urged. 'Can't you see it's the only way out for you?'

'You asking me to put those things on?'

Thérèse could hear the cold hate in his voice. For a moment he scared her, then she forced a little laugh. 'Now don't get mad,' she said, 'these soldiers ain't looking for a girl. You'll be able to get away easily. Can't you see that?'

The boy knew she was right. But the thought of putting those things on struck at his little manhood. He told himself that he'd rather be found and killed than put them on. But when Thérèse started pulling off his coat, he just stood frozen and let her.

'Come on,' she said impatiently, 'don't stand there like a dummy. Help yourself. Get your pants off, don't mind me. I've seen all you've got, an' it don't worry me any.'

As if in some repulsive nightmare, the boy stripped. He stood on the coconut matting, thin, a little dirty, and shuddering.

Thérèse looked him over with a kindly, mocking smile. 'You ain't much of a picture are you?' she said, lightly. 'I guess you want buildin' up.'

The boy told himself that when all this was over he'd come back and kill her. Right now he couldn't do anything. He had just to suffer his humiliation.

Thérèse pushed him on to the bed and tossed the knickers in his lap. 'Get 'em on,' she said, 'then I'll fix your front up.'

The feel of the silk against his bony thighs broke the last shred of his self-control. He sat there, his fists on his knees, and his eyes wild, swearing softly through his full lips. Even Thérèse was shocked at the things he said.

'If you don't shut that foul little trap of yours,' she snapped at last, 'I'll toss you out of here as you are.'

The boy stopped swearing and looked at her. She felt a little shiver run through her as she met his vicious hating look. She knew then that he was bad – that he would always be bad. But he had shot de Babar, and that was enough for her to help him.

She put the brassière on him and padded it out with two small towels. He stood there, looking horrible. Thérèse felt an insane urge to laugh at him, but she knew he would do something to her if she did. Her hands snatched the dress from the bed and pulled it roughly over his head; then she stepped back to see the effect. She thought he looked like a lost soul out of hell.

'Try those shoes on,' she said.

He stooped awkwardly and fitted his feet into the high-heel shoes. Although they fitted him, he couldn't walk in them. She had to hunt again under the chest of drawers and find him a pair of sandals. A big, wide brim hat completed the picture. In the dark he'd pass anywhere. She nodded her approval. 'You'll do,' she said. 'You don't have to worry your head no more.'

She wrapped his suit in a gaily coloured shawl and made

a bundle of it. 'Now,' she said, 'we'll get goin'. Where are you headin' for?'

All the time she had been putting his things together the boy had just stood and watched her. All the time she had been supervising his dressing, he had said nothing. When at last he did speak, his voice was so harsh and brittle that it quite startled her. 'You ain't coming with me,' he said. 'I'm goin' alone.'

She shrugged, suddenly feeling tired of him. She had risked a lot, and she knew every second he stayed with her the risk increased.

'Then go,' she said. 'I guess you're big enough to take care of yourself.'

He shuffled to the door, hating her for putting him in this position. He no longer had any confidence in himself. To be dressed like this took from him his sense of manhood. Somehow the clothes made him feel helpless, and the thought of the darkness outside terrified him.

Thérèse watched him go. He had no word of thanks for her. He didn't even look at her again. With his hand on the rail to guide him he edged carefully down the wooden stairs, his knees shaking as the sandals threatened to pitch him forward.

The moon hid behind cloud and he could see nothing. When he reached the bottom of the stairs he had to wait until his eyes grew accustomed to the darkness. Then, when he could just make out the roof-tops against the sky, he moved slowly away from the house.

He had not gone far before he ran into a group of soldiers who had been watching him approach. They had been out in the darkness a long time and they could see, whereas he was still nearly blind.

It was only when they crowded round him that he realized that he was trapped. He stood very still, terror completely paralysing him.

In the darkness, the soldiers took him for some unprotected girl, and anxious to relieve their boredom, began to quarrel amongst themselves. He had to stand helpless, while they drew lots for him.

It would have been unfortunate if he had been a girl. But when they discovered his identity there was a long pause of terror while they persuaded the soldier who had dragged him away from the rest of them not to kill him immediately with his bayonet. They pointed out, reasonably enough, that there was at least one subtle thing to do to him before they finally finished with him.

THE MAGNIFICENT OPPORTUNITY

The Mexican General, Cortez, and two officers of his staff sat at a big table covered with maps and papers. The two officers sat very still and upright, their eyes fixed in a blank stare at the map which the General was examining. They had already reached a decision, and the tight tenseness of their muscles indicated their impatience for the General to speak.

The sentry, posted at the open door, watched the little group at the table with bored eyes. Those three had been sitting round the table for four hours, whispering together, and now for the past half-hour they hadn't even spoken. A fine way to win a revolution, the sentry thought, and spat contemptuously into the courtyard.

Holtz, the younger of the staff officers, shifted suddenly in his chair. His companion, Mendetta, looked at him with a scowl, moving his head warningly, but Holtz's movement had already distracted the General, who pushed back his chair and stood up.

The sentry pulled his long, slack body away from the doorway, and his eyes looked a little less bored. Perhaps something was going to happen at last, he thought hopefully.

Cortez walked away from the table and paced the length of the room. His big fleshy face was heavy with thought. He said abruptly, 'The situation is bad.'

The two officers relaxed a trifle. They had arrived at that decision more than a half an hour ago.

Holtz said: 'Your Excellency is right. It is very bad.'

The General looked at him sourly. 'How bad?' he demanded, coming back to the table. 'Show me here.' He put a thick finger on the map. 'How bad?'

Holtz leant forward. 'This is how I see it,' he said. 'The enemy are in considerable strength. They are well mounted and they have artillery. If we attempted to make a stand here we could be surrounded. We are outnumbered by four to one and our men are tired. They are even disheartened. We have been retreating for the last two weeks.' He tapped the map. 'Against artillery we could not hold this position long, then it would be too late to fall back. I think we should withdraw immediately.'

The General ran his fingers through his close-cropped iron-grey hair. 'And you?' he said, looking at Mendetta.

'We would have to leave the gun,' Mendetta said slowly, knowing that he had touched the point on which the whole situation hinged. 'We should not have time to get the gun up the mountain-path to the hills. The enemy are hardly three hours' ride from here. If we retreated now, the gun would have to be abandoned.'

Cortez smiled. 'The gun goes with us. Make no mistake about that. We have taken that gun from the enemy and we have dragged it for three hundred miles. We will not abandon it now.'

The two officers glanced at each other and shrugged. It was to be expected. They had anticipated that, sooner or later, the accursed gun would endanger the safety of the tattered, retreating army. It was not as if they had any shells. The gun was useless. It was, however, a symbol of the only victory General Cortez had scored against the enemy in a lightning raid, and under no circumstances was he parting with such a symbol. If he was driven back over the mountains, he was determined that the gun should go with him.

Holtz said, 'Your Excellency has no doubt made his plans?'

There was no longer a bond of sympathy between the two officers and the General. Let the old fool get out of this if he could. They had no wish to endanger their lives for the sake of a captured, useless gun. They were young enough to accept defeat, knowing that they could win perhaps fresh glory another day, but Cortez was getting old. His time was nearly past.

The General felt their antagonism. He knew they would willingly leave the gun to save their skins, but as long as he was in command they would do as he said. He knew them well enough for that. They might think he was a crazy old fool, they might even grumble, but if he told them the gun was to go, they would obey.

He sat down at the table again. 'One of you will take four men and hold up the enemy's advance. You can have the Lewis gun and four rifles. With the Lewis gun you should be able to hold them back long enough to let the remaining troops get clear. Do you understand?'

The two officers sat there stupefied. He was asking one of them to sacrifice himself for the gun. Not only that, but he was throwing away the only Lewis gun they had ever possessed. A gun of the utmost value because they had a large quantity of ammunition to go with it. All for a stupid, rusty, useless field-gun, the symbol of his only victory.

Mendetta said: 'The enemy can certainly be delayed, Your Excellency, but eventually they must break through. It will then be too late to retreat. The loss of the Lewis gun will be serious.'

Cortez shook his head. 'Once we are across the mountains, Pablo will not follow us. The fighting will be over. We shall no longer require the Lewis gun. It will have served its purpose. We shall have to re-equip the whole of the army before launching a new offensive.'

There was a long silence. Neither of the two officers wanted to speak. They waited for Cortez to tell them who was to go. Cortez waved his hand. 'Time presses. The officer who undertakes this operation may not be able to retreat. It is a dangerous, but, at the same time, a glorious opportunity. It would not do for me to choose which of you shall do this. I have great faith in you both. Will you gentlemen kindly withdraw and decide between yourselves who is to go?' I shall expect your decision in ten minutes.'

Mendetta got to his feet, saluted and walked out of the room, followed by Holtz. The bright hot sunlight nearly blinded them as they stepped into the courtyard, and without a word they walked stiffly to the small out-house that served as their quarters.

'He is crazy, the mad senile fool,' Mendetta burst out, as he shut the door behind them. 'He is throwing away the lives of four men and an officer, as well as the Lewis, to save his unprintable vanity.'

Holtz lit a cigarette with a hand that shook a little. He was tall, very dark and handsome. Although he was only twenty-six, he looked a lot older. In spite of the heavy going of the past two weeks, he was smart and his white uniform very neat and clean. A heavy gold chain encircled his brown wrist, and on the second finger of his right hand he wore a curiously fashioned green jade ring. He looked at Mendetta, who was six years his senior. 'We haven't long,' he said. 'I suppose you will take on this operation?' There was a little mocking smile on his lips that infuriated Mendetta.

'I am married and I have two children,' Mendetta said. Sweat came out in little glistening beads on his forehead. 'I thought that you—' He paused and looked away.

'I see,' Holtz said slowly. 'Will your wife miss you so much?'

'It would kill her if anything happened to me,' Mendetta said. He had not seen his wife for three years, but he was very fond of life, and he felt this was the only card that he could play honourably. 'If it were not for my family,' he went on, drawing himself up, 'I would seize this chance. It is a magnificent stroke for the revolution.'

Holtz said, 'I am married too.' This was not strictly accurate, but he couldn't let Mendetta off so easily.

Mendetta went very pale. 'I didn't know that,' he said. 'You never said.'

Holtz got to his feet. 'We have two minutes,' he said. 'Shall we cut cards?'

Mendetta became very agitated, and although he opened and shut his mouth several times he could not speak.

Holtz took a soiled pack of cards from a drawer and tossed them on the table. 'Lowest card has the magnificent opportunity,' he said, and flipped a card from the pack. It fell face upwards. It was the four of spades.

'Not very difficult to beat,' he said, shrugging. 'Come, Mendetta, the General is waiting.' He went to the door and stood with his back to the table.

Mendetta pulled a card from the pack. His hand shook so that the pack became scattered. He looked with horror at the two of diamonds he had drawn. Snatching up another card, he found the six of spades and ran with trembling legs over to Holtz. 'The six of spades,' he managed to gasp.

Holtz looked at him, the mocking smile again on his lips. 'How fortunate you are. To be lucky with cards and to be lucky in love.'

Mendetta saw that Holtz knew he had cheated, and he went white with shame.

Holtz said: 'The General may wish to see you as well. Let us see him together.'

Cortez was waiting for them impatiently. 'Well?' he snapped.

Holtz saluted stiffly. 'I am ready to take your orders, Your Excellency,' he said.

Cortez nodded. He was pleased. Holtz was young. He had a stronger nerve than Mendetta, and, what was more important, he was proud. He would not fall back.

Cortez looked across at Mendetta. 'Make immediate preparations for the withdrawal. Do not forget, the gun goes first. Have everything ready to leave within the hour. You have no time to lose.'

Mendetta saluted and stepped to the door. He looked back at Holtz, then said, 'My best wishes, Lieutenant. May we meet again.'

Holtz bowed. 'Remember me to your wife, Mendetta, remember me to your children,' he said. 'You fortunate man.'

Mendetta went out of the room and shut the door behind him.

The General looked at Holtz searchingly. 'I did not know he had any children,' he said, pulling a map towards him.

Holtz came close to the table. 'They are always convenient,' he said with a little grimace. 'What are my orders, Your Excellency?'

The General looked at him sharply. He didn't like bitterness and he could not understand sarcasm. With an effort of will, he drew his attention to the matter in hand. 'This place can be held with courage,' he said. 'You will have four men. I cannot spare more. Choose whom you like. I take it you will handle the Lewis gun yourself? The enemy are unlikely to use their artillery, once they have ascertained that this place is held only by a few. Shells are costly. You are to delay them as long as possible. As long as you are alive, they cannot pass. You are not to expose yourself, and you are to be very careful not to waste ammunition. I will leave the details to you. Is there anything you do not understand?'

Holtz shook his head. 'You have made it very simple, Your Excellency. How long am I to keep up the resistance?'

'I want at least twelve hours to get to the mountain road. Once I have got beyond the pass I do not think Pablo will follow any further; it would be too dangerous. We leave immediately. Pablo may not attack. In which case you will withdraw after twelve hours have elapsed from the time we leave. If he should attack, then you must hold him off until . . .' he glanced at the small clock on his desk, 'four o'clock tomorrow.'

Holtz nodded. 'I understand perfectly. If you will excuse me, I will make my preparations and choose my men.'

The General waved his hand. 'I shall see you before I go,' he said. 'Make your preparations with all speed.'

Outside in the courtyard there was tremendous activity. Horses were being saddled. Packs slung. Men, running to and fro, shouted orders excitedly. In the centre of the commotion stood the big, rusty field-gun. Men were already fastening thick ropes to it, and even as Holtz approached, the gun began to move slowly down the uneven road towards the distant hills.

He stood for a moment watching it go. Then he turned with a shrug of his shoulders. Time was pressing. He knew the four men he was going to choose. He knew they were reliable, although, of course, they had no wish to throw their lives away. Still, as long as he was with them, they would see it through. He was sure of that.

He caught sight of Sergeant Castra, who was walking towards him. 'Sergeant,' he called. 'Here, I want you.'

Castra increased his pace. He was a tall, thick-set man, with hard eyes and a firm determined jaw. He had been in the service for a long time, and Holtz knew him to be a soldier in every sense of the word.

'I want Golz, Dedos, Fernando and you to remain behind. We are to hold this position until the army has had time to withdraw. Will you get the other men?'

Castra saluted. 'Yes, Lieutenant,' he said, 'at once.'

Holtz watched him hurry away and nodded, satisfied. Castra had shown no surprise, no disappointment. He had accepted the order without question. It was a good beginning.

A few minutes later the four men came hurrying up. They stood before Holtz, their eyes apprehensive. Castra was the only one who looked unmoved.

Without wasting time, Holtz told them what was expected of them. 'The enemy may not attack,' he concluded. 'If they don't, then we shall have won distinction easily; if they do, we shall hold this position to the last man. There can be no retreat, do you understand that? I have chosen you four because of your records, but if there is any man among you who wishes to step down, he can do so. I do not want half-hearted support. There is a small chance of withdrawing as we shall have the Lewis gun, but if you feel about the revolution as I think, then you will not hesitate to do your duty.'

He felt suddenly ashamed when he had spoken, because he knew it was only his pride that made him stay. It was no blow struck for the revolution. Rather it was for the pride of the General. The whole situation really turned on pride, and he felt a hypocrite talking such drivel to these men.

It had the required effect, however. The four men stiffened and did not move.

'Very well,' Holtz said, 'let us prepare. Take your men and get the Lewis gun. Get all the ammunition and report back to me here.'

When they had gone away, he stood watching the army move off. It was quite remarkable, he thought, how quickly they had prepared for the withdrawal. He felt them looking at him as they marched off in ragged lines. He felt their looks of sympathy mixed with derision, and he drew himself to his full height, feeling just for the moment a surge of emotion that comes to a man at this time.

The General came out and Holtz walked over to him. Cortez returned his salute and then abruptly held out his hand. 'I'm sorry, Holtz,' he said in a heavy voice; 'you will be decorated for this. I am certain that you will not fail me, so certain, that I will not add to what I have already said. Should anything happen to you, can I write to anyone for you?'

Holtz thanked him. The lines round his mouth hardened and he took from his breast pocket an envelope. 'Your Excellency is very considerate,' he said. 'If I should be killed, and not before, it would be a great kindness if you would have this letter delivered.'

The General took the letter. 'I will take it myself,' he said; 'that is the least I can do.' He glanced at the address. 'Señorita Nina Howard. She is *Inglès*? Your friend?' He looked hard at the Lieutenant.

Holtz nodded. 'Yes, Your Excellency, my very dear

friend.' He spoke very slowly, and the General was startled at the emotion that shook his voice. 'If you should see her – perhaps you could say that . . . that I was doing my duty . . . I think it would please her.'

The General put the letter in his pocket. 'Of course, of course,' he said, suddenly impatient to be off. 'You can rely on it. I will tell her you died a brave man. You did your duty and you saved the gun. There, that should please her.'

Holtz took a step forward and put his hand on the General's arm. 'Not the gun,' he said earnestly, 'don't tell her about the gun. You see, she would not understand. She values me more than a gun. Just tell her I was doing my duty. That will be enough.'

The General suddenly flushed. He nodded abruptly and rode away. He did not look back.

The courtyard was nearly empty now. Holtz felt lonely. He walked slowly across to where Mendetta was waiting for the last of the men to march out. Mendetta saw him coming and scowled. He did not relish any further sarcasm from Holtz.

Holtz, however, came up to him and held out his hand. 'Good-bye,' he said quietly, 'I'm afraid you're going to have a very hard time getting the gun over the hills. I would rather be here than work so hard.' He gave a little laugh. 'It would be a fine thing if you let the goddamned thing fall over the pass, wouldn't it? I mean after all the fuss that has been made about it.'

Mendetta looked at him suspiciously. 'That won't happen, you can rely on me not to do that. It would be a bad thing after sacrificing so much.'

Holtz kicked a stone. 'I'm afraid I hurt his Excellency's feelings just now,' he said. 'Never mind, he is not likely to worry me much longer, is he?'

Mendetta saw the last man walk through the gate and he gathered up his reins with relief. 'Good-bye,' he said, 'you will come through all right. I am sure of it.'

'Good-bye,' Holtz said; 'you must hurry.'

Mendetta rode after the army and Holtz turned to look for his men. They were waiting for him in the shade of the farmhouse. The Lewis gun and a large wooden box stood near by.

Holtz went over to them. 'We will fortify the house,' he said. 'No one can pass so long as the Lewis gun can fire.

Have it taken to the top room, and board up the windows. I will leave it to you. It is where we will make our stand. Take water and food there. You know what to do. Leave Dedos with me, and take the others.' He turned to Dedos, who was very young, but his thin cruel mouth, and hard flat eyes, flat like those of a snake, made him look a lot older than he was. 'You understand dynamite?'

Dedos nodded. 'Yes, Lieutenant,' he said, 'I understand it very well.'

'Over there is dynamite; fetch it. You will find also an exploder and some caps. Bring a spade too.'

Dedos went over to the farmhouse and came back soon with a big sack on his back and a spade in his hand. Holtz took the spade from him. 'Come with me,' he said.

They walked a short distance down the rough road, away from the farm and in the opposite direction to the way the army had gone. At two hundred paces, Holtz stopped. 'Here, you will prepare a mine,' he said. 'You must be very careful that it is not seen easily. Use all the dynamite. When you have done this, lay a cable back to the farm. I don't know how much wire you have there, but I think it will reach the farm all right. This you must do very quickly. There is no time to waste. Do you understand?'

Dedos smiled. The idea pleased him. 'Immediately, Lieutenant,' he said.

Holtz hurried back to the farmhouse. Rather to his surprise, he found that he was enjoying this. He felt that, after so many dreary days of retreat, this new activity acted as a tonic to his depression.

Upstairs in the farmhouse, Castra had set up the gun. Fernando was boarding up the remaining window, and Golz was staggering to and fro with buckets of water.

The walls of the farmhouse were thick, and unless Pablo brought his artillery into action they had a very fair chance of holding the place for some hours.

Holtz checked over the stores that the General had left for them. There were sufficient rations for four meals. It was enough. Holtz had no intention of holding the place longer than necessary. Not that he was going to surrender; he made a little face at the thought. Pablo was noted for his cruelty. He would have no mercy on prisoners.

There was a story told about this Pablo. Holtz had heard

it several times. He remembered quite well the first time he heard it. It was while he was spending a few days away from the actual front line preparing for an offensive which proved later to be unsuccessful. He had spent the day inspecting horses, guns and men, and in the evening he was glad to sit by the fire, relaxing his aching limbs. It was Santez, his brother officer, who began talking about Pablo.

'I have studied this man,' Santez said, holding two bony hands towards the fire. 'He interested me. I wanted to know why he is so successful in the field. Why it is that Cortez has tried so often to trap him and has failed each time. So, for some time I made it my business to find out things about him, and although I never succeeded in finding out why he is a better general than Cortez, I heard a little story about him which supports my theory that a General who is feared is more successful than a General who is merely admired.'

Holtz had said, rather impatiently: 'But no one admires Cortez. Are you comparing these two men?'

'No. Cortez is a fool. Comparison is out of the question between them.'

'I have heard it said that Pablo is very cruel,' Holtz said. 'He has done many barbarous things in his time.'

Santez nodded. 'Yes,' he said, 'I will tell you. I have heard it from a good source. It was told me by one of Pablo's men who fell into our hands a few weeks ago. It happened like this. There was an engagement; Pablo's advance was checked by a small band of our troops who had become separated from the main body. Pablo was very annoyed that such a small band could hold up an army as large as his. At the same time, he was determined that he would not lose any more men attacking this band who were on the top of a rocky hill which afforded excellent cover.

'Not very far away there was a colony, and Pablo sent some of his soldiers and brought from this colony a large number of old men, women and children. These he forced to approach the hill with his own men sheltering behind them. Our men, of course, were very unwilling to fire on these innocent people, but as they kept coming closer they had no alternative. It is a bad thing to see women and children fall before a volley of rifle-fire. After the first volley the remaining soldiers refused to fire any more and they stood up and surrendered. The officer in charge begged them to continue the fighting, but the soldiers would not do so. They were not to know that some of these people were their own relations. It was a very difficult situation. So they surrendered, and they were brought before Pablo. There were sixteen of them. They were brave men and they had done their duty. Pablo decided that they should all die. They stood before him in two rows, waiting for him to decide how they were going to die.

'The officer was a very brave man and he stood stiffly to attention, looking at Pablo with scorn in his eyes. Pablo ordered sixteen horses to be brought and each man was tied by the feet to the horse's saddle. Then, at Pablo's command, the horses were ridden across the rough country at a furious pace, dragging these men behind them. It is not a nice death, and it is only one example of Pablo's cruelty. Perhaps the wickedest thing he ever did was when he took a small village and slaughtered everyone. The women had a very bad time. When his men had finished with them, he made them parade naked in the village street, and he flogged them with barbed wire until they died. The children were all thrown into a large fire, where they perished, screaming for their mothers; and the men were buried in the sand, alive, and left to suffocate. That indeed was a black day in Pablo's life.'

Those and other stories Holtz had heard about Pablo. It would not do to surrender, rather to keep a bullet for himself, if the worst came. He wondered if he would have the courage to kill himself if the time came for him to do so; he didn't know. He thought that he would; but until he had to press the cold barrel against his temple he really didn't know. He hoped that he would find the courage, anyway.

His thoughts were interrupted by Sergeant Castra, who came in at that moment. 'The gun is set up, Lieutenant,' he said. 'Shall I post one of the men as sentry?'

Holtz nodded. 'Yes,' he said; 'send Golz. Send him down the road where he can observe for some distance. If he sees the enemy advancing, he is to come back here immediately. See how Dedos is getting on. I left him with the dynamite.'

Castra went away. Holtz felt satisfied with him. He could be relied on to take the responsibilities of preparing for the attack.

Holtz checked over the Lewis gun and then went to the window and peered through the small opening that commanded an uninterrupted view of the road. He could see Dedos kneeling in the dust, his hands busy. Further on, Golz was moving towards the slight crest to take up his posi-ition as sentry.

The sun was very hot and threw sharp black shadows. Overhead there were no clouds. It was an unwarlike day, and looking across the courtyard Holtz felt a sudden pang of nostalgia. How absurd all this was. What a farce. At that moment his white-and-gold uniform meant nothing to him. He wanted, very badly, to see Nina again. He could see her very clearly. Tall, dark and vivacious. Yes, you would say she was vivacious. She had a tremendous spirit of gaiety. He had only seen her sad once, and that was just before he said good-bye to her. Neither of them knew when they would meet again. It was the knowledge of not knowing that was the canker of war. Holtz knew that it was she who must suffer in his absence. The privation of her company and of her love were as nothing to the long days of suspended waiting that she must endure. Long before the news could reach her, he would have passed through his pain, and would have been beyond the reach of anything that could harm him more.

He wondered how long she would remain faithful to his memory. It was absurd to expect her to give up her life in mourning for him. He would not like that, or would he? He didn't know. If he had been like Mendetta, he would not be thinking of her at all. Mendetta had never really loved anyone. He had not a lover's vulnerability. He could go into action caring only for himself. He had no haunting thought that with his death someone else would die a little too. It was an added responsibility, this being in love. Yet he had no regrets. He would not have had it otherwise. When one loved as he loved, the pattern of life was sharp-etched. The lines ran sharply and life for him had intensified. Within him dwelt a rock-like feeling of security. He was sure of something. Yes, that was it. In this world of uncertainty, of revolution, of distrust and violent death, he was sure of one thing. He knew that Nina loved him and that he loved her. It wasn't a passing moment of heady, ecstatic love, but a genuine feeling between them that made them as one. That established an affinity between them, binding them close and giving to their love an understanding that is very rare.

Why had he bothered about this stupid revolution? Why

had he taken sides in such a hopeless, unequal struggle? Perhaps it was that he wanted to justify himself by taking the hardest road. Nina had listened to him talk, night after night. They sat in the cafés or in their big bedroom, talking and discussing the revolution. She could see him gradually moving in his mind towards the moment when he had to rejoin his regiment. They could have slipped away easily enough over the border into America and have left this all behind. But she knew he wouldn't do that. She knew he would be unhappy unless he stood with his General. Not that he thought a great deal of Cortez – he didn't; but he felt that, as an officer, he had no right to shirk his responsibilities, and, finally, he went.

They parted at night. She joined some friends not far from Cortez's headquarters, and he reported to Cortez with the knowledge that no matter how well they fought, Pablo was certain to prove too much for them. It was an uneasy beginning, but that did not matter. He knew that he was doing right by himself.

He had to stop thinking about the past, because Dedos had finished his work and was coming back to the farm. He moved slowly backwards, unwinding the coil of wire as he went. Holtz turned and went down the uneven stairs and crossed the courtyard to meet him.

'The wire reaches so far,' Dedos said, stopping a few feet beyond the farm gate.

Holtz considered that it would do. 'You will have to conceal yourself here,' he said. 'As soon as the enemy passes over the mine in sufficient numbers you are to explode it. Then come back to the farmhouse as quickly as possible.'

Dedos smiled. His thin, cruel little face looked quite animated. 'It is well, Lieutenant,' he said. 'That I will do very well.'

Holtz inspected the mine and found that Dedos had done very well. There was nothing more he could do to better it. He said as much to Dedos, who again smiled. Today had been kind to him.

Holtz helped him connect the wires to the exploder. 'You will wait for my signal,' he said. 'Sit here in the shade. When Golz signals the enemy are approaching, you must take up your position by the exploder. When I blow a blast on my whistle you must explode the mine. Do you understand?'

Dedos nodded. 'It is very simple,' he said, and went to sit down as if he had not a care in the world.

Holtz went back to the room where the Lewis gun was and sat down behind it. He checked over the ammunition belt and rejected three cartridges that he thought might jam, then he lit a cigarette and relaxed. It was always the same in war. Long hours of nothing to do, waiting for orders, or for the enemy, or to go home on leave. That was the sweetest wait of all. He had not seen Nina for three months; it was a long time. His body ached for the moment when he would hold her again in his arms.

Usually, long spells of celibacy did not affect him, but that was before he had known Nina. Now, this privation was hard to bear. Not because his body clamoured for relief; it was not that. Nina was so lovely. Lying with her was an experience that no other woman had ever offered him. It was as if he had been swept up by an angry sea. The roar of the surf pounding in his ears, and he could let himself relax to her without reservation. That was it. He could relax whereas, before, he was always a spectator, nervous of criticism, anxious that he should be a great lover. And it was so hard to bear, this privation, because it might never happen again. It was precious, because he did not know when he would see her again. He did not even know if he would ever see her again.

He glanced at his wrist-watch. Cortez had been gone an hour. Eleven more hours to wait, and then he could go too. Suppose Pablo didn't attack? Suppose, after all, he could get away from this farm and follow Cortez into safety over the hill. If that happened, he would not risk another day like this. He would go immediately to Nina and together they would slip across the border and forget all about the revolution. They would live, then, for themselves. Hadn't he done enough for the revolution? One man couldn't make it a success. No matter how hard he fought, it wasn't enough. No, he would go with Nina and forget about it for ever.

Golz on the crest of the hill, was standing very still with his back turned to the farm. Holtz watched him idly. Then his heart gave a sudden lurch as Golz spun on his heel and began to run towards the farm. Holtz could see the dust spurting up under his feet as he came. He beat the air with one hand and held his rifle a little away from his body with the other.

Holtz knew what it meant. He felt a cold sweat break out under his arms and his mouth went very dry. He sat by the gun, holding the shaped firing lever tightly. Golz pounded past Dedos, and Holtz heard him shout something to him as he passed. Dedos scrambled to his feet and ran over to the box-exploder. Holtz could see the flash of his teeth as he grinned delightedly. He didn't care about Pablo. He had no fear. Perhaps, when he was killed, he had no one who would die a little because of his death.

Golz had reached the farm, and Holtz could hear him speaking to Castra. The sergeant came upstairs. His face was immovable as he saluted stiffly. 'A body of horsemen are approaching,' he said. 'They are some way off. Am I to go forward and ascertain their strength?'

Holtz nodded. 'Report to me immediately,' he said. He hoped Castra hadn't seen fear in his face. 'Be careful that they do not see you.'

It was an absurd thing to have said, but he wanted to show Castra that he was intent on the operation, instead of wishing that he was miles away from it.

Castra came back after several minutes. 'It is a patrol,' he said; 'about fifteen men. There is no sign of the main body of the army.'

Holtz got to his feet. This was unexpected. He had laid a big mine, expecting the whole of Pablo's army. How long it would be before Pablo arrived on the scene he couldn't guess, but it was useless to use the mine on a mere handful of men. He told Castra to recall Dedos. 'The Lewis gun will be enough for them. Take your rifles and cover the road as well. When they come within range, I will do what I can to wipe them all out, and then you can finish the rest by rifle-fire.'

He watched Castra place his men under cover. Dedos had taken his rifle and had gone behind a large iron barrel which had been used to store gasoline. Holtz could see him quite clearly. There was a heavy, savage frown on his face, and Holtz guessed he was very disappointed that he was not to fire the mine.

Holtz laid the Lewis gun's sights directly on the middle of the road. He hoped the approaching patrol would be massed together. He mustn't take any chances. He knew that he might have Pablo's main army to deal with very shortly. The patrol would have to be wiped out immediately and no one to escape to warn Pablo.

It seemed a long time before the horsemen suddenly appeared over the crest of the hill. They came down the road in two files. They seemed in no hurry and they sat their horses easily. Their rifles were across their backs, and they seemed to be quite unaware that they might run into an ambush at any moment.

Holtz adjusted the sight of the gun. Two long bursts ought to do it, he thought. He was aware that his heart was bounding and fluttering against his ribs. He was holding the firing lever so tightly that his hands ached. He would wait until they were within twenty feet of the mine. It wouldn't do for them to disturb Dedos' work. He could see them quite plainly now. They were all very young looking, hard and cruel. One of them was singing in a mournful way as he jogged along. The horses looked as if they had come far. Their black hides glistened with sweat and they kept tossing their heads impatiently. They were good horses, and Holtz automatically shifted the sights of the gun a little higher. He loved horses and it meant more to him to kill a horse than it did to kill one of Pablo's men.

Another four paces. His hands began to draw in the slack on the firing lever, then the Lewis gun suddenly began firing. The noise was very violent in the still, silent room. Four of the horsemen fell from their saddles like badly stuffed dolls. The rest of the patrol was thrown into utter confusion. Horses reared. Men struggled to draw their revolvers and control the horses at the same time. The dust in the road swept up under the plunging feet and Holtz could hear the sharp crack of his men's rifles as they began to fire also. He hastily shifted the gun a little and kept firing. Three horses went down in a screaming, kicking heap. The riders were thrown under the hoofs of the other horses and were kicked and trampled to pulp. Holtz drew his lips off his teeth and concentrated the murderous fire on the remaining eight men. These had recovered from their surprise and had thrown themselves off their horses and down on to the road.

As Holtz swept the gun-sights over them the Lewis gun suddenly stopped firing. A misplaced cartridge had jammed the feed. Feverishly, Holtz tugged and jerked, his fingers slippery with sweat. The cartridge was jammed tight. Jerking his revolver from his holster, he hammered at it with the butt and managed to clear it. All the time he was working he could hear the sounds of rifle-fire, and prayed that his men had achieved what he had failed to do. As soon as he had cleared the feed, he swung the gun up into position again. There were only five horses and seven men lying in the road, the others had disappeared. He stood up and yelled through the window to Castra. After a moment, Castra slid from cover and wormed his way across to the farmhouse. From the opposite side of the road, under cover of the thick desert shrubs, two rifle-shots rang out. Holtz saw little puffs of dust spurt up close to Castra, who sprang to his feet and darted into the farmhouse. Holtz swung the Lewis gun and fired a short burst at where the shots had come from. He could see the shrubs shudder under the hail of bullets, but there was no sound to tell him that he had hit anyone. There was now complete silence over the farmhouse and the road. They had all gone to ground and were waiting for each other to show themselves.

Castra came up the stairs and into the room. He saluted stiffly. 'It was the horses,' he said; 'eight of the patrol are over there in the thicket. We tried to shoot them down, but the horses got in our way. What shall we do now, Lieutenant?'

Holtz got up from the gun. 'Take this over.'

Castra sat down behind the gun, looking at Holtz enquiringly.

'Where are the rest of our men?' Holtz asked aloud.

'Dedos is behind the barrel over there. Golz and Fernando are together behind that wagon. They have all a good view of the road, Lieutenant.'

Holtz wiped the sweat from his face with a soiled handkerchief. He was worried. 'They had better all come in,' he said. 'We are too small to be scattered. Pablo's army may be here at any moment.'

Castra shrugged. 'It would be dangerous to move them now,' he pointed out. 'There is no cover for them to get to the house, Lieutenant. They may all be hit.'

Holtz knew that he was right. He cursed the Lewis gun savagely. 'If that goddamned thing hadn't jammed, we should have wiped out the whole patrol. As it is, we are in a difficult situation.'

Castra nodded. The expression on his face was very resigned. He was so used to Cortez's misfortunes that this new difficulty had not surprised him.

A sudden volley came from the thicket and Holtz could hear the bullets smack against the walls of the house.

'They have automatic rifles,' he said, staring at Castra, who nodded again. 'Blast them out of the thicket,' he went on. 'It is the only way.'

Castra turned the sights of the gun on the thick shrubs on the opposite side of the road and swept it with a hail of lead. The noise of the gun set Holtz's teeth on edge. Again the silence that followed did not indicate that anyone had been hit. Holtz stood undecided staring out of the small loophole that had been made. He thought he saw a slight movement over to the right and, drawing his revolver, he sighted carefully and squeezed the trigger. Above the sharp crack of the gun a sudden wail came to them, and a man staggered up from the long grass, took two tottering steps forward and fell on his face.

Castra glanced at Holtz. There was a look of surprise and admiration on his face. 'That was good, Lieutenant,' he said. 'That was very good.'

'Seven more, unless they have withdrawn to get help.'

'I think not. The horses ran away from them. It is too hot to walk far. No, I think they all remain.'

A round, black object suddenly sailed up in the air. Holtz couldn't be sure just where it came from. He watched it make a slow and graceful parabola and he shouted, 'Look out, down there, look out.'

The hand-grenade must have been a very good one. It went off with a vicious explosion just by the cart behind which Fernando and Golz were sheltering. Two terrified yells followed the explosion and Golz came running out behind the cart, holding his hands over his ears.

Holtz yelled, 'Get back, you fool! Get back, under cover!' But Golz was too frightened to listen. The automatic rifle barked twice from across the way and Golz fell backwards, clutching at his chest.

Holtz said, 'The mad, undisciplined swine.' He peered through the loophole, trying to catch a glimpse of

Fernando. He thought he could make out one of his boots just by the cart-wheel, but he couldn't be sure. 'Do you think he's been hurt?' he asked Castra anxiously.

'Stunned, perhaps,' Castra said, fiddling with the firing lever. 'That was a very good bomb, Lieutenant.'

'Yes, yes, but Fernando—' Holtz took a step to the door and then paused.

Castra shook his head. 'No Lieutenant. You should not take risks. If he has gone, it cannot be helped.'

Holtz turned miserably back to the loophole. A large red stain had appeared by the cart-wheel. 'Look, he has been hit. Look, he is bleeding to death.'

Castra said, 'We cannot do anything.' His face had become very grim and hard. Two men in less than a half an hour. That was very bad.

Holtz said: 'Watch very carefully. If they throw another grenade, fire immediately.'

Castra slouched lower over the gun. He swung its sights slowly backwards and forwards, covering the thicket, waiting.

A long silence ensued. Neither of the men spoke. They remained tense and watchful. Then, quite close to the road, away to the left, another grenade came sailing across to the farmhouse. Castra whipped the gun round and fired a long, raking burst. They had no time to feel jubilant as another of Pablo's patrol suddenly sprang to his feet, only to fall over on his face, because the grenade struck the wooden planks they had nailed across the window and burst with a shattering roar.

Holtz felt the rush of air as bits of wood and shrapnel flicked past him, and the violence of the explosion threw him on his knees.

He heard the Lewis gun crash over on its side and Castra rolled over on his back, his face a spongy mass of blood. He lay there moaning.

Holtz crawled over to him, feeling horribly sick. Castra had received the full force of the splinters from the shutters as well as bits of shrapnel from the grenade. His face looked as if it had been crushed by a heavy weight.

Holtz knew that he couldn't do anything, but he took Castra's hand in his. 'I am here, Sergeant,' he said, 'have courage. I am with you.' Futile words, but what else could he say?

Castra drew in a shuddering breath and gripped Holtz's hand hard. 'The gun,' he whispered. 'Watch out they don't throw again. Those grenades are very good, Lieutenant.'

Holtz pulled off his white tunic and made a little pillow of it for Castra's head. 'I am quite near to you,' he said. 'But I must right the gun.'

Castra released his hand. 'I have lost my eyes,' he said, 'I can't help you any more, Lieutenant. I have lost my eyes.'

'No, no, don't say that,' Holtz said, jerking the gun upright. The grenade had torn a large hole in the wooden shutters, and as Holtz stood up to put the gun into position he heard a rifle crack and a bullet whizzed very close to him, flattening itself against the wall behind him. He ducked down, swearing softly. No wonder Pablo was winning this revolution if all his soldiers were as good as these, he thought.

Keeping flat, he manoeuvred the gun into position and then ran back to Castra. He knelt by his side. 'Can I do anything for you, Sergeant?' he asked, taking his hand again.

Castra showed his teeth in a horrible effort to smile, which made Holtz feel very bad. The big, even teeth were bright red from the blood that filled Castra's mouth, and as he lifted his lips, blood ran out of the side of his mouth on to his soiled white tunic. 'Don't let these bastards beat you, Lieutenant,' he said in a thick, choked whisper. 'Avenge me.'

Holtz could not bear to look at him any longer. He went back on hands and knees to the gun. He wondered where Dedos was. There was no sign of him behind the barrel. He lay flat, his hands on the firing lever, waiting.

There was a long silence and then, cautiously, from behind a tree one of the patrol appeared. He stood looking up at the farmhouse, his long, automatic rifle held stiffly at the ready. Before Holtz could fire at him, a rifle barked just beneath and the patrolman staggered back behind the tree. Holtz was fairly certain that he had been hit.

So Dedos was still alive, he thought with satisfaction. He had managed to get as far as the farmhouse. Perhaps he would get inside. He dare not go down to let him in. Any moment Pablo's men might try to rush the house.

Again a grenade was thrown. This time it was obvious to Holtz that it was aimed at Dedos below. Holtz heard his yell of terror as the grenade exploded, and the whole house trembled with the force of the explosion.

Holtz fired a furious burst through the thicket and then shouted down to Dedos, but no one answered him. 'I think they have Dedos too,' he said to Castra. 'It is well that Pablo's army didn't attack in the first place. These men are very good.'

Castra didn't hear him. He had died very quietly just before the grenade had exploded. Holtz turned his head to look at him, and as he realized that Castra was dead the sound of something falling at his feet made him jerk round.

A long black grenade lay close by him. It had been very skilfully thrown through the hole in the shutter and now it lay there within a few feet of him. He had no time to flatten out or make any effort to protect himself. The word 'Nina' came to his lips, but he hadn't time to say the word before the grenade exploded.

He was conscious of a bright yellow flash and a lot of noise. Then he sat up on his elbow and stared at the Lewis gun that had fallen over on its side again. He had been thrown right across the room and his hand rested on the spongy pulp that had been Castra's face. Shuddering, he jerked his hand away and tried to get to his feet. As he moved, a wave of pain lurched into him, cutting his breath and bringing a scream fluttering in his mouth.

He held himself very still. Down the front of his tunic he could see a number of blood-stained little holes and he knew that his chest had been riddled with small splinters of shrapnel.

He lay on his elbow, waiting for the pain to go away. As he lay, he said in a low, sobbing whisper, 'Look what they have done to me, Nina.' Then, because he was alone, hurt and rather frightened, he began to call to Nina as if she could hear him.

The pain that kept lurching in and out of his chest finally brought him to his senses, and he suddenly remembered the patrol outside. They would be coming to the farmhouse in a moment or so, to make sure that they had killed him. He must get the gun into position and settle them once and for all.

He knew that it would hurt if he moved, but he mustn't mind a little pain, he told himself. Come along, he said to himself, come along. Now, move your arm. Sit up slowly. That's right. Hell! It does hurt, doesn't it? Hell! Hell! Hell! He began to cry, but he got his body upright and turned on to his hands and knees. Blood began to drip from his chest on to the floor. He remained like that for several seconds, his head hanging, almost touching the floor. Then he crawled slowly over to the gun and sat down heavily beside it.

The pain took hold of him with steel fingers and ripped into him savagely. A feeling of nausea brought him out into a cold sweat, but he took hold of the gun and dragged it into position. The movement made him lean over the gun and vomit. He was aware only of thinking how glad he was that Nina couldn't see him now. How shocked and horrified she would have been. He pulled the gun carefully round so that the sights covered the road, and then he eased his body against the gun. Sooner or later they would come. If they waited until dark, it didn't matter, because Cortez would be far away. If they came now, he would be able to stop them. Yes, it was going better than he had hoped.

How are you, Nina? What are you doing now? You really mustn't worry about me, because I am quite all right. You might not think so, if you saw me, but I am really. It is dying alone that frightens people. To be left quite alone. I can understand it, can't you? But I am not alone. I have never been alone since I met you. You are here in my head and my heart and I am not afraid to die. It is you that I grieve for, because you will be left. If you have loved me as I think you have, you should not be alone either. I shall be with you long after I have ceased to walk and talk and laugh with you. Nothing can really part us, not after the things we have done together, and the nights we have spent together.

I hope the General is kind when he tells you. That will be the worst moment, but when you are alone again, you will find that there is no pain that is too great to bear. You will have courage because if our love has meant anything at all it will be as a shield in your hour of need.

You won't have regrets, will you? I don't think you will, but I should be very unhappy if you did. No, there must be no regrets. We must be satisfied that we were happy and we have always been kind to each other. That is so very important, isn't it? You can look back on our life together without any reproach. You have denied me nothing, and I know that I also, so far away from you and so soon to die, have been steadfast to you. I hope you don't hear about the gun, but that is the way of war. You die so seldom for what you are fighting. War is made up of errors and pride and rashness. If Generals are proud or make mistakes, they have tomorrow to try again. So I hope you don't hear about the gun, which was very silly to die for.

I know you will be lonely. That is a very sad word. I know how I should be if you were taken from me, but that is the price you have to pay for the past, which was so lovely.

And, Nina, thank you for everything. Yes, really thank you. I am so grateful for what you have given me, and this I promise you. There will come a time when we shall meet again. It may be years and years, but it will come, and we shall be together again. We shall be able to take up our love again. We shall find that our love has not rusted even from your tears. And when we meet again, let life be free from war and hate and uncertainty and distrust. You will not find me changed. So be patient, and although the wait may be long, it will come right in the end. I know it will come right, and because I am so sure, I am not frightened any more.

Two of Pablo's men appeared cautiously from the thicket and looked up at the farmhouse. Holtz watched them through a haze of pain. Come along, he said softly, all of you. Not just two, but all of you. It is quite safe for you because we are dead in this house, so come quickly and keep very close together.

Three others seemed to materialize out of the ground and the five of them stood hesitating, their rifles advanced, staring up at the shattered window. Still Holtz sat there, holding on to the gun and breathing with great difficulty. This time there must be no mistake. He willed them to come to him, exerting his mind as the blood continued to drip from him, with an irritating sound, on to the floor.

They finally made up their minds that it would be safe to approach, and in a body they began to move. Holtz waited until they were in the middle of the road, then, with his remaining strength, savagely, and with deadly precision, he cut them to pieces.

WALK IN THE PARK

The park stretched away into distant flower-beds, trees and heavy shrubs. Near the main gates was a large boating-pond. A number of brightly painted boats rested at anchor in the middle of the pond. Tennis-courts to the right of the pond were deserted. The nets hung slackly, and the white lines stood out sharply against the green grass.

It was early. If it had been a Sunday, no doubt even at that hour, the park would have been crowded, but it was only Thursday, and there was work to be done.

So, for over an hour, the park was very peaceful, and the only sign of movement was from the birds that sang in the sunshine, and flew from branch to branch, or suddenly swooped to the ground. Then two young men walked through the main gates and moved down the centre avenue. They looked very much alike. They were both dressed in shabby blue suits, pinched in at the waist, and very baggy in the trousers. They wore pointed shoes that they hadn't bothered to clean, and black, slouch hats worn tilted on the bridge of their noses. Cigarettes dangled from slack lips, and their hands were thrust deeply into trouser pockets, hunching their shoulders.

Although they were shabby, there was a rhythmic smartness in their movements. Their walk and their balanced poise was similar to the movements of a tiger treading softly through a dense thicket.

They walked past the boating-pond, leaving a wispy trail of tobacco smoke that floated in the still air behind them. On, past the flower-beds, through the avenue of trees and then, branching off the main avenue, they walked along a smaller path that led to the woods.

They didn't speak to each other, but their bright bird-like eyes, moving in quick little darts, missed nothing. The path twisted through the woods, mounting gradually to a high mound which overlooked the whole of the park. Walking, now in single file, they finally reached the top and stood motionless, their eyes darting to the right and to the left. The park seemed quite deserted. Except for these two young men, and the birds, nothing moved.

The two young men remained standing motionless for some little while, their cigarettes bobbing now and then, as they drew in a lungful of smoke. Then one of them nudged the other. A long way to the right he had seen a movement that had caught his eye. His companion's eyes darted in the direction that the other had indicated. He could just make out someone moving towards them, appearing and disappearing behind the screen of trees. Both of them became very intent. Their heads thrust forward and their eyes narrowed.

After a short while, a girl came out of the wood and moved towards them up the twisty path.

They looked at each other and nodded, then they separated and vanished into the bushes.

The girl came on slowly, unconscious that she wasn't entirely alone. She wore a cheap print dress that had once been very pretty, but constant washing had faded its large flowered pattern. She was bareheaded, and carried a perky little straw hat in her hand. She was above the average height and slender. Her figure was rather childish, and she had soft, smudgy curves as if she had never worn a restricting garment.

She was not exactly pretty, because her features were irregular and her expression vague, but the two young men, watching her, thought she was attractive enough.

She came on slowly, swinging her hat carelessly, and singing softly. She reached the top of the mound and looked a little vaguely round the park. Then she sat down with her back to a tree, stretched out her long legs and adjusted the dress with a prim little movement.

The two young men gave her a few minutes to settle down, then they made a quick, silent detour and came out on to the path where she was bound to see them. They walked towards her silently, and without appearing to notice her.

Under their hat brims they saw that she was startled. In fact, for a moment, their sudden appearance nearly panicked her. She started up as if she were about to spring to her feet, but seeing that they were so close she turned her head, as if she hadn't seen them, and relaxed once more against the tree.

One of the young men said, 'Do you think we ought to speak to her?"

'Aw, Jakie, why not? She looks sort of lonely all by herself.'

The girl kept her head turned from them, but they could see by the way she stiffened that she had heard what they had said.

The young man addressed as Jakie moved closer to her. 'It's a nice morning, isn't it?' he said. His voice was very flat, cold and unmusical.

She didn't say anything.

'It's swell to walk in the park on a mornin' like this, ain't it?' he went on, gently kicking a root of the tree with his soiled shoe. 'There's no one about. You can just wander around an' do what you like.'

The other young man suddenly giggled.

Jakie frowned at him. 'Gee, Pugsey, can't you behave? Ain't nothin' to laugh about.'

Pugsey giggled again. 'She ain't takin' any notice of you,' he said. 'Don't look like you're gettin' places so fast.'

Jakie turned back to the girl. 'You mustn't mind him,' he said. 'You see, he don't know how to handle dames. I do.'

She still said nothing.

Pugsey said, 'Maybe she's deaf,' hopefully.

Jakie shook his head. 'Naw,' he said, 'she ain't deaf; she's just a little dumb.'

Pugsey gave a sudden squeal of laughter. 'Gee!' he said. 'I bet you read that somewhere. That's pretty smart.'

The girl suddenly looked at them. Her eyes were scared, not because she was frightened of them, but because she was scared that they were making fun of her. 'Go away, please,' she said, 'I don't want to talk to you.'

Jakie took a step back. 'Did you hear that, Pugsey? She don't want to talk to us.'

'Too bad,' Pugsey said, squatting on his heels and staring at the girl. He kept his distance and was to the rear and to the right of Jakie. 'Can you think of any reason why she wouldn't want to talk to us?'

Jakie shook his head. 'Naw,' he said. 'Suppose you ask her?'

'You're a smart guy,' Pugsey said. 'Isn't he a smart guy?' he went on to the girl. 'Jakie always gets to the root of anything. You see, he wants to know why. You tell us.'

The girl looked away without speaking.

'She's in a trance again,' Pugsey said, shifting a little nearer. 'I don't think she likes you, Jakie.'

Jakie sat on the ground and leant back on his elbows. The girl was between the two of them. He selected a long blade of grass and put it between his teeth. 'What the hell's the matter with me?' he asked. 'Why shouldn't she like me?'

Pugsey considered this. 'Maybe you smell or something,' he suggested, after some thought.

Jakie picked his nose. 'Ask her,' he said.

'What's wrong with Jakie?' Pugsey asked, looking at the girl. 'That's a fair question, ain't it?'

She made a move as if she were going to get up, but the two suddenly became very tense, looking at her coldly with their hard little eyes, and she relaxed again against the tree. She looked rather desperately across the park, but she could see no one.

The two followed her gaze. 'Too early,' Jakie said. 'We're lucky to find you, I guess. Do you know, Pugsey, she reminds me of that little judy we ran into a couple of weeks ago on Franklin Street.'

'The one we took into that empty house?' Pugsey asked.

'Yeah.'

Pugsey looked at the girl again. 'Maybe you've got something there. Yeah, I think you've got something there.'

'She ain't so fair, is she? Still she's about the same age. Jeeze! Didn't that one squawk when we – you know.'

Pugsey giggled. 'It don't matter a great deal if this one squawks here, does it? I mean, there ain't anyone around to come bustin' in. Maybe she'll be sensible.'

The girl had gone very white and her eyes opened wide. She put one hand on the ground and struggled up on her knees.

Jakie said, 'Looks like she's goin' to take a powder.'

Pugsey edged a little nearer. 'Naw,' he said, 'she's going to be sensible, ain't you baby?'

The girl said: 'Leave me alone. I don't want to talk to you. Go away. Please go away.'

Jakie put his fingers into his vest pocket. 'Hear her talk,' he said, his dark little eyes darting over her. 'Think I ought to try and persuade her?'

Pugsey nodded. 'Yeah, we better hurry. Look, it's gettin' late.' He produced a cheap watch and waved it in front of Jakie.

Jakie took a little green bottle with a glass stopper from his pocket. He said to the girl: 'It's acid. Burns, you know; eats into things. Makes holes in your skin.'

The girl crouched back. She tried to speak, but she could only make a terrified whimpering noise.

'If I throw this at you,' Jakie said simply, 'it'll spoil your pretty face. I just want you to be sensible and do what you're told. If you try and get tough, then you'll get this in your mug, see? Otherwise, you'll be all right.'

Pugsey giggled again.

'Maybe we'd better toss for it,' Jakie said, taking a dime out of his pocket.

Pugsey called and won. Jakie got up and dusted down his suit. He put the little bottle in his pocket. Then he looked at the girl with his cold, unfeeling eyes. 'I got it here,' he said, patting his pocket, 'be good. I ain't tellin' you a second time. One dame didn't believe me. Remember how she ran down the street with the stuff stripping the meat off her face? She was a dope, wasn't she? Be smart sister. We ain't going to be long.'

Pugsey walked over to her and pulled her to her feet. She cringed from him, but she didn't try to run away.

Jakie sat with his back to a tree, his black hat over his nose, and a cigarette dangling from his thin lips. His little eyes kept watch over the park, missing nothing.

When Pugsey got through, Jakie went over to the girl, and Pugsey kept watch. Pugsey had to stuff his handkerchief in his mouth to stop his giggles when the girl began crying. He was mighty glad that she hadn't done that when he was with her. Jakie had betted him a dollar that she would be too scared to cry. It amused Pugsey to think he'd won a dollar from Jakie, because Jakie hated giving money away.

They left the girl on the mound and walked back to the boating-pond. Jakie gave Pugsey the dollar rather sourly.

Pugsey didn't want him to feel bad about it, so he said: 'You're a smart guy, Jakie. I didn't really think it would work.'

Jakie took the little bottle out of his pocket and fondled it. 'I knew it would,' he said, with a thin grimace that served him as a smile. 'But it was a good thing she didn't look too close, the bottle's empty.' He went to the edge of the pond and carefully dipped the bottle in, filling it with the muddy water. 'It wouldn't do to make the same mistake twice.'

Pugsey said: 'Naw, but these dames are pretty dumb. They wouldn't notice nothin'.'

Together they went out of the park, moving slightly less rhythmically than they had when they came in.

THE PLACE OF LOVE

1

She lay very still on the bed, vaguely conscious that she ought not to be there; that she ought to be doing something very important, but what it was she couldn't remember.

She moved her long legs, feeling the smooth linen sliding over her flesh. What had she to do? Something . . . What was it? She couldn't remember. It was all too much trouble. Everything was too much trouble.

In the distance the note of a ship's siren sounded, a soft, gentle wail. Her heart missed a beat, but still she didn't move. Now, she remembered. The ship, of course. It sailed at two o'clock. They had said repeatedly that they were not waiting for anyone. Something was going to happen in Havana. They didn't say what it would be. They didn't even admit that it was going to happen, but by a little gesture, by the apprehensive look in their eyes, by the flurry they all were in, one gathered that something was going to happen that couldn't possibly be pleasant.

The little, pock-marked steward, when he had given her her coat, had emphasized the necessity of being on board by midnight. He was nice, in spite of his pock-marks, and she made a point of assuring him that she would be back before then. She would have been if she hadn't met Lacey.

She moved restlessly. Lacey. She saw him as he was the previous night. Tall, very clean-looking in his white evening clothes. He was good to look at. Any woman would have thought so. His lean face, his full lips, and the jeering, cynical look he had in his eyes.

He had joined the boat at Bahama. As soon as he came on board the women began to talk about him. He was that kind of a man.

She pressed her fingers to her aching head. God! She

must have been tight, as tight as she had been crazy – that must have been very, very tight. She wanted to go to sleep again, but she began remembering, and as the memory of the previous night built up in her mind, sleep retreated.

Oh yes, he had been awfully nice. It was by the sheerest coincidence that he happened to be going ashore as she stepped on the gang-plank. She had planned to see Havana with a Mr. and Mrs. Skinner. They were nice people, elderly, kindly and safe – nice people.

Lacey had jeered at them. He had shaken his head at her, behind their backs, as they prepared to take her away on a stately little drive along the brightly lit Havana waterfront. Then he had stepped forward. It was all done so smoothly. She couldn't remember what he had said, but it must have been horribly smooth and just right, because the Skinners went away, smiling. They even looked back and waved, leaving her alone with him. Oh yes, she had to admit that it was all very neat and clever. He had taken her into the heart of Havana. He seemed to know all the unexpected places. He didn't take her to the show places, but to all the exciting little cafés and houses, as if he owned the place.

He talked. She began gathering the top of the sheet unconsciously into a tight, long rope. Yes, he had talked. At first, he said amusing things. He did what very few people could do, he made her laugh. Then later, in the evening, after they had a few drinks, he began to flatter her. It wasn't eye-talk stuff. It was shockingly personal, and it made her go hot, but because of the velvety strength of the drinks he had given her she didn't go away from him as she ought to have done. So it went on until she suddenly realized that she was getting dangerously light-headed. She stopped drinking, but she couldn't stop him talking. He said, in a charming way, the most outrageous things. She felt herself being drawn to him entirely against her will. It was as if something inside her was going out to him, leaving her weak and without resistance.

She remembered wondering when he would touch her. She knew, beyond any doubt, that he would touch her. Why else did he continue to stare at her with such intentness?

He seemed in no hurry. That was because he was so confident. Even in small things he was always confident. Small things, as lighting a cigarette, walking through a crowded room, or ordering a meal.

She remembered thinking that in an hour, or less, he was going to possess her. He would take her as confidently as he took everything. She was going to do absolutely nothing about it. She knew that before he started. Absolutely nothing, because she had no resistance. She felt almost as if she were asleep, dreaming that this was happening to her.

There – he had touched her. He had reached out and put his hand firmly on hers. She was quite sure that he would reach out his hand in the same way, steadily and confidently, to pat the head of a snarling dog.

At his touch her blood ran hot in her veins. She remembered thinking, at the time, that such a thing only happened in novels, but she actually felt a sudden surge of warmth go through her.

He went on talking, holding her hand lightly in his. Meeting his eyes, she saw that he had finished playing with her. He was serious now. She saw an eagerness that had pushed the jeering look into the background.

He rose to his feet abruptly, and took her through the back of the restaurant, through a doorway screened by a bead curtain. Together they went down a dim corridor that smelt faintly of sandalwood.

She followed him, her knees feeling weak, into a little room which was beautifully furnished, lit by rose-coloured lanterns. She was quite unable to say anything.

As she lay there in bed she could see those lanterns very clearly. She shut her eyes and she could see them even more clearly. She could feel him drawing her down on the divan, his hands taking the weight from her breasts. His hands there made her suddenly want him with an urgency that terrified her.

She had said, a little wildly, 'Be kind to me – be kind to me,' and she remembered trying to find his mouth with hers.

She did not know how he undressed her. She was conscious of her clothes leaving her smoothly as he did everything. Then he suddenly lost all his smoothness, and treated her shamefully.

She lay staring at the rose-pink lanterns, feeling a sick loathing of herself. Her desires had gone away from her the moment he took her. It was all so sudden, so brutal, so unexpected – so filthily selfish. So she lay looking at the rose-pink lanterns until he stood away from her.

He had said, a little impatiently, 'It's getting late, we had better go back to the boat.'

She had said nothing. She couldn't even cry.

'Don't you hear?' he said. 'It is nearly twelve.'

Without looking at him, she said: 'Does it matter? Does anything ever matter to you? Go away. Go back to the boat. I've nothing else to give you. Why don't you go away?'

He said impatiently, 'For God's sake stop talking and get dressed.'

She shut her eyes and said nothing, so he left her. He walked out of the room with his confident tread and left her there.

When he had gone she got up and dressed. She remembered that she couldn't look herself in the face as she stood before the mirror. She remembered thinking that she had behaved like a bitch, and she was ashamed.

She went back to the restaurant. The waiter who had served them looked at her curiously when she sat down at the table they had previously occupied. She didn't care what he thought. She didn't care about anything. She just felt a cold fury with herself for being such a bitch. She didn't even think of Lacey any more. All she could think was that because this was Havana, because of the great yellow moon, and because of the blue-black water, studded with thousands of lights from the waterfront, she had behaved like a bitch with a horribly smooth ship's Romeo. She deserved to be treated as a whore. She hadn't even the satisfaction of knowing that she had been as efficient as a whore – she hadn't. She had just wanted to be very sick and to cry, but she had done absolutely nothing.

She had ordered a lot of drink from the waiter. She had to get tight. She could do that. There was nothing else she could do. She couldn't sit in the restaurant, knowing the ship was sailing with all her clothes, leaving her in Havana, where something was going to happen, without getting good and tight. So she got good and tight, and she might have been still sitting there if the waiter hadn't very tactfully put her in a taxi and told the driver to take her to a hotel. She would go back one day and thank the waiter. It was the first act of kindness she had received in Havana.

At the hotel they didn't seem to notice how very tight she

was. The manager seemed to have something on his mind. He wasn't even sorry when he heard that she had lost the boat. He just raised his hands, saying, 'That is a very grave misfortune for you, señorita,' and gave instructions for her to be taken to a room on the third floor overlooking the waterfront.

She sat up in bed and ran her fingers through her thick wavy hair. She must do something now. She couldn't stay in bed nursing her cold hatred.

Reaching out, she rang the bell at her side violently.

2

It was hot. Too hot to stay in bed Quentin thought, pushing the sheet from him and sliding on to the coconut matting.

The sunlight came through the slots in the shutter and burnt his feet. He scratched his head, yawning, then reached under the bed for his heelless slippers. He sat there, staring at the wall, feeling lousy. It must have been the rum he'd belted the previous night. That guy Morecombre certainly could shift liquor. He might have known what kind of a party he was sitting down to. These press photographers spent most of their time on the booze. He pressed fingers tenderly to his head and then wandered over to the chest of drawers and found a bottle of Scotch. He put a little ice water in a glass and three fingers of Scotch to colour it, then he went back and sat on his bed.

The drink was swell, and he dawdled over it while he considered what he had to do that day. There wasn't much he could do, he decided, except just sit around and wait. Well he was used to that. He could do that fine.

He reached out with his foot and kicked the shutter open. From where he sat he could see the harbour and a little of the bay. By leaning forward he could see the old *Morro Castle*. He drew a deep breath. The place was pretty good, he decided. Very, very nice to look at. He got up and wandered to the open window. Below him the hotel grounds stretched away to the waterfront – flowers, trees, palms, everything that grew so richly in the tropical heat spread out before him. He hunched his muscles and yawned. Not bad, he thought, not bad at all. The Foreign Correspondent of the

New York Post staying in the dump that millionaires condescend to be seen in. He finished the Scotch. All the same, he wouldn't mind betting there was no one in the hotel except Morecombre and himself and the General. He grinned a little sourly. From where he stood he could see the waterfront, which looked ominously deserted. The hotel grounds were deserted too. 'The word's got round all right,' he thought; 'rats leaving the sinking ship.'

He wandered over and rang the bell, then went on into the bathroom and turned on the shower. He stood watching the water hiss down, still holding the empty glass in his hand. He eyed it thoughtfully, decided he wouldn't have any more, put the glass down and slid out of his pyjamas.

The shower was fine. The water pricked and tingled on his skin. Raising his head, he began to sing, very low and rather mournfully.

When he came back to the bedroom he found Anita standing looking out of the window.

Anita was the maid in charge of the third floor. She was very dark, small, very well built. Her breasts rode high, firm . . . audacious breasts. They looked like they were proud of themselves, and Quentin himself thought they were pretty good.

'Hello,' he said, wrapping a towel round his waist, 'don't you ever knock?'

She smiled at him. She had a nice smile, glistening white teeth and sparkling eyes. 'The water,' she said, lifting her hands, 'it makes so much noise. You did not hear me knock, so I come in.'

'One of these days,' Quentin said, pulling on a silk dressing-gown and sliding the towel off, 'you're going to get an unpleasant shock when you walk in like that.'

She shook her head. 'This morning I had it – it was not so bad.'

Quentin looked at her severely. 'You're not such a nice little girl as you look. You know too much.'

'It was Señor. Morecombre,' she said, her eyes opening. 'He is a beautiful man – yes?'

'Suppose you get me some breakfast, and stop chattering,' Quentin said. 'Get me a lotta food, I'm hungry.'

She made a little face. 'There is nothing,' she said. 'Coffee . . . yes, but the food . . . it is all gone.'

Quentin paused, his shaving-brush suspended half-way to his face. 'I don't get it, baby,' he said. 'This is a hotel, ain't it? This is *the* hotel, ain't it?'

She smiled again. That smile certainly had a load of come-hither hanging to it. 'But the strike,' she explained, 'it is the strike. No food for four days. All out of the ice-box. Now the ice-box is empty.'

Quentin resumed his shaving. 'So I'm going to pay a small fortune to stay in this joint and starve – is that it?'

'But, señor, everyone has gone away. There is only you and Señor Morecombre left.'

'And the General,' Quentin reminded her. 'Don't forget the General.'

Anita pulled a face. 'I don't forget him,' she said, 'he is a bad man. He has everything; he has food. He knew what was going to happen.'

'Maybe he'll consider sharing his breakfast with me,' Quentin said. 'Suppose you run along and ask him. Tell him George Quentin of the *New York Post* would like to breakfast with him. See what happens.'

She shook her head. 'No,' she said, 'I do not ask favours from such a man; he is bad. Soon someone will kill him, you see.'

Quentin put down his shaving-brush. 'Then get me some coffee. Now beat it, baby; you're in the way. I want to dress.' He put his hand under her elbow and took her to the door. She tilted her head and smiled at him. 'Señor is a very fine man, yes?' she said. She offered him her lips, but Quentin shook his head. 'Go on, dust,' he said a little irritably, and drove her out with a smack on her behind.

When he was half dressed, Bill Morecombre came in. He was a tall, loosely built guy, a soft hat worn carelessly at the back of his head, and a cigarette dangled from the side of his mouth. He draped himself up against the door-post and waved a languid hand. 'Hyah, pal,' he said, 'anythin' happenin'?'

Quentin shook his head. 'Not a thing except there's no breakfast.'

Morecombre shrugged. 'I expected that, didn't you? Hell, the strike's been on a week now. This joint's going to be plenty tough before it gets better. I brought some stuff along with me. When you're ready come on over. I guess the manager will be up too. I got plenty.'

'You guys certainly look after yourselves,' Quentin said, fixing his tie. 'Sure I'll be over.'

Morecombre was in no hurry to leave. 'See Anita this morning?' he asked, flicking ash on the floor.

'I have,' Quentin returned grimly. 'That baby's wearing a pair of very hot pants.'

'You're right, but what else has she got to do? I'm sorry for that judy.'

Quentin slipped on his jacket. 'The trouble with you,' he said dryly, 'is that you're always sorry for dames. Then, eventually, they get sorry for themselves.'

They crossed the corridor into Morecombre's room. 'Do you seriously think anything's going to happen?' Morecombre asked, diving under his bed and dragging out a large suit-case. 'I mean big enough to justify all this fuss and expense?'

Quentin sat on the bed and eyed the suit-case with interest. 'I don't know,' he said, 'but when you get into a country as hot as this, packed with people who've been pushed around and treated as these people have been, it's a safe bet that the lid will come off sometime. And when it comes off a lotta guys are going to be hurt.'

Morecombre opened the suitcase and sat back on his heels. 'Looks good,' he said, examining a big array of brightly labelled tins. 'What shall we have?'

A discreet knock sounded. Morecombre looked at Quentin with a grin. 'Vulture number one,' he said, going across and opening the door.

The hotel manager was a short, rather pathetic-looking little Cuban. He bowed very stiffly at the waist. 'I've come to present my apologies—' he began, looking at the tinned food with a sparkle in his eye.

'Forget it,' Morecombre said, stepping to one side. 'Come on in and have a spot of something. You can take it off the bill.'

The manager came into the room very quickly, a smile lighting his face. 'That is generous,' he said. 'American gentlemen are always very generous.'

Quentin looked up. He was busy opening a tin. 'You know why we are here, don't you?' he asked abruptly.

The manager looked confused. 'You come to see our beautiful city . . . yes?' he said, fidgeting with his small white hands.

'We are here to report and obtain photographs of a coming revolution,' Quentin said impressively. 'How long do you think we'll have to wait before it begins?'

The manager looked helplessly at the tin in Quentin's hands. 'I could not say,' he said. 'I know nothing about a revolution.'

Quentin glanced across at Morecombre and shrugged. 'They're all alike,' he said a little bitterly. 'I guess we've just got to be patient and wait.'

Another knock sounded on the door and Anita came in with a tray. She, too, regarded the tins with interest.

'Coffee, señor,' she said.

Morecombre took the tray from her. 'Come on in and join us,' he said. 'This is no time to stand on ceremony.'

The manager scowled at her, but she sat down close to Morecombre, taking no notice of him.

Suddenly the manager clapped his hands to his head. 'I forget,' he said, 'the señorita who came last night. What has become of her?'

Anita frowned. 'I gave her coffee,' she said. 'She wishes to sleep again.'

'Who's that?' Quentin asked. 'What señorita?'

'Beautiful American lady lost the boat last night. She come to this hotel. I am very worried, but I give her a room. I only just remember.'

'You let her stay here?' Morecombre exclaimed angrily. 'What the hell did you do that for?'

The manager looked distressed. 'I was not thinking. I was very worried.' He broke off and looked pathetic again.

'I guess you were tight,' Quentin said angrily, getting to his feet. He turned to Anita. 'Go and wake her at once. Tell her she had better pack and clear out of this joint. Explain that trouble is likely to happen here.'

The manager started up. 'No, no!' he said. 'Nothing is going to happen to my beautiful hotel. You must not say such things.'

Quentin looked at him grimly. 'That's what you say. If a revolution does start, this is one of the first places they're coming to. You don't think they'll let General Fuentes get away after what he's done to them, do you?'

The manager looked as if he were going to faint. 'You must not say such things,' he said in a hoarse whisper. 'It is very dangerous to talk like that.'

Quentin jerked his head at Anita. 'Go and tell her,' he said, 'this is no place for American women.'

Anita scowled at him. 'It is all right for me . . . yes?' she said. 'It doesn't matter about me . . . no?'

Quentin climbed out of his chair. 'Go and tell her,' he said. 'Never mind about yourself. You'll be all right.'

She went out, closing the door sharply behind her. Quentin glanced at Morecombre, who was setting the table. 'Rather complicated if we've got to look after some American girl, huh?' he said. 'If things do start happening, I want to be free to move from here quickly.'

Morecombre grinned. 'No woman has ever complicated my life,' he said. 'If she's a looker, you don't have to worry. I'll look after her.'

The manager wrung his hands. 'This is a terrible thing that you do, señor,' he said, 'turning my guests from my hotel.'

Quentin poured out some coffee. 'Don't talk a lotta bull,' he said. 'You know as well as I do that all your guests have gone. If anything happens to this girl, I'm going to report the matter to the consul.'

The manager looked at him sulkily, and helped himself to a cup of coffee. 'Nothing will happen,' he said; 'I assure you that nothing will happen.'

Just then Anita came back. Her black eyes sparkled with satisfaction. 'The señorita says she stays,' she said. 'She has no place else to go, so she stays.'

Quentin groaned. 'As if I haven't got enough to worry about,' he said. 'You gotta go and see her,' he went on, turning to the manager, 'tell her that there is likely to be a disturbance in the town and she had better go.'

The manager shook his head. 'I cannot say such a thing. It is not true.'

Quentin got to his feet. 'Then I'll see her,' he said. 'I'm not taking the responsibility of her being here if things get hot. She can take a car out of town and the sooner she's out the better.' He went to the door. 'What room is she in?'

Anita's eyes opened. 'But, señor, she is in bed. You cannot go to her.'

Morecombre got to his feet hurriedly. 'Just a minute, pal,' he said. 'This sounds like a job for a man of the world. Just step on one side and let me handle it.'

Quentin eyed him coldly. 'Sit down and shut up! What room is she in?'

Anita told him, looking furiously at Morecombre, and Quentin went out, crossed the corridor and knocked sharply on the door indicated. He heard someone say something inaudible, so he turned the handle and went in.

Standing by the open windows, looking on to the hotel grounds, was a tall girl, dressed in a white silk evening wrap. She turned sharply as Quentin entered. 'What do you want?' she asked.

Quentin regarded her with interest. He was more interested in her expression than her actual beauty. He was curious about the hurt, sullen look in her eyes and the little frown that increased as their eyes met.

'I'm sorry to come barging in like this,' he said, standing just inside the room, holding the door handle, 'but I thought you ought to be told that this hotel is not the place for any unattached girl. There is going to be a bad disturbance— '

She interrupted him. 'I don't know who you are,' she said, 'but the maid has already told me that I ought to go. This is a hotel, and I intend to stay. Anyway, for the time being.' She turned back to the window, dismissing him.

Quentin felt a strong desire to reach out and turn her over his knee. He came further into the room and shut the door. 'Maybe I had better introduce myself. I'm Quentin of the *New York Post*.'

He saw her suddenly stiffen, but she didn't turn from the window.

He went on: 'I'm down here because my paper expects trouble. All Americans, except the residents, have cleared out. The residents have gone over to the consul's house under guard. I guess you're about the only white woman foot-loose around this town. If you'll pack, I'll take you over to the consul myself.'

For a moment she hesitated, then she turned and faced him. 'I don't understand what you're talking about,' she said sharply. 'What trouble? What can happen here?'

Quentin grinned sourly. 'Plenty,' he said. 'Maybe you don't know anything about Cuban politics?' He came and joined her at the window. 'A grand-looking joint, ain't it?' he said, looking across the flaming flower-beds, the green lawns and across the bay. 'Sure, it looks all right, but underneath it is a mass of seething misery. The graft that goes on here would make Chicago look like a virgin's tea-party. The President in power right now is one of the meanest guys alive. All the punks who work under him run their own little graft on the side. This has been going on some time, and I guess the natives are getting tired of it. The trouble came to a head last week over transport dues. The guy who handles that has put a tax on every truck, pushing up the freight rate. Everyone knows that it will go into his own pocket, so they've got wise to him. They've come out on strike. These higher-up guys are crafty, and they guessed what would happen, so they've laid in a good stock of food and are sitting pretty. The rest of Havana is going without. No boats bring stuff in, no trains, no lorries, no nothing. Food is running short. It won't be long now before the natives get mad. When those guys get mad, they're likely to cause a heap of trouble. Now that's why you ought to get out or at least go over to the consul's place.'

The girl had stood very still while he was talking, watching him closely. When he had finished speaking, she seemed to relax and the frown disappeared. 'I'm afraid you must have thought I was very rude,' she said, 'but I'm in rather a difficult position.' She paused, looked at him rather helplessly, and then turned to the window again.

Quentin felt her embarrassment. 'I heard you missed the ship,' he said casually. 'I suppose you left all your things on board – clothes, money and so on, huh?'

She turned eagerly. 'Yes, I did. I've got nothing to wear except this. I've got no money – what – what do you think I can do?'

'You'll be all right. I'll get a car and drive you over to the consul. I guess the manager of this joint has got a car. The consul'll fix you up for dough. It's his job.'

She looked relieved. 'It's very kind of you, Mr. Quentin,' she said. 'I hope you'll forgive me. I'm afraid I was very rude just now.'

Quentin gave her a lazy grin. 'That's all right,' he said, 'you ain't got anything to worry about. All the same, I'd like to see you out of here. Just to get the records straight, will you tell me your name?'

She reacted immediately to his question by stiffening once more and regarding him suspiciously.

Quentin was in no mood for mysteries. Far more important things were about to happen. He said rather sharply: 'Listen; I know what you're thinking. I'm a newspaper man. The fact that you're in this hotel, without an escort, in evening dress, in the middle of a coming revolution, is news. So it is, but not now. A nice-looking dame who for some reason or other gets herself mislaid ain't the kind of news my chief is expecting me to turn in. He wants a full-blooded revolution, so relax. I ain't printing anything about you, but if you want me to help you you gotta give me your name. What is it?'

She said a little sulkily, 'Myra Arnold.'

Quentin nodded. The name meant nothing to him. 'O.K., Miss Arnold, if you'll wait here, I'll arrange to get a car for you – unless you'd like to come over to my friend's room and have some breakfast.'

She shook her head. 'I'll wait here,' she said.

Quentin shrugged. 'O.K., I won't keep you long.'

He went back to Morecombre's room. Anita, the manager and Morecombre were busy with tins when he entered. Morecombre said, 'What's she like?'

Quentin made curves with his hands. 'Very nice, but very cold and up-stage,' he said, taking a cup of coffee from Anita. 'Listen,' he went on to the manager, 'you gotta car? I want to run her over to the consul's place. I guess that'll be the best place for her.'

The manager nodded. 'I have a car,' he said. 'She can go in it by all means, but there is too much fuss; there will be no trouble, you see.'

As Quentin turned to leave the room, the door was thrown open and two Cuban soldiers with rifles and fixed bayonets slid in, taking up positions each side of the door.

The manager went very white and sat petrified. Anita's big eyes opened and a tiny scream fluttered at her mouth.

Quentin said coldly, 'What the hell's this?'

In the passage, just outside the door, stood a thin little man, dressed in the white-and-gold uniform of a Cuban general. His coffee-coloured face reminded Quentin of a vicious, startled little monkey. One claw-like hand rested on a revolver strapped to his waist.

The manager said faintly, 'Can I be of any service, General?'

The little man didn't even look at him. He was staring at Quentin very thoughtfully. Then he walked into the room and one of the soldiers carefully shut the door.

The little man introduced himself. 'General Fuentes,' he said, clicking his heels. 'Who are you?'

'My name is George Quentin of the *New York Post*. This is my colleague, Mr. Morecombre, of the *New York Daily.* This is a very fortunate meeting.'

The General raised his eyebrows. 'That is a matter of opinion,' he said tartly. 'What are you doing here? I understood all visitors had left the town.'

'You're probably right,' Quentin returned, 'but we are on business here.'

'So I thought.' The General's eyes gleamed. 'I'm afraid you both must consider yourselves under arrest. It is not good that newspaper men should be here at this time.'

'Really, General,' Quentin said, shaking his head, 'you can't do that. We are American citizens, and we are entitled to remain here as long as we like. You have no power to arrest us, and I think you know it.'

Fuentes touched his neat, close-clipped moustache with his fingers. 'Owing to the present emergency,' he said, 'the Government have special powers. I repeat, you both are under arrest. You are not to leave the hotel without permission. Should you fail to obey this order you will be shot without mercy.' He looked at the other two. 'And this also applies to you.'

Morecombre pushed himself out of his chair. 'Say, listen, General,' he said, 'you can't pull a thing like this. We're here to represent our papers, and we've got to have our freedom of movement.'

Fuentes shrugged. 'You can please yourself about that,' he said dryly. 'I shall regret any accident, but you can't say that you were not warned.' He looked across to the manager. 'Any other Americans in this hotel?' he demanded.

The manager hesitated, but Quentin moved forward. 'I can answer your question, General,' he said quietly. 'There is a lady here, under my charge. She is going to the consul this morning.'

Fuentes shook his head. 'I don't think so. She will stay here. Where is she?'

Quentin kept his temper with difficulty. 'This attitude you're adopting isn't going to get you anywhere,' he said. 'The lady missed the ship last night. She is entitled to go to the consul without interference.'

Fuentes turned on his heel. 'Come,' he said to the soldiers, 'find this woman.'

Quentin followed him out into the corridor. 'As you're determined to play this little drama to its conclusion, I'll take you to her.'

Fuentes eased his revolver slightly in its holster. 'You have a great deal to say for yourself, haven't you?' he said. 'I should be careful how you choose your words.'

Quentin walked across to Myra's door and knocked. She came immediately, and stood looking first at him and then at the little General.

Quentin said: 'I'm afraid you will have to alter your plans, Miss Arnold. This is General Fuentes of the President's Army. He has just told me that all Americans in this building are under arrest and are not at liberty to leave. He has made it quite plain that should they do so, they will be shot.'

Fuentes had been looking at Myra steadily. He made no attempt to disguise his admiration. He drew himself up and bowed. 'I am exceedingly sorry that I must insist on you remaining in the hotel, señorita, but I shall be delighted to offer my services as host, if you will permit me. I understand the hotel is short of food, and I have plenty. It would afford me great pleasure if you took your meals with me.'

Myra moved her head slightly, bringing the General in line with her vision. She studied him, her blue eyes slowly growing cold and her mouth hardening, but before she could speak, Quentin said gently: 'I think that is generous of you, General, but Miss Arnold is in my charge. We are fortunate to have a stock of food, and she has her meals with us.'

Fuentes smiled. He looked genuinely amused. 'I am busy now,' he said, 'there is much to be done. When I have a little spare time, I shall ask the señorita again.' He bowed, then added, 'It would be absurd to refuse.' He turned on his heel and stalked down the passage. The two soldiers followed him and took up positions at the head of the stairs.

Quentin pulled a face. 'I'm afraid that guy is going to be difficult,' he said.

Myra said: 'But can't we 'phone to the consul? Surely we can't be held long!'

'We couldn't get any calls through,' Quentin returned. 'No doubt he has a man on the switchboard. I think, Miss Arnold, it would be safer for you if you came over and joined us in the other room.'

Myra picked up a little white satin handbag. 'I'm afraid I'm being a fearful nuisance,' she said; 'it is very kind of you to bother with me.'

Quentin eyed her thoughtfully. She didn't realize just how much of a nuisance she was going to be. Fuentes had obviously fallen for her in a big way, and when Cuban generals fall for nice-looking girls, they don't stop at patting their hands. At the best of times a swell looker is out of place in a revolution, but when she's parked right in the stronghold of one of the big shots, the mug who undertakes to protect her might just as well make out his will. There wasn't much Quentin could do. They were all in the hotel as prisoners, so he might just as well offer her his protection as not. There was no side-stepping the issue.

He introduced her to Morecombre, who seemed rather awe-struck at her beauty. Anita went over by the window and watched Myra out of the corner of her eye. She was smart enough to know that she didn't stand much chance with the two Americans as long as this girl was around.

Quentin poured Myra out a cup of coffee and Morecombre hastily prepared breakfast for her. She sat in a chair, rather tense, rather hostile, and a little frightened.

'I don't know how long we shall be here, but we must watch the grub,' Quentin said. He looked over at the manager. 'You'd better get downstairs and see if they've taken over the hotel services. If not, see what you can do about hustling up some more grub.' He swung round to Anita. 'I want an outfit for señorita right away. She can't live in these clothes she has. Go and rake up something.' He went over and slipped twenty dollars into Anita's hand.

She looked at it, bit her lip and then handed it back. 'I don't need the money to do that,' she said. 'She can have some of my clothes. Would that do?'

Quentin hooked his finger in the front of her dress and dropped the note into the hollow. 'Yeah,' he said, with his big, lazy grin, 'that'll do fine. Take the dough, baby; you might need it one of these days.'

She went out of the room without smiling at him.

As soon as she had gone and they were alone, he said: 'Now we've got a moment to ourselves, we might as well consider our position. Quite frankly, I don't like it too much.'

'What are you beefing about?' Morecombre asked. 'We're all right, ain't we?'

'For the time being,' Quentin agreed, 'but if trouble starts we shall be between two fires. If the natives come here and succeed in forcing an entry, everyone will be knocked off, including we three. If they don't get in, Fuentes might think it a good idea to get rid of us rather than risk us raising the dust about being arrested like this.'

'For Gawd's sake,' Morecombre said, staring, 'he wouldn't do that?'

Quentin shrugged. 'He might. Then there is Miss Arnold here. She's in rather a difficult position. Apparently the General has got ideas about her – ideas which will take a little checking.'

Myra shivered. 'What am I going to do?' she asked.

'That's what we've got to think about. Did you bring a gun with you, Bill?'

Morecombre nodded. 'Yeah,' he said, 'I always carry one. Did you?'

Quentin patted his pocket. 'I don't say we'll get anywhere with rough stuff, but it's nice to know, in case we have to start something.' He went to the window and looked down at the deserted waterfront. 'No one about,' he said. 'It looks as if something is blowing up. You can't hear a sound. I'm willing to bet that any moment the lid's coming off.'

Morecombre crossed over and stood just behind him, looking over his shoulder. Myra hesitated, put her coffee-cup down and joined them.

Quentin said unemotionally, 'Look, it's starting' – he pointed down. 'Good God, Bill, we ought to be down there. We ought to get to a telephone. Look over there. Do you see those guys coming out of that house? Look, they're carrying rifles. They're not soldiers . . . they're dockers. Dockers with rifles . . . I told you how it'd be. There they go. Nothing's going to happen until they run into the soldiers . . . that's when the lid will come off.'

'Anyway, I can get pictures,' Morecombre said. 'I'm mighty glad I brought the telescopic attachment with me.' He rushed across the room and feverishly began setting up his camera.

Myra edged closer to Quentin. 'Do you really think there will be fighting?' she asked.

Quentin didn't take his eyes off the little group of men making their way cautiously along the waterfront. 'I guess so,' he said shortly. 'Those guys are itching to let those cannons off . . . I don't blame them really.'

Morecombre came back and set up the camera on a short-legged tripod. He hastily made adjustments, focusing on the men below. From where they stood they had an uninterrupted view of the whole of the winding waterfront.

Quentin stepped back into the room. 'It would be as well to keep out of sight as much as possible,' he said to Myra. 'These guys are going to shoot at anything.'

From just inside the verandah they watched the small group of men move slowly along the waterfront. They moved very cautiously, pausing outside each café, their rifles at the ready. No one disturbed them. Whether the word had gone out that they were starting something, Quentin didn't know, but no one interfered with them; even the dogs slid into the dark alleys at their approach. Finally, they turned off the waterfront and made their direction inland. The three watchers lost sight of them.

Quentin went over to the sideboard and poured out three long gin slings. He handed them round in silence.

Morecombre sat back on his heels; he kept near the window. 'Fell a little flat, didn't it?' he said. 'Thought this was where it was going to start.'

Quentin shook his head. 'It's started all right,' he said. 'In a day or so there'll be as much trouble as anyone can handle here. That little gang will be wiped out. Then a bigger gang will turn up and they'll go the same way. Then a bigger gang still will appear, and maybe a number of them will get away and join the next band. It takes time to get a real revolution going. These guys don't have much chance to organize.'

Morecombre got up and stretched his legs. 'Maybe we're in the safest spot. I don't fancy running around the streets with that sort of stuff going on.'

Quentin didn't answer. He glanced over at Myra, and his

lips tightened. If she wasn't there, he would have been a lot happier. Maybe Fuentes would have left them alone but for her. There was always trouble when a woman turned up in a spot like this.

A tap sounded on the door and Anita came in. She carried a bundle of clothes over her arm. 'Señorita is welcome to these,' she said, looking first at Myra and then at Quentin.

Myra took them from her. 'It is very kind of you,' she said.

Anita shrugged. 'They will not make señorita less attractive,' she said. There was a malicious look in her eyes as she said it. She went out without looking back.

Morecombre ran his fingers through his unruly hair. 'That dame is mad about something,' he said. 'I didn't like the dirty look, did you?'

Quentin went over and opened the bedroom door. 'You can change in there,' he said. 'I'm sure you will feel much more comfortable out of that evening affair.'

Myra said: 'I will. Please don't worry about me any further. You must have a lot to think about. I can manage now very well.' She went into the room and shut the door.

Morecombre heaved a sigh. 'That's very nice, isn't it?' he said, jerking his head towards the door. 'A little cold and standoffish, but she'd make a swell tumble, huh?'

Quentin lit a cigarette. 'I don't think you're the only guy with that idea,' he said.

'Fuentes?'

'Yeah, that's where the trouble's going to start for us. We can't very well stand by and let that punk go for her, can we?'

'Like hell,' Morecombre said. 'If he starts anything like that I'll knock him into next week.'

'At least, that's what you'll try to do,' Quentin said dryly. 'Actually, the guy has some forty soldiers to help him.'

Morecombre sniffed. 'Oh, I guess we could manage them together. I wouldn't like to try it on my own, but, with you, I guess we'd get by.'

'Sure,' Quentin said dubiously. 'But all the same, I wish she hadn't turned up like this.'

He went back to the window and continued to stare into the deserted streets. Morecombre joined him, and for a while they stood silent, watching the sun gradually fall behind the horizon.

3

In the evening it became cooler. The slight breeze coming in off the bay stirred the net curtains of the verandah window.

Morecombre sat by the window, smoking a pipe, his eyes never shifting from the deserted waterfront. Quentin lay on the divan with his eyes shut, and an open book lying across his chest. Myra sat away from them, trying to read, but every sound from outside, and every step in the corridor, made her stiffen.

They had just finished a snack meal from the assortment of canned food, and Quentin was mentally calculating how long that small store would last them. He opened his eyes and glanced across at Myra. She was looking away from him, unaware that he was watching her. He thought she looked absurdly young in the short, black silk dress Anita had lent her. Her long legs in shiny black stockings and the touch of white under the dress, which he could glimpse from the angle he was lying, brought a frown to his face. She was too good, he decided. Her fair hair, like a sheet of shining metal, reflected in the soft light of the reading-lamp. He liked her long, thin fingers, and the curve of her arms. He studied her face thoughtfully. The hard curve of her mouth puzzled him. The expression on her face made him grope for the right word – disillusion. Yes, that was it.

He found himself wondering what had happened on the previous night. Why she was unescorted. How she came to miss the ship. All day she had been very silent. Obviously she was grateful to them for offering her hospitality, but there it ended. She had erected a barrier which neither Morecombre nor he could break through. In the long hours of waiting and listening for something to happen, both the men would have been glad to have been on their own. This constant small talk that led nowhere and social politeness which neither found to his mood had become irksome. Quentin found himself wishing that she would go away, but she had sat quietly in the chair all the long afternoon, speaking when spoken to, but otherwise retaining a brooding silence.

Both the men had given up finally in despair, and for the past hour there was a heavy strained silence, broken only by the rustle of a turning page and the creak of a chair, as

Morecombre shifted from one position to another.

Suddenly from out of the darkness came three rifle-shots. They sounded very close. Morecombre sprang to his feet. 'Did you hear that?' he asked, rather unnecessarily.

Quentin was already up and crossed the room to turn out the light. Then he stumbled over to the window and peered out. But for the flickering lights on the waterfront he could see nothing. They listened in the darkness. Faintly they could hear someone shouting, and then two more shots sounded. This time they caught a glimpse of the flash from a rifle. It was just outside the hotel.

'Maybe the sentry's gettin' the wind-up,' Quentin said. 'I noticed a man at the gate this afternoon.'

Morecombre fumed. 'He must be shooting at something,' he said, going out on to the verandah.

Quentin reached forward and jerked him back. 'Keep off there, Bill,' he advised. 'In this moonlight you'd be quite a target.'

Morecombre hastily stepped into the room and put on the light again. 'Well, I suppose this is about all we can do,' he said irritably, 'just sit around and wonder. I tell you I'm getting mighty fed up with doing nothing.'

The door jerked open, and a young lieutenant walked in. Behind him stood two soldiers, their rifles hovering in the direction of the two Americans. 'You'll pardon me,' the Lieutenant said in careful English, 'for interrupting you.'

Quentin said, 'What was that shooting?'

The Lieutenant shrugged. 'A little disturbance. It is purely a local affair. I assure you it is well in hand by now.'

Quentin concealed his impatience. 'Well, Lieutenant, what can I do for you?'

The Lieutenant glanced round the room until his eyes rested on Myra. A thin little smile came to his sharp-featured face, and he bowed from the waist. 'General Fuentes presents his compliments, and wishes you to dine with him,' he said.

Myra lifted her chin. 'Will you thank the General and tell him that I have already dined?'

There was a long pause. The Lieutenant stood, the thin smile still on his mouth, his eyes slowly travelling over her with an appraising, insolent stare.

Quentin said quietly, 'Is that all?'

The Lieutenant ignored him. He said to Myra: 'Señorita doesn't understand. This is – how shall I put it? – a command invitation, yes?'

Quentin eased his way between the Lieutenant and Myra. 'Perhaps I could make things a little easier for you, Lieutenant,' he said. 'Miss Arnold does not wish to dine with the General. She has already dined and she prefers to stay here under my protection.'

The Lieutenant appeared to see him for the first time. He gave an elaborate start. 'Señor would be advised not to interfere in this matter,' he said. 'Escaping prisoners are unfortunately shot.' He looked significantly at the two soldiers. 'I am sure señorita would not wish to be the cause of such a distressing occurrence?'

Quentin said: 'You're bluffing. Miss Arnold stays here with me.'

Myra suddenly stood up. 'No,' she said, 'I will go. He is quite right. It would be absurd for you to be hurt because of me. You have important work to do. I will come with you,' she said, turning to the Lieutenant.

At a sign from him, the two soldiers took a step forward, bringing their rifles to the ready.

'One movement from either of these men,' the Lieutenant said sharply, 'you are to shoot them like dogs. Come, señorita, let us have no more of this play-acting.' He stepped to the door and jerked it open.

Myra hesitated, then walked out quietly. The Lieutenant followed her, shutting the door behind her.

He overtook her in the passage. 'The General has a suite on the second floor to this,' he said; 'you would be advised to be as accommodating as possible to the General. He is a man who has what he wants and it is unfortunate that he has – what shall I say?' – he flicked his fingers impatiently – 'no finesse, is that the word? You understand, señorita?'

Myra stopped and faced him. 'Am I to understand that you are acting in the capacity of a procurer, Lieutenant?' she said coldly.

The Lieutenant started as if she had struck him. His yellowish skin darkened. 'You will find that an unfortunate remark,' he said, his eyes gleaming angrily. 'Since you prefer such candour, I see no reason why you should not realize the position you are in. The General will not tolerate any nonsense from you. Unless you are prepared to be entirely passive, you will be held to the bed by soldiers. Now do you understand?'

Myra didn't flinch. She said quietly: 'Please take me immediately to General Fuentes. I am sure he will be interested to hear what you have just said.'

The Lieutenant went very pale. 'But, señorita – surely . . .' he stammered.

She walked past him and mounted the stairs. Her face was set in a cold, hard mask. The Lieutenant ran after her and caught her at the head of the stairs. 'Señorita, I have to apologize. My remarks were entirely out of place. I wish to withdraw them.' Sweat had started out on his face, and he endeavoured to smile, succeeding only in making a terrified grimace.

She took no notice of him at all, but continued to walk down the corridor to where a soldier stood with fixed bayonet. He saw her as she approached, and a little smirk crossed his fat, oily face. He rapped on the door and threw it open. 'The señorita,' he said.

The General stood by the open french windows. He looked up eagerly as Myra came in. 'This is going to be a beautiful evening,' he said, advancing with his hand outstretched. There was no smile on his face. His eyes, like little glass pebbles, took in her beauty possessively.

Myra ignored his hand. She said: 'Is it true, General, that you employ your soldiers to assist you in your love-making?'

The General stood transfixed. Blood mounted to his face, and he half raised his hand as if he was about to strike her. She met his furious eyes without flinching. For several seconds he was so nonplussed that he could only make little spluttering noises, then he jerked out, 'How dare you say such a thing?'

'I thought there must be some misunderstanding. Your Lieutenant told me that I was to expect no mercy from you, and that if I did not submit to you, I was to be held down on your bed by your soldiers.' The scorn and contempt in her voice nearly drove the General crazy. She stood very erect, her eyes flashing and her hands clenched by her side. She knew that everything depended on keeping the General angry. 'I am relieved you are angry, General,' she went on. 'I did not believe for a moment that a man who has risen to your high rank would tolerate such an insufferable insult to a woman. Perhaps you will correct your Lieutenant's conception of you. It is not flattering.'

Fuentes took a quick step forward and gripped her wrist. His face was white with fury. 'Did he really say that?' he demanded.

Myra, feeling a little sick, said: 'I have had enough of Cuban hospitality for tonight. Would you please take me back to my room.'

She turned to the door and opened it. The soldier on guard gaped at her, and made a half-hearted attempt to stop her, but she brushed past him and walked down the passage. She heard the General's light step behind her and she had to make an effort not to break into a run. He overtook her at the head of the stairs. 'It is most unfortunate that you should have received such treatment. Will you reconsider your decision and return to my suite? I can assure you of my protection. As for Lieutenant Cartez, I shall discipline him severely.'

Keeping her voice steady, Myra said: 'You must excuse me, General, but I have had a considerable shock. Your generosity, when you have me entirely at a disadvantage, is worthy of the highest traditions of your race. Please don't think that I'm ungrateful.' She gave him a frightened little smile and ran downstairs. The General watched her go. He was like a stupefied bull in the ring, transfixed by the sudden flip of a matador's cape.

He stood very silent at the head of the stairs until she had gone from his sight. His face was twisted with vicious fury, then he jerked round and barked to the sentry, 'Send Lieutenant Cartez to me at once.'

The sentry, round-eyed with fear, moved hurriedly to obey. Fuentes raised his hand. 'Wait,' he said. 'In an hour's time I want a woman brought to my suite, do you understand? The maid who works here will do. Get her at once and bring her to me in an hour's time.'

The sentry grinned uneasily. 'Yes, Your Excellency.'

Fuentes looked at him. 'If you touch her during that hour I will personally attend to your punishment. See that she is clean and wearing clean clothes when you bring her. Now, send the Lieutenant to me.'

He turned and walked back to his room with quick, impatient steps.

4

The small ornate clock on the mantelpiece struck nine o'clock sharply. Faint sounds of distant shouting and an occasional shot drifted in through the open windows. Morecombre sat on the floor, his back to the room, looking into the darkness. He had not moved for half an hour.

Quentin, in shirt-sleeves and his collar open, paced the room with long strides. Cigarette-butts piled in the fireplace. Every now and then he glanced across at Myra, who lay asleep on the divan. He thought she looked very tired, drawn and defenceless, now that her features were relaxed. He crossed over to Morecombre and stood behind him, looking out into the night.

'We're in a jam, Bill,' he said, very softly; 'we've got to do something before the night's out.' He looked over his shoulder at the sleeping girl. 'She was lucky to get away with it this time, but tomorrow will be a different story. We ought to try to get her out of this.'

Morecombre grunted. 'You mean shooting our way through hordes of soldiers like they do on the movies?'

'Along those lines.'

'We two mugs protecting her from a hail of lead with our big, sunburnt bodies – huh?'

'Something like that.'

'O.K., if that's the way you feel. I guess I've had enough of newspaper work. Maybe heaven won't be so bad,' he laughed. 'I wonder if angels take their wings off when they go to bed. It would rather restrict one if they didn't.'

Quentin lit a cigarette. 'The consul's about a half mile from here. It will be tricky going, but that's where we've got to take her.'

Morecombre stood up. 'When do we go?'

'After midnight, I think. We might stand a chance of surprising the guards.'

A sudden wild frightened scream made them swing round. Myra also sat up with a start. 'What was that?' she asked, her voice going off key.

Quentin went to the door and jerked it open. As he did so

the scream was repeated. It came from upstairs. The sentry outside the door threatened him with his rifle. 'Get back into your room,' he said.

Quentin took no notice, he stood staring upwards. At the head of the staircase, with her back to him, stood Anita. She was naked.

Facing her was a gigantic negro soldier. He held a rifle and face almost split in two by a jeering grin. He held a rifle and bayonet and the long glittering blade hovered within a foot of her.

Before Quentin could move he heard a voice say impatiently, 'Go on, you fool, finish her.' He recognized the dry, harsh voice of Fuentes. His hand swung to his hip pocket, but the sentry hit him very hard on his chest with the butt of the rifle, sending him staggering back against Morecombre, who had crowded up behind him.

They heard Anita give another terrified scream. They saw her catch the blade as the negro drove at her. They saw her hands sliding along the blade and the blood, as the sharp bayonet opened her palms, running down her wrists, then the point of the blade struck her in the middle of her chest with incredible force, and three inches of red steel protruded from her back. Still grinning, the negro held the rifle steady so that she could not fall. Her knees went and her hands beat feebly against the barrel of the rifle, but he still held her, rolling his great black eyes and laughing at her.

Quentin regained his balance. The sentry had drawn back, his finger curled round the trigger of his rifle. 'Get back!' he said savagely. 'Get back!'

As Anita fell, the negro shoved out his foot and kicked her off the bayonet. It was a tremendous kick and it sent her crashing down the stairs. Her body thudded to the floor almost at Quentin's feet. The sentry took his eyes off Quentin for a moment to gape at her. Quentin didn't hesitate, his hand flashed to his pocket and with one movement shot the sentry between his eyes. The big negro, hearing the shot, came charging to the top of the stairs and Quentin fired again. The negro gave a startled grunt, put both his hands to his belly and sat down heavily on the floor.

One glance at Anita was sufficient. She was pathetically, horribly dead. Quentin spun round. 'Let's go,' he said; 'no time like the present.'

'I'll take the rifle and go first,' Morecombre said, stepping forward. 'You bring Miss Arnold and cover the rear.'

Before Quentin could protest, Morecombre was already off down the corridor.

Quentin said sharply, 'Come on, we've got to get out of here.'

Myra came to the doorway, very white, but steady. He grabbed her arm and bustled her past the two bodies. His face was set and grim. He knew this wasn't going to be a picnic.

Morecombre had already reached the head of the stairs. Faintly they could hear the General shouting, and as Morecombre took one step down, a soldier came dashing to the foot of the stairs. Holding the rifle at his waist, Morecombre fired at him. The rifle kicked up and the bullet swished over the soldier's head. As Morecombre fumbled at the bolt, Quentin came up behind him and shot the soldier as he was about to fire in his turn. 'Use your gun,' he snapped. 'You ain't used to a rifle.'

'You're telling me,' Morecombre said, wiping the sweat from his face. He dropped the rifle with a clatter, and pulled a police .38 special from his hip pocket. They got down the next flight of stairs into the lobby of the hotel before three soldiers and a sergeant appeared from out of a side room. Two of the soldiers fired point-blank at them. Quentin felt the wind of a bullet against his face, and he fired with Morecombre. Two of the soldiers pitched forward, and the sergeant was shot through the arm. He turned and ran back into the room, shouting at the top of his voice.

Morecombre said: 'Go down to the cellar – you won't get out any other way. They can't get you there . . . I've seen it.' He swayed on his feet.

Quentin ran to him. 'Are you hurt?' he asked, taking his arm.

Morecombre's legs folded up under him and Quentin had to lower him to the floor. 'What is it?' he asked, bending over him.

'Go on – go on, you nut,' Morecombre said faintly, 'don't worry about me. Get the girl away.' He pressed his hands to his chest and Quentin could see blood oozing through his fingers.

'Keep your hair on,' he said gently. 'We'll go together. Put your arm round my neck.'

'For Christ's sake leave me alone,' Morecombre said, his voice breaking into a sob. 'Clear off – they can't do anything to me . . . Get the girl . . .'

'Damn the girl!' Quentin said savagely. 'I'm not going to leave you.' He stooped, and with a tremendous effort lifted Morecombre and took two staggering steps towards the back elevator which screened the service stairs. 'Get down quick . . . go first,' he gasped to Myra.

She snatched up Morecombre's gun which had fallen on the floor and stood watching the door through which the soldier had disappeared. Quentin staggered on. He knew it would only waste time if he argued. Morecombre suddenly stiffened in his arms and then went limp, upsetting Quentin's balance and bringing him to his knees. One look at Morecombre's face was sufficient. Quentin laid him on the floor gently, and then, rising, ran back to Myra. 'He's gone,' he said. 'Come on, for God's sake.'

Together they ran down the dark stairs into the basement. As they reached the bottom of the stairs they heard a heavy pounding of feet overhead. Taking Myra's arm, Quentin hustled her along the stone corridor, down another flight of stone steps into the cellar. The entrance to the cellar was low and narrow. Only one person could enter at a time. It was an ideal place for a siege.

'We'll be all right here for a time,' Quentin said, producing a small flashlight and examining the low-roofed vault. It was very large and full of wine barrels. 'Doesn't look as if we'll go thirsty, either,' he added with a crooked grin.

He found the switch of the pilot light and a dim glow appeared in the ceiling when he turned down the switch. 'If we can shift a couple of these barrels over to the door we can hold this place until the cows come home.'

Myra helped him get the barrels into position and then she sat down limply on the stone floor. Quentin was too occupied to bother with her for the moment. He made certain that there was no other exit and then took up a position by the door. He could hear movements going on upstairs, and then a sudden clicking of heels. He heard Fuentes say, 'Where are they?'

There was a murmured reply which Quentin could not hear, then Fuentes said: 'We can pick them up later. Put two men at the head of the stairs. Tell them to shoot at sight.'

Quentin made a little face. 'He's got us there,' he said. 'They can't get in, but we can't get out. We'll have to wait until someone comes along and chases these guys away.'

Myra said: 'If it wasn't for me, this would never have happened.'

'Forget it. What's the use of talking like that? If we get out of it, I've got a grand story to write. If we don't, some other guy's got the story – so what?'

'Your friend lost his life because of me.'

Quentin's face hardened. 'This ain't the time for that kind of talk. It won't get you anywhere. Bill was unlucky. If you hadn't been here, you don't think we would have let the General push Anita around as he did, do you?' He shook his head. 'No, I guess we were mugs to come to this joint. We wanted to be in at the death, now it looks like we're going to attend the wrong funeral.'

Myra sat limply, her hands folded in her lap and her long legs tucked under her. Morecombre's death had shocked her badly.

He got to his feet and went over to the wine-bins. After careful scrutiny he selected a couple of bottles and drew the corks with the corkscrew on his knife. 'Have you ever tried drinking a nice light wine from the bottle?' he asked her. 'I want you to have some of this stuff. It'll do you good.'

She hesitated, then took the bottle. The wine was strong and sweet. They were thirsty and they both drank deeply. He sat by the door again. 'Not bad stuff, is it?' he said, feeling the wine surging through him. Potent stuff, he thought, and put the bottle down. It wouldn't do to have a muddled head in his position.

Glancing at her, he saw that her face was a little flushed and her eyes brighter. She drank from the bottle again. 'It is strong, isn't it?' she said, after a moment, and then laughed. She stared at him thoughtfully for a few minutes. 'You know, I'm scared being on my own like this,' she said abruptly.

Quentin could see she was getting a little tight. 'You don't have to be scared of me,' he said quietly.

'No, I know that.' She turned the bottle slowly in her hands. 'You know when I said it was my fault that your friend was killed?'

'We don't have to start that all over again.'

'But it's true. It began with Lacey. You wouldn't know about Lacey, but he and the moon began it.' She put the bottle to her lips and tilted her head. Quentin made a little move to stop her, then thought she might just as well get tight and talk.

She put the bottle down. 'I was crazy. Have you ever been crazy? Have you ever felt that you'd give anything in the world for a really fine man to sweep you off your feet?' She looked at him, and shook her head. 'No, I guess you'd never feel that way. I did. I wanted love. I wanted someone to sweep me off my feet. I was so sick of New York. I came to Havana because I heard it was the place of love. I wanted to believe it so badly that I kidded myself to death. I wanted it so badly that I let a down-at-heel ship's Romeo seduce me. That is the type of double fool that I am. That was Lacey. Tall, beautiful and terribly, terribly cheap, and I thought he was the real thing. I couldn't go back to the boat after that, could I? I mean, I couldn't take that long trip back, scared that I might run into him at any moment. No, I couldn't do that. So I decided to stay. Do you see now? If I hadn't been such a bitch, you wouldn't have annoyed the General, your friend wouldn't have died . . . and I shouldn't be here. You do see that, don't you?'

All the time she had been talking, Quentin stared at his highly polished shoes. This sudden outburst rather shook him. She didn't look the type to go off the rails. He said at last: 'It's damn' queer how things happen, isn't it? I mean, maybe, when you get out of this, and look back on it, you'll be able to see why it had to happen.'

Myra screwed up her eyes as if to see him more clearly. 'You think it had to happen?'

He nodded. 'Sure, I think these sort of things are planned to happen to you. Sometimes you think that life is giving you a hell of a belting, but when you've had time to get away from it, and you look back, you see why it happened. Most times you realize that it was the best thing that could have happened.'

She frowned. 'Can you see any redeeming feature in being shut up in a cellar with a good chance of losing one's life?'

Quentin smiled. 'Right now I can't, but maybe in another six months' time I might be glad to have had the experience.'

'No, that couldn't work with me. Why should it happen to us? Why must it be us, down here?'

'Why should it be anyone else? I'm not scared what will happen to us. Are you?'

Her face suddenly twisted, and she began to cry. 'Yes, I'm scared. I feel that we'll never get away. It is because I was such a fool. You've got to suffer because of me.'

He went over to her and sat by her side. 'It's not like that,' he said, giving her his handkerchief; 'you'll come out of it all right and so will I. In a few days you'll be looking back on this as a swell adventure and something to tell your friends about.'

His arm went round her and she relaxed against him. They sat like that for a long time until she fell asleep.

5

It was just after midnight when things began to happen. The sound of shooting and distant shouting became ominously nearer. Myra woke with a start as three rifle-shots crashed out above them. She gave a little scream and looked wildly round the dim cellar. She could just make out Quentin kneeling at the door, watching the stairs; the light reflected on the barrel of his .38. She scrambled over to him. 'What is it?' she asked.

'Something's happenin',' he said. 'Maybe the natives have found out that Fuentes is here.'

Again rifle-shots came from upstairs, and they could hear someone shouting orders feverishly in Spanish. Heavy boots thudded as soldiers ran about taking up positions. Sudden yells and shouts came from the garden. Quentin eased his position. 'Yeah,' he said, 'I guess they've come to smoke him out. Listen to that.'

The distant noise was rapidly swelling into a tremendous uproar as the crowd outside approached. The cellar shook with the noise of rifle-fire as the soldiers poured volley after volley into the crowd. More yells and screams followed, then suddenly someone screamed like a frightened child, and a tremendous explosion brought plaster and dust down on top of the two crouching in the cellar.

Myra was thrown off the box she was sitting on on to the floor.

'Some guy threw a bomb,' Quentin gasped, helping her to her feet. 'Are you all right?'

She brushed her dress with her hands. 'Yes . . . Will they do that again? Is it safe here?'

'Sure, these cellars can take a lot of that. I wonder how the General liked that little packet.' He went over to the door and peered up the staircase. Plaster lay in great pieces all the way up the stairs, and the air was thick with dust. Shooting began again, but this time the volleys were very ragged. 'I guess these guys won't hold out much longer. I think that bomb killed a lot of them.'

Two soldiers suddenly came running down the stairs, their scared faces coated with white dust, and their eyes filled with terror. Quentin fired at them. He hit one, who pitched forward, rolling down the rest of the stairs. The other soldier gave a yell and bolted upstairs again.

Myra flopped on the floor, putting her hands over her ears. The noise of the surging crowd and the tramping of feet overhead told them that the natives had entered the hotel. 'They're in now,' Quentin said. 'We've got to keep out of sight. They'll go for us if they see us. Once they have finished Fuentes they'll probably clear off, then we can beat it when it gets quieter.'

The uproar continued upstairs. Shots, yells and tramping of feet. Suddenly a full-throated roar went up, followed immediately by a high scream of terror.

'They've got him,' Quentin said, running to the doorway and leaning over the barrels, trying to see up the stairs.

Myra crouched lower on the floor, shutting out the snarling roar of the crowd as it surged forward. Then, above the noise, she heard Quentin shout, 'Look out . . . look out!' She saw him trying to get away from the door, his hands shielding his face. She could see his eyes, very large and frightened. Then a blinding flash came just outside the door and she became enveloped in dust and bricks. She was quite conscious of what was happening around her. She saw Quentin's body lifted as if by a giant's hand and tossed across the cellar. She went to him on her hands and knees. When she got close, she stopped, her hand going to her mouth. The bomb had made him like some horrible nightmare of torn blood and flesh. She scrambled to her feet and ran away from him. The force of the explosion numbed her mind. She couldn't think. She just wanted to get away from that poor, mutilated body. She found herself crawling up the broken staircase. The woodwork creaked under her weight, but she kept on until she reached the top. The hall was in a complete shambles. Soldiers lay about the floor in big crimson pools.

She wandered into the lounge. One of the bombs had exploded in there. Furniture was scattered and broken. Glass from mirrors and windows lay on the floor. Plaster and dust covered everything with a coat of white. Opposite her, pinned by bayonets to the door, was the General. His head hung on his chest, and the front of his white uniform was blotched with blood. She put her hands to her face and ran blindly out of the room.

At that moment a small party of natives, bent on loot, came in from the garden. They closed in on her like a hungry pack of wolves, their hands seeking and their eyes maddened with lust for her. She was more aware of the overpowering reek of their bodies as they struggled round her than her own terror. She was conscious of thinking: 'So he was wrong. I knew he was wrong. This couldn't have been planned. God wouldn't let this happen to me if He could stop it.'

One huge native managed to pull her away from the others and he tossed her across his back, threatening the others with the General's revolver. He began edging away towards the stairs.

She said to herself: 'He is only going to do what Lacey did. Only this time it will be more sincere. He won't pretend that he is a beautiful man, and I shan't pretend that Havana is the place of love.' She watched the floor move swiftly under big, black, naked feet. Dangling over his shoulder, almost upside down, she had a unique view of the hotel lounge. She found that she was laughing, because it was all rather funny. The group of natives huddled together, their eyes hungry and disappointed. All wanting her, but because this big one had the gun, they just had to stand back and do without.

She said to the black feet: 'I know what you want. I am a woman of the world. I had to come to Havana to find out about it, but I know. I know exactly what you will do to me when you have got me alone. It won't be long now.' Then she thought hopefully: 'I wonder if I shall die tonight?'

Obviously no one will blame her for thinking and talking like this, as the accumulation of circumstances had been too much for her reason.

VIGIL

George came in around two o'clock. He stood just inside the little room with the door open behind him.

Alfy sat on the one chair in the room, close to the empty hearth. He sat very limply, with his hands thrust deep into his trouser pockets. He didn't look up when George came in. More than anything, he wanted to be alone. He didn't have to pretend when he was alone. George made it difficult for him. It wouldn't do to let George see that he couldn't take it. Anyway, it was getting a little too much for him to pretend any more, even with George in the room.

George came in and shut the door. It wasn't that George wanted to stay, he didn't; but his conscience wouldn't let him go. He sat on the edge of the table and fumbled for a cigarette. The scrape of the match on the box made Alfy turn his head a little.

He said, 'You needn't bother.'

'I guess I'll hang around. It don't seem right to go,' George said ponderously, dragging down a lungful of smoke. 'It's long, ain't it?'

Alfy moved his feet restlessly. He wanted to avoid talking about it. 'Listen,' he said, 'you don't have to tell me. You don't have to say anything about it. If you think for a moment, you'd know that nothing you say could be new to me.'

George looked at him and then shifted his eyes. There was a long pause, then Alfy said, 'I'm sorry, I didn't mean that.'

'Sure, that's all right,' George said hurriedly. 'I guess I wasn't thinking.'

'That's right. Your weren't thinkin'.'

'Maybe I'd better go,' George said. He sounded so miserable that Alfy couldn't send him away.

'No, you stay. It's all right that you stay.'

'Well I'd like to. I wouldn't care to be far away in case—'

Alfy winced. This was going to be worse than he thought.

He said: 'No, I can see that. Yeah, I can see that all right.'

George looked at him again uneasily. He stubbed out his cigarette and took another. He hesitated, then he offered the packet to Alfy. 'You'd better smoke,' he said.

Alfy took a cigarette out of the carton. He didn't do it easily because his hand was shaking, but George pretended he hadn't noticed. When he lit their cigarettes he was annoyed that his own hand was very unsteady.

Alfy looked at him across the tiny flame of the match. There was a look in George's eyes that startled him. George looked away immediately, but it gave Alfy quite a shock. He realized, not without a stab of jealousy, that George was suffering just as much as he was. This discovery rather pulled him together and he slumped back in his chair to consider it.

Well it was understandable. George had always got on well with Margie. He'd been in and out most days since they were married. Wasn't George his best friend? It was swell of George to feel bad about it, or was it? He frowned down at his feet. This won't do, he told himself. He'd got quite enough on his mind right now. It wasn't the time to think up new worries. Maybe he was being a little too hard on George. Maybe, if he got his mind to thinking about George, it'd help him forget what was going on.

He said with a little burst of confidence: 'I don't like that croaker, George. There's something about that guy.'

George ran his thick fingers through his hair. 'Yeah?' he said. 'What's the matter with him? Ain't he any good?' There was an anxious note in his voice.

'Sure he's good. The best croaker in the town, but he ain't got any feelin'. A while back I heard him laughing.'

'Laughin'?'

'Yeah, and the nurse laughed too.'

There was a long pause. Then George said, 'That's a hell of a thing to do.'

Alfy went on: 'He's a cold guy. I bet nothing would move that guy.'

George said, 'He's been here an awful long time, ain't he?'

Alfy looked at the clock on the mantelshelf. 'Four hours,' he said, then, as if to give himself courage, he added: 'He said it would take a while.'

'He said that, did he?' George wiped his face with a handkerchief. 'Ain't nothin' gone wrong, do you think?'

Unconsciously he put into words what Alfy had been thinking for the past half-hour. It didn't do Alfy much good. He said, 'For God's sake, must you take that line?'

George got off the table and wandered across to the window. He leant against the wall, holding back the curtain to look into the street. 'The moon's still up,' he said unevenly; 'high as hell that moon is.'

Alfy said: 'We'd planned not to have kids, George. Somethin' must've gone wrong. Margie wanted a kid, but I said no. You can't have a kid an' a boat. Not these days, you can't. Margie was nobody's dope. She'd got her mind fixed for a kid, George. You know how women are, but I watched it. How the hell it went wrong I don't know.'

George stood very still and silent by the window. He didn't say anything.

Very faintly, from somewhere upstairs, someone screamed.

George beat Alfy to the door. They stood in the passage listening. The only sound they could hear was the faint roar of the overhead trains.

George said, 'Ain't you goin' up?'

'Best not. I can't do anythin'.'

They stood there listening for several minutes, and then, as they turned to go back to the room, the scream came again. Both men stiffened.

Overhead a door opened and light streamed on to the stairs. Heavy deliberate footsteps came down the passage and the doctor appeared at the head of the stairs. He stood looking down at the two men in the hallway. He was wiping his hands on a towel. He came down slowly, still using the towel.

Silently the two men backed into the sitting-room as he approached, and the doctor came in and half shut the door behind him. A nerve in his face kept twitching, and his cold eyes were dreadfully bored.

He said to Alfy, 'Your wife's havin' a bad time.' Carefully he began to fold the towel. 'She ought never to have had a child. Too narrow. I don't think I can save the child. I could try, but it would be very dangerous.'

A low sigh from George caused the doctor to look at him

sharply. He said impatiently: 'Hold up, man, hold up. I've got enough on my hands without looking after you.'

George sat down and put his hands over his face. Alfy looked at him very strangely.

The doctor said impatiently again, 'What do you want me to do?'

Still Alfy looked at George, a little white ring round his mouth.

The doctor put out a long thin hand and shook Alfy's arm. 'Can't you hear what I'm saying?' he said sharply.

Alfy turned his head. His eyes were very blank. 'I guess you'd better do what you think,' he said slowly. 'Yeah, do what you think.'

'You haven't understood,' the doctor said. 'I can try and save the child—'

Alfy nodded. 'Yes, sure, I understood,' he broke in, 'save Margie. It doesn't matter about the kid. She can have another some other time. Yeah, save Margie.'

The doctor gave them both a hard, puzzled look, and then went upstairs again. They heard him walk along the passage and go into Margie's bedroom.

Alfy said, 'So it didn't go wrong, after all.'

George said, without looking up: 'No, it didn't go wrong. We were crazy to have done it, Alfy. We didn't think you'd know. Margie wanted the kid. I wanted Margie. There was nothing else in it. Honest to God, Alfy, you've got to believe that. We were just crazy. It was when we all went up river. When we fished the swamp. You didn't make camp until late. It was a hell of a thing to have done. Honest, Alfy, I've felt bad about it. You were crazy not to have given her a kid; that was all she wanted. Look, I'll get out of here. There was nothing else to it, Alfy. She's yours; she'd never be anyone else's. It was just the river, the moon, and her wantin' a kid. You believe that, don't you?'

Alfy sat down on the edge of the table. He felt slightly sick. He wanted Margie more than he wanted anything else in the world. He didn't want her to die. He was surprised that he felt nothing about George and Margie. He could understand that. She did want a kid. She'd fixed her mind on a kid. Hadn't George said that there was nothing else behind it? He hadn't lost Margie's love. It was just that those two had been crazy. He could understand that. If he hadn't been such a dumb bastard and put his boat before giving her a kid, this would never have happened. When Margie was all right, he'd fix things for her. He wasn't going to be a dope any more.

George got slowly to his feet.

'It's all right,' Alfy said. 'You wait, we'll see this thing through.'

He was suddenly terribly, terribly glad that the kid was going to die. He hated himself for feeling that way, but it would mean that he could start again from scratch.

George sat back in the chair with a little sigh. He said, 'You're a swell guy taking it like that.'

They sat there for a long time in silence. The more Alfy thought about it, the more eager he was for Margie to get well so that they could start things properly. Maybe it would be fun having a kid. Maybe, if he worked hard enough, he could keep the boat and the three of them could go up the river together. Even George could come along. No, not George. It was a pity about George, but he couldn't be around any more. Not that he'd mind, but Margie would. No, George would have to go, but the little 'un would take his place.

The door opened and the doctor came in. The two men looked at him. His face was expressionless. He said: 'I'm afraid things have gone wrong. She didn't try.' The nerve in his face continued to twitch. 'She was very disappointed, you see.'

Alfy got slowly to his feet. 'Won't she—?'

The doctor shrugged a little. 'Not long now. She's asking—'

Alfy made for the door, but the doctor stopped him. 'Not you,' he said, almost kindly, 'she's asking for George.' He looked at George with faint curiosity. 'You had better hurry.'

The two of them went out of the room quickly, leaving Alfy alone.

NIGHT OUT

Jason arrived at the Gaucho Club a few minutes before midnight. He stood hesitating on the sidewalk looking up at the brilliant array of neon lights that flashed and flickered on the outside of the building.

The taxi-driver who brought him leant out of his cab and stared too. 'Quite a joint, ain't it?' he said. 'Plenty of class. I bet you have to pay to breathe in a dump like that.'

Jason groped in his pocket and found some small change. He paid the taxi-driver. Then, because he was in two minds about going into the club, he said, 'I don't know why I came here, do you?'

The driver shook his head. 'Now you're talking sense,' he said. 'Most folk just go in there. They don't ask themselves why. Personally, I wouldn't be seen dead in a joint like that.'

Jason put his foot on the running-board. 'Maybe you've got somewhere else to go,' he said. 'Maybe you're married or something.'

The driver nodded. 'Yeah, I'm married all right. I don't see what that's got to do with it.'

'Oh, it has. It makes all the difference. You see, I've got no one at the moment. I only got into New York a few hours ago. I've got a room about ten floors up, which seems to me completely isolated from any earthly contacts. I was told that the Gaucho Club was the place to find company, but I'm not at all sure that it looks quite what I want.'

The driver regarded him thoughtfully. 'It depends on what you want, boss,' he said. 'If you're looking for someone to sleep with, I should say that you've come to the right spot.'

Jason shook his head. 'I hadn't that in mind at all,' he said, 'although the suggestion is worth considering. I'll go in, anyway. If I don't like it, I can always come out again, can't I?'

The driver engaged his gears. 'It's your evening,' he said, and set his cab in motion.

Inside the club, Jason found the lights were soft, coloured and concealed, and the carpets very thick and springy to the feet. A number of impressively dressed flunkeys stood about doing nothing in particular, obviously too magnificent to be approached. They merely directed him towards a very crowded lounge simply by indicating the direction with their eyes. Feeling extraordinarily unimportant, and wishing that he had someone to share this initial ordeal with him, he went into the lounge and looked around for the cloakroom.

The lounge, however, was much more human that the entrance. A girl, wearing an extremely short white frock, a pale blue frilly little apron affair, and a large blue bow in her hair, suddenly appeared from nowhere and took his hat. She gave him a check and then, seeing he was unusually good-looking, added quite a nice smile.

Jason said hurriedly: 'Wait a moment. Don't run away. Whatever you do, don't put that hat where I can't get it quickly. I may not stay. My nerves are fluttering right now. I suppose you're used to this – this magnificence? You would be. Yeah, no doubt I could get use to it. But right now I'm shaken. Those guys down front certainly made me nervous. I don't think it is a smart idea having those guys. I guess they turn away a lot of business.'

The girl looked at him closely, rejected the idea that he was drunk, and decided that he was just a little soft. 'You don't have to worry about them,' she said. 'Most of our clients come here tight and they never notice them.'

Jason considered that. 'To hell with that for an idea,' he said finally. 'However, now I'm here, what do you advise?'

'If I were you,' she said seriously, 'I would go to the bar and buy myself a lot of drink. Then I should go into the restaurant, get a table close to the band, buy myself a small but carefully selected supper and enjoy myself.'

Jason fingered his white tie. 'You think it is necessary to break down my repressions with drink, do you?'

She giggled. 'I think it will help an awful lot.'

'Very well, I'll do exactly as you suggest. I'll let you know how I get on. Thank you very much.' Jason smiled at her and walked into the bar.

Here again everything was remarkably tasteful and luxurious. The bar was very long and somewhat crowded. Jason climbed on to a high stool, carefully spread his dress tails, and sat down.

Next to him was a tall man, going grey at the temples, who was talking in a completely inaudible voice to a very young egg-yolk blonde, who appeared to be wearing nothing at all under an extremely tight-fitting bottle-green gown. The gown, in itself, was modest and smart. It was modest because it was high at the throat, long in the sleeve and reached to the floor in a very graceful sweep.

The tall man prevented Jason from seeing as much of the

girl as he wished. By leaning forward, Jason could see her head and a little of her figure; by leaning back, he could just see her neat little behind, perched on the stool. He wished the tall man would go away.

The barman raised his eyebrows and Jason ordered Scotch-and-ginger. 'Make it a triple Scotch,' he said, 'it will save time.'

The barman looked at him sharply and then turned to his bottles.

The tall man stopped whispering to the egg-yolk blonde and glanced at Jason curiously.

Jason smiled at him. 'Do you favour Listerine for infectious dandruff?' he asked pleasantly.

The tall man started. 'Dandruff?' he repeated, rather stupidly.

'Sure, dandruff. I understand that the bottle-shaped bacillus known as Pityrosporum Ovale is now considered by leading authorities as the real trouble-maker.' Jason leant forward and removed an invisible hair from the tall man's coat. 'Maybe the subject doesn't interest you. If that is the case, think no more about it.'

The tall man seemed quite dazed. He said, uneasily, 'Please excuse me.' Then he whispered to the egg-yolk blonde, who leant forward and gave Jason a searching look.

Jason smiled at her. 'How do you do?' he said. 'They tell me that race-horses are to wear straw hats this summer. Absurd, I think, don't you?'

The tall man and the egg-yolk blonde left the bar. Jason watched them go rather sadly. He said to the barman: 'I don't think I made a big hit with those two, do you?'

The barman put a large glass down before him and splashed in the ginger ale. 'It ain't true about the straw hats, is it, mister?' he asked.

Jason shook his head. 'I don't think so. I thought the little girl might find that amusing.' He lifted the glass and swallowed the Scotch. He then handed the empty glass to the barman. 'Fill it up,' he said. 'I shall continue this performance until I feel I have enough to see me through what appears, at present, to be an exceedingly sticky evening.'

The barman put the bottle at Jason's elbow. 'Suppose you help yourself?' he said.

Jason thanked him. 'Would it be against the rules if you joined me?' he asked.

The barman shook his head. 'I gave up drinking three years ago,' he said.

'How extraordinary. You must tell me about it one of these days.' Jason filled his glass. 'Before you go away I should like your opinion.' He leant forward. 'The blonde that went out just now. Did she seem to you a trifle undressed under her gown?'

The barman's eyebrows lifted. 'I really didn't notice, sir,' he said stiffly.

Jason nodded understandingly. 'I suppose you gave that up also, three years ago,' he said. 'It is really quite astonishing to meet such an iron will. I must congratulate you.'

The barman said, 'You'll excuse me, sir,' and went away down to the far end of the bar.

After several more drinks Jason felt it was time to go into the restaurant. He climbed off the stool, paid his check and went through a glass door into another large room where suppers were being served. A small dance-band played in the far corner of the room, and several couples were dancing on a pocket-handkerchief-size floor.

The head waiter took him to a table set for two near the band. He sat down. 'This is my first visit here,' he confided to the waiter. 'Is it possible for a lady to join me? Do you do that sort of thing here?'

The waiter said rather stiffly, 'I'm afraid not, sir.'

Jason sighed. 'I just asked. Some places do, you know.'

The waiter dismissed the subject with a flick of his napkin. 'What would you like?'

Jason ordered supper without enthusiasm. He felt the evening was going to be a complete flop.

While he waited for his first course he looked round the room with a speculative eye. There were a number of smartly dressed women who appealed to him, but in every case they were all attached to large parties. He noticed that at the table next to him a girl sat with her back to him, and opposite her was a young man who looked as though he were permanently drunk. He was talking to the girl in penetrating tones. Jason listened with interest.

The young man said: 'I know you want to. You're just

being superior. For God's sake, don't sit there looking like a graven image.'

Jason couldn't hear what she said, but the back of her head interested him. She had very beautiful, soft brown hair.

When the band stopped playing, the young man went over to them and had a long conversation with the pianist. The pianist shook his head and then whispered to the other three players. They all looked across at the girl and whispered some more. Then the pianist stood up and the young man went back to his table.

Jason was quite interested. He saw the girl take four rings off her fingers and give them to the young man, then she got up and went over to the band.

Jason thought, 'Social butterfly inflicts talent on the joy-weary,' and prepared to be critical.

She sat down at the piano and the rest of the band stood up and grouped themselves round her. Jason could just see her tiny hands on the keyboard.

The trombone player turned his head and called to the young man: 'Miss Gellert would like a drink first.'

The young man got rather unsteadily out of his chair and brought over a glass of champagne. 'Do get on with it,' he begged; 'people will think you're showing off.'

The glass of champagne disappeared behind the group of musicians, and a moment later reappeared on top of the piano, empty.

Then, with her two tiny hands, she hit four chords all in the bass. Jason sat up in his chair, and people stopped talking.

She played for exactly five minutes, then she got up and went back to her table. People clapped very loudly and shouted, but she wouldn't play again. Jason was so impressed that he said to the young man: 'That was simply terrific. Pass on my congratulations.'

The girl turned and looked at him. Jason thought how like Hepburn she was. She said, 'Thank you, very much.'

The young man scowled at Jason and broke in: 'Will you get your things? We ought to be moving.'

She got up and went away to the ladies' cloakroom.

Jason said to the young man, 'Do you know her very well?'

'A lot better than you are likely to know her,' the young

man said angrily. 'Will you keep your snout out of my affairs? She's my girl and I'm a very tough guy.'

Jason smiled. 'I don't think so. You just smell strong.'

The young man got unsteadily to his feet.

Jason said hurriedly: 'Not here. Let's go to the toilet.'

'O.K., I only just wanted to show you that I can take you and think nothing of it.'

Jason settled his check. The waiter glanced at the uneaten meal, but didn't say anything. He seemed quite pleased with the tip Jason gave him.

'Come along,' Jason said to the young man, 'let us see who is the better man.' He had to support the young man, who seemed to have considerable difficulty with his legs.

The toilet was empty, and Jason had no difficulty in overpowering the young man. He tied his hands and feet together with towels and put him in one of the closets. The young man wept with humiliation, but Jason really couldn't be bothered to console him.

He hurried back to the restaurant, but he couldn't see the girl anywhere. However, after what seemed to him to be hours of suspense, he caught sight of her waiting in the lounge.

He went over to the cloakroom and gave up his hat check. The girl found his hat and asked him how he was getting on.

Jason gave her five dollars. 'You were absolutely right,' he told her, 'everything is building up beautifully.'

He went over to Miss Gellert. 'I've just left your escort in a room of meditation,' he said. 'He asked me to look after the rest of the evening with you.'

She didn't seem very surprised. 'Did he?' she said.

'My name is Howard Jason,' he went on. 'I have a lot of money and this is my first night in New York. What shall we do?'

She thought for a moment. 'Have you really got a lot of money?' she said at last.

Jason assured her gravely that he had.

'Have you plenty on you right at this moment?'

'At a rough guess I have about a couple of thousand bucks, all in very nice new notes.'

She sighed. 'It must be nice to have as much as that.'

'Can't we get off money?' Jason asked. 'Why the interest in money? Don't you think it is a trifle sordid talking about money as we are?'

She said: 'Oh no, because where we are going you have to have lots of money or else they get very fierce and throw you into the street.'

Jason smiled. 'Now that sounds exciting. Let's go.'

In the taxi he said: 'You play the piano awfully well. What else do you do?'

She looked out of the window at the bright lights as they flashed past. 'Oh, things, you know. I don't do anything so well as the piano. I'm lucky there, I suppose.'

'I wouldn't say that. You must have worked hard at the piano to be able to play like that.' He twisted round in his seat so that he could look at her properly. 'I think I'm going to like you quite a lot,' he said.

She leant her head back against the side of the cab. 'I suppose you're now laying the foundation?' she said.

Jason considered that. 'Isn't that frightfully cynical and elderly?' he said.

'I don't think so. You see, I often go for rides in taxis with men I don't know very well. It interests me to see the first initial moves.'

Jason felt in his pocket for his cigarette-case. 'Strictly, from your angle, it must be interesting,' he said, offering her his case. 'Do you go to bed with any of them?'

She took a cigarette and leant forward as he thumbed his lighter. 'No,' she said, 'it's ethically wrong, I think.'

Jason filled his lungs with cigarette smoke. After a moment he said, 'I see.'

'You can take me home now if you like,' she said. 'I mean, there is still plenty of time to find someone else. If this is your first night in New York, perhaps you want that sort of thing.'

'You know you're being awfully superior,' Jason said severely. 'I'm enjoying myself enormously. I wish you would tell me where we are going.'

'Oh, you'll see in a moment, we're just there.'

The cab drew up outside a tall building that looked like a private dwelling place. Jason paid off the taxi and together Miss Gellert and he ascended the crescent-shaped steps to the front door.

She rang the bell and after a moment's delay the door was opened by a short, dapper little man wearing heavy horn-rimmed spectacles. 'Why, hello, Mary,' he said, 'aren't you very late?'

He stood on one side to let them in.
Miss Gellert said, 'This is Mr. Howard Jason.'
The little man shook Jason's hand cordially.
'Dr. Kaufman works harder than any other man in New York,' Miss Gellert said to Jason. 'May we come in for a few moments, Doctor?'
'Why, sure, come in. Take your things off, young man.'
Miss Gellert said seriously: 'I want him to see everything. Will you take him round? You will find he is very intelligent.'
Jason stood frowning slightly. 'Could you explain what all this is about?' he asked politely. 'I really believe I could appreciate things so much better if I knew.'
Dr Kaufman took his arm. 'Of course,' he said; 'Mary is so impulsive. She brings all sorts of people here. I am very grateful to her, but sometimes I feel she brings them on false pretences.'
Miss Gellert said: 'Take him round, Doctor, then we can have a talk. I'll wait in the library for you both.'
Kaufman said: 'Will you be patient? I want to show you the work I am trying to do. Will you come?'
Jason said, 'Why certainly,' and went with him, feeling somehow that the little man was too sincere to be refused.
Miss Gellert waited for over an hour before Jason came into the library. He came alone. She was sitting by a big fire, very serene and relaxed. Jason came and sat down opposite her. In the firelight he looked very pale.
She said: 'I can't say I'm sorry. You see, unless I do this sort of thing, I can't get people to take any interest.'
Jason said, a little bitterly, 'I suppose he wants money?'
'Don't you think he deserves to have it? Would you like to do what he's doing?'
Jason took out his wallet and pulled out some notes. He put them on the table. 'I think I'll go now,' he said, getting to his feet.
She touched the money with a long slender finger. 'It is an awful lot, isn't it?' she said. 'Thank you so much. I'm afraid I've completely spoilt your evening.'
Jason looked at her. 'How the devil did you get mixed up with such foulness?' he asked abruptly.
She looked into the fire. 'I guess it was because someone I loved a lot died of it. Dr Kaufman is the only man here who

really understands its cure. But it costs so much. He can't make progress without money. So I help him as much as I can.'

Jason said: 'I see. I think you're very clever. Do you always take people from places like night-clubs?'

'You mean I'm taking an unfair advantage?'

'It does make one think how much nicer it is in a crowded restaurant than it must be in those wards.' Jason wandered over to the door. 'Perhaps you'll give the doctor my best wishes.'

She got up and went with him to the front door. 'I have spoilt your evening, haven't I?' she said.

He looked down at her thoughtfully. 'You know you completely deceived me. I thought it was just a gag about your ethics.'

She said again, 'I'm awfully sorry.'

He smiled. 'I suppose you'll take that other guy some other night?'

She nodded. 'Oh yes, he has a lot of money too.'

He opened the front door and looked up and down the street. 'Well, good night,' he said, and almost ran down the steps.

A taxi slid out of the shadows and the driver leant forward to jerk open the door. 'Where to, boss?' he asked.

Jason looked back over his shoulder, but Miss Gellert had shut the door. He looked up at the tall building and frowned.

Then he turned his attention to the driver. 'Listen,' he said, 'I've only been in New York a few hours. I've got a room about ten floors up which seems to me completely isolated from any earthly contacts. I want to find company. What do you suggest?'

The driver thought for a moment. 'The Gaucho Club is a good spot for a pick-up, boss,' he said. 'If you're wanting someone to sleep with, I'd say that's your spot.'

Jason raised his hat. 'Never mind,' he said politely, 'I think I'll walk.'

SKIN DEEP

You know how it is when you keep sticking your thumb up,

and the cars go on by, just like you weren't there. You think, 'O.K., I'll let this flock through and wait for a truck.' Then you pound away on your dogs, hoping for a truck to show up, but it doesn't.

That's the way it took Hienie. Not that Hienie was a bum, he wasn't. Fate, or what ever you like to call a lousy break, had dealt him one from the bottom of the deck. He and Johnny Frost had got together to do a job. It was simple enough. Hienie had seen to all the details and that meant something. Hienie was a smart guy when it came to details.

All they had to do was to walk into a café, show the guy behind the counter a gun, open his cash-box, and beat it. Hienie knew this guy took the cash round to the bank every Friday. During the week the cash-box got good and full. The guy was crazy to have a system like that, but then, Hienie and Frost lived on crazy guys.

You'd think you couldn't go wrong on a simple set-up like that – you couldn't, but Frost got it into his nut that you could. He started making plans and getting smart, until Hienie got sore.

Hienie kept telling him all they had to do was to blow in, show the gun, and collect. You didn't have to hang around checking the time when the coppers would be around. You didn't have to turn your clothes inside out, so you wouldn't be spotted, or do any of the other cock-eyed ideas Frost kept squawking about.

Frost wouldn't do the job the easy way. They were still arguing when they set off by road to Jefferson City. Finally, Hienie got mad, and that's where he came unstuck. Frost was a big guy and he owned the car. He listened to Hienie for a couple of minutes and then hoofed him out of the car. 'O.K., smart guy,' he said, letting the clutch in with a bang, 'go bowl a hoop. I'll handle the job myself.'

Hienie was so mad that he let him go. He had a childlike faith that he could collect a lift from one of the many glittering cars that continually roared past. He'd get a lift to Jefferson City and beat that hophead to it.

It was only after the sixteenth car had ignored his frantic signals that doubt began to cloud his optimism. After the twentieth car had choked him with dust, he gave up and decided to wait for a truck.

He sat by the roadside and lit a cigarette. He cursed Frost

viciously, groping far back in his loose mind for suitable terms. If ever he caught up with that guy he'd give it to him. He'd walk right up to him and say, 'Hello, pal,' and then he'd let him have it in the guts. He'd stand over him and watch the heel croak.

As he sat there brooding, he noticed a car approaching in the distance. One glance made him get to his feet hurriedly. It wasn't a private car; from where he was standing it looked mighty like a hearse.

'This guy ain't passin' me,' Hienie thought, moving out into the middle of the highway. 'He'll have to run me down first.' He began waving his arms violently.

As the car approached, he could see a small red cross painted on the front, and for a moment he almost stepped aside; but the thought of Frost made him stand firm.

The ambulance made as if to swerve, then slid to a standstill. A little guy in a white coat, and wearing a peaked cap, rolled down the window and looked at Hienie with interest.

'What's bitin' you pal?' he asked, resting two powerful fists on the wheel.

Hienie took off his hat and blotted his face. 'Jeeze! I was just givin' up when you blew along.'

The little guy shook his head. 'You can't ride on this wagon,' he said. 'Don't get me wrong. I'd give you a lift, sure thing, but I'm on duty. I gotta patient.'

Hienie didn't care if he'd got elephants on board. He was going to ride now he'd succeeded in stopping something on four wheels.

'Forget it,' he said sharply, his thin wolfish face going hard. 'There's room in the cab. I don't want to get inside.'

The little guy shook his head again. 'Can't do it, pal. I'd lose my job. Some other guy will be along soon. I gotta get on. Maybe you'd like a smoke or somethin'?'

Hienie stepped round the ambulance, jerked open the offside door and got into the cab. He slammed the door shut.

'I'm ridin',' he said briefly. 'Get goin'.'

The little guy twisted round in his seat, so that he faced Hienie. 'Don't let's have any trouble; I may be a little guy, but I'm tough. Beat it, before I start somethin'.'

Hienie could handle this sort of talk. He reached behind him and pulled his gun. He showed it to the little guy. 'I don't have to be tough,' he said.

The little guy's eyes popped. 'Jeeze!'

'That's it,' Hienie said, putting the gun away. 'Let's go.'

The little guy engaged the gears. 'I'm going to lose my job,' he said regretfully.

Hienie leant back against the well-cushioned seat. 'You ain't losin' nothin',' he said. 'You get me to Jefferson and you'll make yourself somethin'.'

They drove in silence for a few minutes, then Hienie said: 'You ain't worryin' about the rod, are you, pal?'

The little guy gave him a quick glance. 'Sure, I ain't,' he said hastily.

'You're O.K. with me,' Hienie assured him, 'it's just the way I've got when guys get tough. I just gotta pull a rod. Maybe it's goin' to get me into a little trouble one day.'

'I ain't so tough,' the little guy said rather bitterly. 'I oughtta've taken a chance and hung one on you.'

Hienie grinned. 'You're all right. You're a wise guy. It ain't healthy to tap a guy with a rod. Take it from me, pal, I know.' He fumbled for a cigarette and offered one.

When they had lit up, Hienie said, 'What's your name, pal?'

The little guy looked at him suspiciously. 'Joe,' he said, with obvious reluctance.

Hienie grinned. 'A swell name for a swell guy, huh?'

Joe didn't say anything, he kept on driving. Hienie watched the road for a while, then he shut his eyes and dozed. It was hot inside the cab, so he let himself drift for a while. Then curiosity made him ask lazily, 'Say, Joe, what's wrong with the patient?'

'Aw, she's nuts,' Joe said, leaning forward to switch on the side lights.

Hienie sat up. 'You mean she's crazy?'

'Yeah.'

'That's tough. Gee! I'd hate to be a nut.'

Joe shrugged. 'When you're crazy, you don't mind so much. It's goin' crazy that's bad.'

Hienie thought this over. 'Yeah,' he said, 'I guess that's right.' He lit another cigarette. 'Crazy guys give me the heebies.'

'You get used to it,' Joe said, rolling down the window to spit into the dark. 'It's the tough ones I don't fancy.'

'Is she tough?' Hienie asked with morbid curiosity.

Joe hesitated. 'Yeah,' he said; 'I ain't allowed to talk about the patients.' He slowed down as they approached a gas station. 'Keep outta sight, pal,' he said, 'I got my job to think about.'

Hienie sat back. 'I could use a drink. Yes, sir, right now I could use a lotta drink.'

Joe's face brightened. 'I could get you somethin' if you've the dough.'

'The right stuff. I don't want any gut-rot. I want the right stuff.'

'Sure, the liquor's the McCoy. The guy distils it himself right here. It'll cost you a couple of bucks, but it's panther's spit all right.'

Hienie dug into his trouser pocket and found two dollars. 'Get it,' he said briefly.

Joe climbed out of the cab and walked stiffly into the office. He came out after a few minutes, carrying a gallon-size earthernware jar. Hienie reached forward and took it from him.

Joe stood watching. Hienie drew the cork with his teeth and carefully raised the jar to his mouth. He took a long pull and blinked. He coughed, and began to rub his coat front with the palm of his hand. 'Yeah,' he said, when he could get his breath, 'it's the McCoy all right.'

Joe shifted about, anxiously eyeing the bottle, but Hienie paid no attention. He took another long pull from the jar, then hurriedly handed it to Joe. 'My Gawd,' he gasped, 'it went down as far as my boots that time.'

Joe wrapped himself round the jar lovingly and kept it glued to his mouth.

After almost a minute, Hienie leant forward. 'Hey!' he shouted sharply. 'Take it easy. Hey! Lay off, will you?'

Joe removed himself from the jar with a little shudder. His eyes swam mistily as he handed it back. 'Pretty nice,' he said: 'that's swell poison.'

Hienie looked at him admiringly. 'You certainly can take it,' he said.

Joe wiped his mouth with the back of his hand. 'Yeah, I can take it all right, but it sortta sneaks up on me and bonk – I'm out.'

Hienie wasn't listening, he was busy with the jar again.

Joe said, when he was through: 'I'm just goin' to look at my patient, and then we'll dust.'

'Sure, give her a drink – it's tough bein' a nut.'

Joe shook his head. 'She ain't to have any liquor. That's her trouble – too much liquor,' he said, going round to the back of the ambulance. When he had paid for the gasoline he climbed into the cab.

Hienie said, 'She O.K.?'

'Yeah, she's asleep,' Joe returned, starting the engine.

Hienie offered him the jar. 'Just one for the road,' he said.

Joe grabbed the jar and took a long pull. He handed it back with a deep sigh. 'Pal,' he said, blowing out his leathery cheeks, 'this is certainly a great little evenin'.'

After a couple more drinks, Hienie felt so merry he began to sing at the top of his voice.

Joe said hastily, 'You can't do that on this wagon.'

Hienie continued to bellow, counting his time by waving the jar to and fro.

Joe got scared and brought the ambulance to a standstill. 'For Pete's sake,' he said urgently, 'pipe down. You'll wake my patient up and maybe get the cops lookin' us over.'

Hienie roared with laughter. 'Forget it, Joe,' he said, taking another pull from the jar. 'Don't be a crab. I bet that nutty dame just loves my voice. Come on, you sing too.'

Joe said angrily: 'Cut it out. No girl's goin' to like the row you're makin' – not even a crazy one.'

Hienie stiffened. His smile slipped into a heavy scowl. 'Yeah? Is that so? O.K., you soft-bellied little runt, we'll ask her and see.'

Joe shook his head. 'Like hell we will,' he said firmly. 'You pipe down, or I'll get tough.'

Hienie reached out and slid back the small panel that divided the ambulance from the cab. He put his head through the foot-square aperture and blinked into the faintly lit ambulance. He touched an electric switch by his hand, and a brilliant light went on.

Joe said furiously: 'Lay off. You can't do this.'

Hienie ignored him. He looked curiously at the bunk that ran the length of the ambulance. Someone was lying there covered by a rug.

He leant further forward. 'Hey!' he called. 'Let's have a look at you.'

The figure stirred and then slowly sat up. Although the applejack had given him plenty of courage, he felt a little chill run through him as the woman moved. He had always had a fear of things he couldn't understand. Madness scared him more than most things. He got a hell of a shock when she sat up. He had vaguely pictured her to be old and horrible to look at, only because he had associated madness with decay.

This dame was something to look at. She was not only a beauty, but she had everything. Her colouring, the sleepy passion in her eyes, the small, full, heavily rouged lips and the soft, golden lustre of her hair. Her beauty hit Hienie like a physical blow. He peered at her, his jaw a little slack and his bloodshot eyes glassy. 'For God's sake!' he said in a low tone.

She looked at him, a puzzled interested expression on her face. 'Who are you?' she asked, then, hurriedly: 'Please get me out of here.'

Hienie was so confused that he jerked back and slammed the panel shut. Feebly, he pulled out his handkerchief and wiped his damp hands.

Joe said angrily: 'What the hell do you think you're doin'?'

Hienie looked at him. 'Wait a moment. That dame's no more crazy than I am. What's the game?'

Joe began to stutter. 'I don't know what you're talkin' about. I tell you she's not only nutty but she's goddam dangerous. You can't go by how a dame looks. It ain't her looks that're wrong, it's her mind – get it?'

Hienie nodded. 'Yeah, I get it,' he said, sliding his hand behind him and pulling his gun. 'Listen, pal, how come you're travellin' alone with this dame?'

Joe hastily shifted his eyes. 'I'm givin' you a lift. That's all that'll interest you.' He reached forward to start the engine but Hienie rammed his gun into his ribs.

'Hold it, lug,' he said viciously. 'Spill it, or I'll start somethin'.'

Joe shifted uneasily. 'The nurse oughtta've come along, but she wanted to make the journey on the train with her boyfriend. So I fixed it for them. It's against regulations, but they knew the girl was safe with me.'

Hienie sneered. 'What a yarn! Say, I could have cooked

up a better tale in half the time. I'm on to you, hophead. This ain't no nut wagon. You ain't no nut hand – this is a snatch, ain't that right?'

Joe's eyes bulged. 'You're crazy.'

'That's what you think. I'm goin' to see what cherry-pie's got to say.' He slid back the panel.

The girl still sat on the bunk. She was looking scared now. As soon as she saw him she said frantically: 'Let me out! Please! I'm not mad! He keeps saying I am, but I'm not. Don't you believe me – do I look mad?'

Hienie shook his head. 'Keep your pants on, sister,' he said soothingly. 'I just want a little talk with this guy here, an' then you'll be O.K. Take it easy. It ain't goin' to be long.' He slid back the panel and looked at Joe. 'So what?' he said.

Joe flapped his hands. 'Don't listen to her,' he said feverishly. 'Don't I keep tellin' you she's nuts?'

Hienie sneered. 'A dish as hot as that ain't bugs,' he said. 'Come on, lug, spill it. This dame ain't crazy. Who is she? Who're you workin' for?'

Joe clutched his head. Sweat ran down his face, and his eyes rolled feverishly. 'For Gawd's sake don't do anythin',' he gasped. 'I tell you she's pullin' a fast one. Don't let her get away. I'll lose my job.'

'Who is she?'

'Marie van Drutten. The banker's daughter.'

'Listen, I've heard of that guy. He never had a nutty daughter, but he's got a load of dough. What's the ransom, buddy?'

'There ain't any ransom,' Joe said earnestly. 'Van Drutten's hushing this up. He don't want anyone to know she's gone nuts. He's given out she's in Europe or some place. Now do you get it?'

Hienie half believed him. His mind began to work from another angle. 'A mighty slick yarn. Listen, Joe, people don't just go crazy. What's it all about?'

Joe shook his head. 'Gee! I can't tell you that. It'd cost me my job.'

Hienie put some more weight on his gun arm. 'You can either spill it or get out an' walk. Suit yourself. If it sounds reasonable I'll take off the heat and you can forget about this; but if you ain't comin' clean, I'll take a chance an' let the dame go – suit yourself.'

Joe groaned. 'Don't do that, I tell you she's dangerous!'

'So is Sally Rand, so is Mae West, so what?' Hienie snarled. 'Suit yourself, but you're goin' to walk if you don't come clean.'

Joe blotted his face with his sleeve. 'You gotta keep your mouth shut,' he said; 'old man Drutten'll go crazy himself if this gets out.'

Hienie raised his eyebrows. 'That would be just too bad,' he said with a sneer. 'I'd hate Drutten to get into a lather. Like hell, I would.'

Joe looked furtively up and down the long, dark road, then he said hoarsely: 'She got mixed up with a playboy.'

Hienie stared at him. 'What the hell are you givin' me? Mixin' with playboys don't make you crazy.'

'Yeah?' Joe's eyes snapped. 'Well, this guy sent her crazy. He'd got a bad mind, this guy. I guess from what I've heard he was a real bastard. He got her to his apartment one night an' he did things to her. I ain't tellin' you what he did – but you can take it from me they were raw. She ran out of the apartment screamin', like hell, without any clothes on, slap into a copper's arms. There was an awful stink. The cops got hold of this guy and his dog—'

'His dog?' Hienie said.

Joe shifted uncomfortably. 'Yeah, he had a dog as big as an elephant.' He lowered his voice. 'I guess it was the dog that sent her crazy.'

Hienie sat back. 'Hell!' he said.

'That's how it went. They got her back home, and they couldn't do a thing with her. She'd just sit around broodin', not sayin' a word. I guess old Drutten had a bad time. Then she got on the booze; she got so she must have a man.' Joe shook his head. 'It was a bad business. They kept her locked up, away from any guy, until one day one of the old man's chauffeurs ran into her just after a drinking jag. Of course, she encouraged him, and after that they put her in a home.' Joe shuddered. 'She's bad when she gets with a man. She fixes him. That dame's got a hell of a way of fixin' a guy. When she fixes him, she fixes him good.'

Hienie wasn't listening. He was already making plans. Boy! What a set-up. He'd only have to take the dame to her pa and tip the old man how much he knew, and he'd be in the gravy for the rest of his days.

He turned and looked at Joe. 'It stinks,' he said. 'I don't believe a word. Joe, you're gettin' out an' you're walkin'.'

'You double-crossin' son of a bitch,' Joe said furiously.

'Cut it out, sucker,' Hienie said viciously. 'Get out or I'll blast you.'

Joe hesitated, then opened the door and slid into the road. Hienie got into the driving-seat and started the engine. 'Take it easy, pal,' he called, 'the first ten miles are the worst.'

Leaving Joe yelling furiously after him, Hienie drove for some time into the darkness. Then he swung off the highway into a dirt road. When he had gone some miles he considered it safe enough to stop. He opened the panel and put his head through the aperture. 'Hyah, Miss Drutten,' he called. 'I guess you're safe now.'

She climbed off the bunk and came over to him. She wore a dark, knitted two-piece suit. Hienie's eyes kept returning to her figure. He thought this dame's certainly got what it takes. Her frontage alone would be worth putting in pickle.

'You mean I can go? I shan't see that dreadful little man again?'

Hienie grinned. 'That's right, baby; I'll take you back to your pa, just as soon as you've given me the address.'

She peered at him. 'I can't see you – who are you? I'm still awfully scared.' Dark eyes looked into his, and he suddenly wanted her as he'd never wanted a woman before. He wanted to reach out and pull her to him. He wanted to feel her softness yield to him.

He looked at her, his eyes stripping her. Suppose she was crazy, that didn't stop him giving her a tumble? She couldn't start anything with him. He was acutely aware of his strength. If she did turn nutty, he could look after himself. He wanted a drink badly. Lifting the jar, he took a long pull. The liquor gave him just the little extra courage he needed. 'To hell with it,' he thought, and climbed out of the cab. He went round to the back of the ambulance, still carrying the jar. He hesitated for a moment, then he undid the latch and turned the spring lock. He pulled open the door and climbed into the ambulance.

She came slowly towards him. She had a slow, almost lazy movement, and he could see her rounded thighs move under the woollen skirt.

He stood just inside the door, staring at her. The back of his throat went suddenly dry. Jeeze! This dame was good. Make no mistake about it. She was a riot. He stepped inside, pulling the door which closed with a faint click.

There wasn't a great deal of room in the ambulance. Hienie said: 'Sit down, baby, an' let's get acquainted.'

Her eyes were on the jar. 'What's that? she asked.

Hienie sat down, holding the jar on his knee. 'It's applejack,' he said, watching her closely.

She sat down close to him and put her hand on the jar, just above Hienie's hand. 'Applejack?' she repeated.

'That's right,' Hienie said, shifting his hand further up the jar. For a moment they touched. He felt the coolness of her flesh against his. Deliberately she took her hand away and put it in her lap. Hienie began to breathe heavily. He was going to give her the works even if she squawked her head off.

She smiled at him. She had a very nice smile. 'I've never had applejack before. It's a nice name, isn't it?'

A tight little grin settled on Hienie's mouth. He got up and went over to the little wash-basin. He took a glass and washed it carefully, and half filled it with liquor. All right, if she was crazy, and she got hot on booze he'd risk the experiment. The longer he was with her the less he thought of Joe's yarn.

'Try it, baby,' he said, 'you'll find it a tough drink all right.'

She looked at the glass, reached out, and again her slim fingers touched his. It affected Hienie like an electric shock. He shivered, standing against the wall of the ambulance, watching her.

She held the glass close to her lips. 'It has a nice smell,' she said. Tilting her head, so he could see the white column of her throat, she began to drink. Hienie stood transfixed. The raw spirit slid down her throat like water.

Hienie said: 'For Gawd's sake – how did you do that?'

She held the glass towards him. 'It's nice. I'm so thirsty. May I have some more?'

He still stood staring at her. 'Didn't it burn you? Jeeze! It must have burnt you!'

A little frown settled between her eyebrows. 'Can't I have some more?' There was a slight grating sound in her voice.

Hienie looked at her sharply, hesitated, then filled her glass. This time he took a long pull from the jar himself. The liquor made him choke and splutter. When he had recovered, he saw she was nursing the empty glass, her eyes on the jar. He put the cork back firmly, and thumped it home with his fist.

'Don't do that,' she said sharply, 'I want some more.'

Hienie shook his head. He felt a sudden confidence. He was no longer nervous of her. He didn't care how mad she might be, he could handle her. 'You've had plenty,' he said, putting the jar by the door, away from her. 'You don't want too much of that stuff.'

She put her hand on his arm, and leant close to him. Her breath, smelling of the sweet sickly spirit, fanned his face. 'There's such a lot left – I'm thirsty.'

Hienie shifted closer to her. She was giving him the works all right. He slid his arm round her back. 'Maybe there is, baby, but we've got a lot of time to kill.'

'But it's so nice,' she giggled suddenly. 'It makes me feel tight.' She leant against his arm.

'Sure it makes you feel tight.' He encircled her waist, letting his hand rest on her hip bone. She looked down at his hand, then swiftly up into his face. He pulled her close to him. 'Your pa's got plenty of dough, ain't he?' he said, waiting for her to pull away.

She didn't move. 'Why did you ask that?'

'I like talkin' about dough.' His hand shifted up, closing over her breast, it felt firm and full, imprisoned in his hand. She shivered and stiffened. Hienie went on talking, trying to keep his voice normal. 'I like hearin' about guys with plenty of dough. It must be a swell feeling to give a dame like you just what you want without wondering where the dough's comin' from to pay for it.' He didn't know what he was saying, but he knew he had to keep on talking. He could feel her relaxing against his arm. 'I've been a bum all my life. Maybe you wouldn't understand what that means.' He shifted his hand, taking the weight of her breast.

She made a little face. 'Now you're being miserable,' she said, her full lips parting a little. Her long slender fingers gripped his wrist and pulled at his hand.

'Let it stay, baby, it feels good.'

She hesitated, keeping her eyes turned away from him,

then her hand fell away. Hienie said thickly: 'You're a swell kid. Gee! You're a swell kid!'

She moved her long legs restlessly. 'You haven't told me who you are,' she said. There was no interest in her voice.

Hienie reached down and put his hand under her knees. 'I'll show you how to be comfortable,' he said, swinging her legs off the ground, so that she was half sitting, half lying across his knees. He expected some resistance, but she lay limply, her hand hanging by her side. He thought, 'It's a push over.' 'Ain't this comfortable?' he said, leaning over her. Her head fell back, her eyes closed, she murmured something that he couldn't hear. He pulled her to him roughly and mashed his mouth down on hers. Her mouth opened and he could feel her breath in his throat. Her arms encircled his neck and she began to moan softly.

His free hand slid over her silken knee, touched warm, smooth flesh, and then she suddenly gripped him, forcing her mouth against his until it hurt. He found it was difficult to breathe and he tried to move his head away, but she moved with him. He jerked his hand from her, trying to push her off, the blood drumming in his head. Her arms were encircling his throat like steel bands, cutting the air from his lungs. In a sudden panic, he began fighting, but he couldn't shift her. Then lights began to flash before his eyes, and he was conscious that she was strangling him, and he couldn't do anything about it.

Long after midnight, Joe and a State trooper found them. The State trooper stopped his car close to the ambulance and they climbed out.

'It looks like he's beaten it,' Joe said, looking into the cab. He climbed in and glanced through the aperture. Then he said, 'For God's sake,' and almost threw himself out of the cab.

The State trooper looked at him. 'What's up?' he asked.

Joe pointed a shaky finger at the ambulance. 'I warned him, but he wouldn't believe me.'

The trooper pushed past him and climbed into the cab. He remained at the aperture for several minutes, then he got down slowly. He looked bad. 'The poor bastard,' he said unevenly. 'The poor bastard. Hell! She didn't ought to have done that. I guess no dame ought to do that to any guy.' He spat in the road. 'It's the only fun some guys have got.'

OVERHEARD

They occupied the end part of the long chromium and mahogany bar. They sat on high stools, their shoulders touching and their concentration on each other intense. For them, the 'Silver Coast' bar did not exist, and Mandell, the barman, listened to their conversation with amused tolerance. He leant against the counter, aimlessly polishing a small square of shiny mahogany very slowly with a soft duster. It was quiet in the bar with only these two and three men in white ducks who stood at the far end of the bar. The sun came through the chinks of the heavy sunblinds, making sharp little patterns on the coconut matting. It was noon, and very hot for the time of year.

Mandell left off polishing the bar and took out a clean white handkerchief to chase away a little trickle of sweat he felt running behind his ears. He put the handkerchief away and glanced over at the two sitting close to him.

She was tall and high-breasted. Her long silky hair was blue-black and hung on her crisp white collar in an ordered upward sweep. Her face interested Mandell very much. He liked her large deep blue eyes and her beautifully painted mouth. Her skin was clear and white, except for a touch of rouge high up on her cheek-bones. Mandell particularly liked her slender, beautifully shaped hands.

Her companion was a heavily built man with a fleshy, strikingly handsome face. His square jaw-line and light blue eyes gave him a look of authority which comes, sometimes, to wealthy men. Mandell envied him his tailor and envied him his figure; he also envied him his companion.

They were drinking Bar Specials, made with rum and absinthe; and Mandell had a large shaker by his side ready to replenish their glasses.

They had been talking about Havana for some minutes, and Mandell gathered that this was her first trip. Her companion seemed to know the place well, and from what he said he must have been living there for some time. Mandell couldn't quite make out when these two first met. He could tell without any difficulty that the man was just crazy about her. He wasn't sure whether it was reciprocated or not.

She said quite suddenly, 'Oh, must we talk geography any more?'

He fiddled with his long, frosted glass. 'I'm sorry, I thought it would interest you. It is so lovely here. I've been looking forward so much to showing you around. I guess I got carried away.'

'Do you like it better than Stresa?'

He seemed undecided. 'It's different. Stresa was lovely, too, wasn't it?'

She moved a little forward on her stool. Her eyes became for a moment very animated. 'Do you remember the little albergo at Arolo?' she asked. 'You couldn't speak a word of Italian – and the fun we had. Do you remember Anita?'

He nodded. 'The innkeeper's daughter? I always think of something rude when I say that. She called me *poverino* because the sun blistered my nose.' He laughed. 'I guess we had a swell time there. She used to chatter away to me in the early morning when you were still asleep, and I didn't know what she was talking about. You know, I must really learn Italian before we go there again.'

'Do you think we'll ever go there again?' she asked, her face becoming sad. 'It seems such a long way off.'

'Of course we'll go there again. Don't you want to swim in the lake once more? Do you remember the time when that old snake fell out of a tree and scared you? We were just going in and you absolutely refused to swim that day.'

She shivered. 'I hate snakes,' she said. 'You know I hate snakes.'

'I was only teasing,' he said quickly; 'I hate things like that too, but I'm glad I came here. There is something solid and primitive about this place that Italy hasn't got. Italy is ice-cake buildings and post-card skies. Here you feel the pulse of the people. The streets have run with blood and the buildings still echo with the groans of the oppressed. Look at it, look at the sea, the flowers, the people. Don't you think they are more solid, more real than Italy?'

She said: 'Yes, everything now is more real and more solid. The touch of fairyland has gone away.'

'Why do you say that?' he asked, turning his head to look at her. 'The touch of fairyland has gone away. That sounds so sad and final.'

She didn't look at him. 'Do you remember the fireflies at Arolo? The banks of the lake in the moonlight with hundreds of fireflies like silver sparks glowing in the grass?'

'There is something wrong,' he said. 'Tell me, isn't there something wrong?'

'Do you feel it too?'

'Then there is something. What is it?'

'I've told you.'

'Please don't be mysterious. Tell me.'

She took a nervous sip from her glass and didn't say anything. Mandell wondered why she looked so tragic. He thought this talk about fairyland was under the arm. He liked straight dealings himself and fancy language gave him a pain.

'Are you sorry you've come?' the big man asked. 'Is that it? Would you rather we had gone to Europe instead?'

She shook her head. 'No, it's not that. You see, the edges are frayed now. Please don't make me say it. You must feel as I feel.'

He stretched out his hand to take hers, but she avoided him. 'Why must you talk in riddles? First, the touch of fairyland has gone, and now the edges are frayed. What do you mean?'

She finished her drink. 'I'm trying so hard to be kind,' she said. 'Can't you see that? Things don't mean the same to me any more – there, I've told you.'

Still he couldn't grasp what she meant. He signalled to Mandell to fill the glasses. Mandell gave an elaborate start, as if he had just noticed them, and brought the shaker over. 'You like these, sir?' he said agreeably.

'Yes, they are very good,' the big man said, smiling vaguely, 'very good indeed.'

Mandell pushed the glasses a few inches towards them and then stood away, taking up his old position.

'What was it you were saying?' the big man asked, taking up the thread of the conversation. 'Are you bored with travelling? Do you want to settle down?'

She said, 'Yes.'

'But where? Here?'

She shook her head. 'No. It wouldn't be here.'

There was a long pause, then he said: 'I love you so much that I will go wherever you wish. Tell me, and we will make plans.'

She faced him. 'Can't you understand' – there was an edge on her voice – 'I can't bear any more of this? I've tried and tried to tell you, but you won't understand. I can't go on with this any longer.'

'Don't get angry. I understand that. I am quite willing to do what you want. Really, you can please yourself.'

She said very intensely, 'We must part.'

He slopped his drink on the mahogany top of the bar. 'We must part?' he repeated. 'You mean you don't want me any more?'

'I tried so hard to tell you nicely, but you are so sure of yourself. You have always been so sure of yourself.'

'No, you have mistaken me if you think that. I have never been sure of myself, but I've been sure of you. It isn't the same thing. I thought your love for me was as enduring as mine for you. You mustn't say I was sure of myself. I trusted your love. I had to have something I need not doubt. Don't you understand! With all this horrible chaos in the world, with lies and envy and sordid business, I hung on to the one thing I thought would never forsake me.'

She said, 'I'm very sorry.'

'Of course' – he passed his fingers through his hair – 'I know you are. When did it happen? Recently?'

She said: 'Now I've told you I don't want to talk about it any more.'

'You can't leave it like that. I'm crazy about you. You know I'm crazy about you. Have I done anything that decided you?'

She shook her head. 'I'm bad,' she said softly; 'I thought I could find the happiness I wanted with you, but I haven't. I must live my life. I have not the courage to pretend. You wouldn't want me to pretend, would you?'

'Why do you say you're bad? Is it because there is someone else?'

She hesitated a moment, then she said: 'Yes, yes. I didn't want to tell you, but I must. You are bound to hear sooner or later.'

With the morbid interest of a lounger at a street accident, Mandell watched the big man dispassionately. He noticed that he had suddenly gone very pale and it was only with difficulty that he controlled himself.

'I see,' he said.

'No,' she said quickly, 'you don't. You couldn't possibly. You are thinking that I have wounded your pride. I know how men feel when this happens. But it won't wound your pride. I'm so glad about that because you have been so very sweet to me. You have, and I have appreciated—'

'Please,' he said, 'don't talk like that. You are making my love sound like a donation to a hospital. It wasn't like that. I gave you everything, and I suppose it just wasn't enough.'

Mandell saw her flinch and he raised his eyebrows approvingly. He thought this big guy was taking it lying down. What this dame wanted was fireworks. He sniffed contemptuously. All this talk about fairyland and frayed edges – it was just so much crap.

'I'm going away with Margaret Whitely,' she said quietly.

The big man's colour came back, making his face congested. 'Who?' he said, staring at her.

'Yes. Oh, I know what you are going to say, but I've thought and thought and thought. I must please myself.'

He seemed now to be quite controlled again. When he spoke, it was in an irritatingly soothing voice that one might use to a child. 'My dear, surely you have got over that nonsense now?'

She shook her head. 'Please don't try and be understanding,' she said. 'I know how you feel about it, but I've really made up my mind once and for all.'

He lit a cigarette, holding the heavy gold case thoughtfully in his hand. 'Does Margaret know about us? Does she know what she is doing to us?'

'She has waited for me. She knew that this would come to nothing. She told me a year ago. She waited and, you see, she was right.'

'Are you being perverted? Isn't it rather a beastly thing to do?'

'I suppose I must expect to hear that sort of thing, but it will not stop me. Margaret and I can't be parted any longer.'

'I think I would rather it had been a man.'

She shook her head. 'No, you are wrong. You would not have taken it as you are taking it now. You wouldn't have been patient. You would have got into a terrible rage and you would have wanted to kill him.'

He made a little grimace. 'I suppose I should,' he admitted. 'This is so out of my hands. I feel there is something so repugnant about it that I don't want to have anything to do with it.'

She reached out and gathered up her bag. 'Good-bye, Harry,' she said; 'thank you for everything.'

'Don't go,' he said quickly. 'You can't leave it like this. For God's sake, think what you are doing.'

She slid off the stool. 'There is really nothing more to be done; it is all settled. I just didn't want to hurt you. I'm so sorry.'

He said very bitterly: 'Then last year doesn't mean anything? It is just so much dust . . . nothing.'

She bit her lip, then put her hand on his arm. 'You see why I ought to go quickly? We shall be saying cruel things in a moment and we shall be sorry. Good-bye, Harry,' and she went out of the bar quickly, moving lightly and gracefully.

Mandell watched her go regretfully. The conversation had amused him. As she passed through the door, a girl came in and stood looking round the bar. Mandell's lips tightened. He recognized the type immediately. That was one thing he wouldn't stand for in his bar. He said to the big man, 'You'll excuse me if I come through the barrier, sir, there's a dame blown in who looks very doubtful. I'm just goin' to tell her to beat it.'

The big man looked over his shoulder at the girl. He got off the stool. 'Doubtful, did you say?' he said. 'Why, you big stiff, she's a goddam certainty,' and he walked across to the girl who met him with a professional smile and they went away together.

THE PAINTED ANGEL

Slug Moynihan eased his weight against the lamp-post and thrust his hands into his trouser pockets. The hard light from the lamp threw his face into dark shadows, hiding his eyes and lighting his square jaw. He was wearing a light sport's coat over a white polo sweater, and his shabby flannel trousers were noticeably frayed at the turn-ups.

People who passed glanced at him curiously, and then, as he turned his head, they looked away hurriedly. Slug was a tough bird and he didn't like people looking at him. He belonged to a team of third-rate boxers who fought at Henklestien's saloon twice a week. He made a little money and took a lot of punishment. He was still under twenty-five, so he found that the punishment didn't affect him. All the same, it sometimes worried him when he watched the older fighters gradually going slug nutty. He could see that happening to him before long.

Right now he wasn't worrying about that. He had other things to worry him. He had got Rose Hanson on his mind. Usually, Slug was particularly callous with women. When he wanted one, he'd find one, take her and then forget her. He generally got what he wanted without any trouble. Chiefly because he was careful whom he chose. There were still a lot of dumb blondes who fell for a fighter, but apart from their physical use, Slug just didn't give them a second thought. Now Rose Hanson had blown along and things were different. Slug didn't realize it, but he had got Rose in his system in a bad way. He had made his usual overture to her, saying: 'Listen, honey, you and me could get places. How about settlin' down in bed together?' which generally proved effective. Rose had looked through him and had given him the air. She didn't even give him the pleasure of embarrassing her as some of the more prudent ones had done. She simply ignored him as if he hadn't spoken, and that certainly had done things to Slug.

He had first met her at the Ciro Dance Hall, which stood at the corner of Forty-third and Western Avenue. She was dancing with a tall, thin guy who looked as if he'd got a lot of dough. Slug considered starting trouble, then decided that it would only get himself in bad with Rose. All the same, his fingers itched to get a grip on this thin guy's neck, and the temptation had been so strong that he had left the hall and gone home.

He thought he could forget about Rose, but he found that she was continually coming into his daily existence. He saw her several times on the street and once in a snack-bar having lunch. The tall, thin guy was with her and Slug saw them come out together.

Every time he saw Rose, his desire for her mounted until he decided that something had got to be done about it. He found out with considerable difficulty where she worked. She was a manicurist at a smart little barber's saloon run by a guy named Brownrigg. Slug decided that he'd go and have a manicure. It cost him a lot to get himself in the saloon. He was sweating visibly to think that his companions might see him undergoing sissy treatment to his broken fists. However, he walked in and nodded ferociously at Brownrigg, who was a little guy, with a lot of black wavy hair and a pencilled moustache.

'You gotta dame here who fixes nails, ain't you?' Slug asked, taking off his cap and mopping his face.

Brownrigg opened his eyes. 'Sure, Mr. Moynihan. Come right in and sit down.'

Slug looked at him suspiciously. 'How the hell do you know I'm Moynihan?' he asked.

Brownrigg smiled. 'I follow your fights,' he said. 'You're goin' to get somewhere one of these days. I know a champ when I see one.'

Slug grunted and sat down. 'Yeah?' he said. 'Well, hustle this dame along. I ain't got all day.'

Brownrigg went behind a curtain at the end of the saloon and then came back after a few minutes. 'Miss Hanson's just comin',' he said. 'Would you like a hair-cut or a shave as well?'

Slug scowled at him. 'No,' he said, 'get out in the front of the shop. I want to talk to this dame.'

Brownrigg hesitated, and then said: 'That's all right, Mr. Moynihan, you go ahead.'

Slug sneered at him. 'Sure it's all right,' he said. 'Get movin', Clippers, an' don't come back till I've gone.'

Brownrigg went into the shop meekly enough, but he left the saloon door open an inch or two. He didn't like the look on Slug's battered face.

Rose Hanson came from behind the curtain, wheeling a little table on which was set out all her manicure paraphernalia. When she saw Slug, her face hardened.

She was a swell-looking dame with curves in the right places and thick auburn hair. 'Oh, it's you,' she said disdainfully. 'What do you want?'

Slug looked at her admiringly. 'Just fix my nails, baby,' he said, 'and I'll tell you some bedtime stories.'

She shook her head. 'You don't want a manicure,' she said. 'You want a pneumatic drill with hands like yours.'

Slug flexed his huge hands and grinned foolishly. 'Listen, baby,' he said, 'these mitts earn me a nice slice. I thought maybe they oughtta have a birthday present. Come on, give 'em a treat.'

She pulled a stool up close to him and sat down, then she crossed her leg, showing him a neat knee. Slug looked openly at her shapely legs. 'That's a grand pair of stems you got there,' he said. 'You're certainly a red-hot number.'

She took one of his hands. 'Don't tell me,' she said, 'I know.'

Slugs pursed his mouth. This dame was hard-boiled all right, he thought. It was going to be mighty hard work to make her. 'Like a ticket for one of my fights?' he said, trying the best trick of all his stock-in-trade. 'There'll be a grand show tomorrow an' I can get you a ringside if you say the word.'

She was looking rather hopelessly at his hand. 'What did you say?' she asked.

Slug heaved a heavy sigh and repeated his invitation.

'I don't like fights,' she said, beginning to work on his nails. 'But I could give the ticket to a friend of mine if you have one to spare.'

Slug blew out his cheeks. The crust of this dame, he thought. 'Is that the long guy you float around with?' he asked.

Rose glanced up at him and then concentrated on his nails once more. 'You seem to know a lot about me,' she said. 'Harry is crazy about fights. He'll be pleased to get the ticket.'

'Maybe he'll get a fight too,' Slug snarled. 'I don't like guys like him.'

Rose arched her eyebrows. 'I could hardly imagine you would,' she said coldly.

There was a long pause, then Slug, feeling that he was not gaining ground, said: 'I'll have a nice roll of dough after tonight, suppose you an' me go somewhere an' spend it?'

'Where should we go?' Rose asked cautiously, still intent on his nails.

Slug thought rapidly. 'Aw, I guess you could fix that yourself,' he said generously. 'Just say where you'd like to go.'

'Well . . .' She paused, then she shook her head. 'No, I guess that place isn't quite what you're used to.'

Slug scowled. 'Come on,' he said, 'where is it?'

'I've always wanted to go to the Miami Club, but that's where all the swells go. You couldn't rise to that, could you?'

With a sinking heart, Slug said fiercely: 'Who says? Let me tell you, baby, there ain't no place that I can't go. If you want to go to that joint it's O.K. with me.'

Rose sat back and looked at him. Her big eyes regarded him almost with admiration. 'Gee!' she said. 'Why, even Harry won't go there. Do you really mean it?'

Conscious of a great victory, Slug committed himself, regardless of the cost. 'Sure,' he said, 'you wantta line up with the big-timers. A baby like you don't want to run around with a lotta dopes. I tell you that sortta dump is just canary seed to me.'

'Why, Mr. Moynihan, I didn't realize that you were such a big-shot. Look, let's not go to Miami Club, let's go to the "Ambassadors". That's a place I've really wanted to go to.'

Slug gulped. He saw too late where his boasting had led him. Miami Club was bad enough, but the 'Ambassadors' was one of the most expensive night-clubs in town. Not only that, but it was a stiff-shirt joint, and Slug hadn't got a tuxedo. He felt the sweat coming out from his body at the very thought of what the evening was going to cost him.

Rose went on brightly. 'Let's make it tomorrow,' she said, 'I haven't a date then. Suppose you pick me up here at nine o'clock. Gee! I am looking forward to that. Do make yourself smart. I must get Mr Brownrigg to give you a haircut.'

Before he could protest she had called Brownrigg, who whipped a snowy white towel round him and, with a cold gleam in his eye, proceeded to give him the works. He had a haircut, a shampoo and a face massage and Brownrigg kept up such an incessant flow of chatter that he had no further opportunity of talking to Rose. After enduring what seemed to him a series of undignified tortures, he found himself in the street, three dollars poorer in pocket, and committed to the most expensive evening of his life.

However, he was grimly determined to see it through. With a furtive step he went into Izzy's dress shop and spent a long time haggling over the renting of a tuxedo. By his usual threatening attitude he managed to obtain the complete outfit at a not too ruinous figure. Gingerly, he tried on an opera hat which Izzy insisted was the thing to wear. He stood before the long mirror and stared at his reflection. He couldn't make up his mind whether or not he liked himself in the hat until he noticed Izzy hiding a grin behind a grimy hand, then he realized just how awful he looked in it. He took the hat off hurriedly and gave it back to Izzy. 'Gimme a black felt,' he said, 'an' take that grin off your mug before I wipe it off.'

The clothes were carefully packed in a large cardboard box and, having paid a substantial deposit, Slug made his way home. He spent the rest of the day at the gymnasium loosening up for the evening's fight, his mind more intent on Rose and the evening he had to face at the 'Ambassadors'.

He took Pug O'Malley, one of his sparring partners, into his confidence. 'Listen, Pug,' he said, offering a cigarette, 'I gotta take a dame to the "Ambassadors" tomorrow night.'

Pug looked at him suspiciously, suspecting that Slug was just blowing off hot air. 'Huh,' he said, 'So what?'

Slug scratched his chin uneasily. 'You ever been there?' he asked hopefully.

Pug shook his head. 'I ain't a sucker,' he said. 'That joint charges you every time you breathe.'

'This dame wants to go,' Slug explained.

'I'd tell her where she got off. Jeeze, that joint is so expensive F.D.R. won't go there. I tell you when the dame takes your hat she charges you so much that you think she'll give you your hat and herself when you leave – only she just gives you the hat.'

Slug became more worried. 'What'll it cost me?' he asked. 'Think twenty bucks will cover it?'

Pug pursed his lips. 'Yeah,' he said, 'I guess so. This dame must be mighty good. Why not give her the twenty bucks and save yourself the trouble of goin'. You could make her for that, couldn't you?'

Slug shook his head. 'She ain't that sort of a dame,' he said. 'She's class, see? When she's had a nice time, then we'll go back to her joint an' have a little tumble, but she likes a nice time first.'

Pug shook his head. 'Looks like you're goin' to ride high, buddy,' he said. 'The "Ambassadors" ain't your style.'

Nothing further was said about it after that, and Slug went through with his fight in rather an abstract manner. He was a good enough fighter, and didn't have to exert himself to beat his opponent. The shouts of appreciation from the crowd did a lot to bolster up his confidence, and when the manager paid him fifty dollars he did not hesitate to demand another twenty-five advance. This he got after some unpleasantness, and he immediately went back to his lodgings, refusing any attempt to persuade him to join in the celebrations that were in progress. He knew that he'd want every dollar he could lay hands on for tomorrow evening, and he was not spending anything until then.

When he got home he searched in the back of one of the three chests of drawers and brought out a further twenty-five dollars, which he always kept handy for emergencies such as this. He now had a hundred dollars and some small change, and he felt confident that he would get by with that amount of money. All the same, it was all the dough he had in the world, and he had got to keep something to live on for the next week or so until he fought again.

'Aw, to hell with it,' he said, and put the small roll in his pocket. He couldn't spend all that in an evening. It was enough for him to live on for a month.

The next evening came round and found Slug struggling with his stiff shirt. With the aid of the landlady and her daughter, who were quite immune to his somewhat obscene ravings, he got his collar and tie fixed at last. When he finally took stock of himself in the glass he was agreeably surprised. The stiff black-and-white effect of the evening clothes softened the brutal coarseness of his features and his great bulk assumed a sharper outline in the carefully cut suit, making him look big and well built.

The landlady's daughter, a monkey-like little creature with a bad squint, declared that he was as handsome as Dempsey, which pleased his vanity.

He pulled on his slouch hat, put his small roll in his trouser pocket and left the house. He stopped at the nearest saloon and had three stiff whiskies, noting with a mixture of pride and irritated embarrassment the nudging that went on amongst his acquaintances.

By the time he reached the barber's shop he was feeling pleasantly tight, and had got fairly used to the collar and shirt which had threatened to strangle him. He found Brownrigg closing up, and he entered the shop with a swagger that was plainly to impress.

Brownrigg looked him over not without a certain admiration. 'Say, Mr. Moynihan, you're looking swell tonight,' he said, 'that's a grand suit you've got there.'

Slug flicked an invisible speck from the coat. 'You think so?' he asked. 'Well, boy, this suit cost plenty. It oughtta look good.' He glanced round the room. 'Ain't she here yet?'

Brownrigg jerked his head towards the manicure parlour. 'She's gettin' ready,' he said with a wink. 'Where are you takin' her, Mr. Moynihan?'

Slug selected a cigar from a box on the counter. 'The "Ambassadors",' he said carelessly. 'I like to take my dames to the right joints.'

Brownrigg whistled. 'Say,' he said, 'you certainly are goin' places.' He hurriedly struck a match and lit Slug's cigar.

Slug didn't offer to pay for it, and Brownrigg, after a moment's hesitation, decided to let it ride. Just then Rose came out from behind the curtained doorway and stood looking at Slug with a little smile.

Slug could hardly believe his eyes, she looked so beautiful. Her dress clung to her figure, revealing curves that he had suspected but was never quite sure were there. It was a bottle-green affair, tight in the bodice and round her neat hips and then flowed loosely to her feet. Her hair was dressed low to her shoulders, and her make-up was flawless, startling and provocative. He thought she looked like a high-class movie star.

'You look swell,' he said, and meant it.

She moved a little to the right and then to the left so that he could admire her more easily. 'You like me?' she asked. 'That's fine. You don't look such a tramp yourself, you know.'

Brownrigg nodded his approval. 'You look a grand couple,' he said. 'Now get along an' enjoy yourselves, I want to shut down.'

Rose moved past Slug and he caught the scent of a heady perfume. He followed her out, feeling a little dazed. It was as if he were experiencing a magnificent dream.

As soon as they were outside, Rose glanced up and down the street and frowned. 'Where's the car? she asked.

Slug, who had every intention of taking a trolley, felt a sudden twinge of apprehension. 'I ain't gotta car,' he said.

'Oh, don't say ain't, it's vulgar,' she said a little sharply. 'I thought you were bound to have a car. Well, get a taxi. It's quite cold standing here.'

Slug said, 'Sure, sure,' rather feebly, and waved at a yellow cab that cruised by on the opposite side of the road.

The driver recognized him and gaped, then he looked past Slug and saw Rose. His eyebrows went up and he pursed his lips. 'Where to, buddy?' he asked. 'A run round the park?'

Slug scowled at him. ' "Ambassadors",' he said shortly, jerking open the door.

The driver whistled. 'O.K., big-shot,' he said, ' "Ambassadors" it is.'

Slug climbed in and sat down beside Rose. She had settled herself in a corner and had arranged her dress carefully on the seat so that Slug had to squash himself up in the far corner to avoid crushing it. Behind this brittle but impassable barrier, she surveyed him with a bright smile.

'Gee! I can hardly believe that we're going to the 'Ambassadors',' she said. 'Harry will be green with envy when I tell him.'

Slug scowled. 'You better lay off seein' that guy any more,' he said. 'You're my girl now, an' I don't like other guys hornin' in on my ground.'

She laughed. 'Don't be silly,' she said. 'I'm nobody's girl. I go where I like and do what I like and no one dictates to me.'

Slug looked at her and decided that it wasn't time to try any heavy stuff. This dame was tough and would want a lot of handling; but looking at her in the flickering lights of the passing street lamps, he decided that any trouble would be well repaid with a dame of this class.

He reached out a hand and tried to take hers, but she avoided him. 'Please don't,' she said a little sharply. 'I don't want my dress to get creased.'

Slug sat back with a little scowl, but she immediately went on to ask him about the fight and talked to him gaily until his good humour was restored.

The cab slowed down and then swung into the kerb. The door was opened by a tall, uniformed porter, who touched his peaked cap respectfully with a snowy white glove.

Slug got out hurriedly and stood in the bright lights from the big neon sign that spelled 'Ambassadors'. He paid the cab-driver and gave the porter some small change. Then he followed Rose through the revolving doors that were kept on the move by two bell-hops dressed in white with scarlet pill-box hats.

The big hall was crowded with people who stood about laughing and talking, waiting for their parties to arrive. Feeling that he would like the earth to open and swallow him up, Slug slunk along behind Rose, who moved across the hall towards the ladies' room. She turned for a moment and said, 'I'll meet you here in a few minutes,' and disappeared through a group of expensively dressed women.

Slug looked helplessly round, conscious that the women were eyeing him with interest. A guy suddenly appeared at his elbow, dressed in what looked like a fantastic fancy dress, and took his hat from him. 'This way, sir,' he said, in a soothing voice, and led Slug over to the cloakroom, where a hat-check girl was checking in a big party of men.

Slug watched with round eyes the casual way these guys tossed dollars into a plate on the counter as each received a check. Finally his turn came and the girl looked at him with a friendly smile as she gave him his number. Slug thought she'd make a nice tumble, and put his dollar in the plate without any regrets.

'Some joint,' he said hoarsely, 'sortta puts the White House in the shade, don't it?'

The girl gave him a quick, puzzled glance, smiled again automatically and went on giving out numbers.

Slug drifted back towards the ladies' room and concealed himself as best he could behind a large clump of palms that swayed a little from a huge brass tub.

He hadn't been standing there more than a few minutes, when a tall, distinguished-looking man, holding an elaborately designed leather folder, approached him. 'You are taking the dinner, monsieur?' he asked, bowing to Slug, who gave ground.

'What the hell's it to do with you what I'm doin'?' Slug asked fiercely.

The man remained quite unperturbed. 'You will pardon me, monsieur,' he said quietly, 'I am merely here to make your visit a pleasant one. Is monsieur alone? Has monsieur booked a table?'

It dawned on Slug that this guy was trying to help him, and he clutched his arm as if he expected him to lose patience with him and go away.

'Listen, pal,' he said urgently, 'you're just the guy I was lookin' for. I gotta dame here, see? She's class, do you get it? I want this little business to go off good. I got the dough, an' I want you to fix the rest for me. O.K.?'

The man bowed. 'Certainly, monsieur,' he said; 'you would like to leave all the arrangements to me?'

'You got it, pal, you got it,' Slug said feverishly. 'Just give the dame a good time.'

The man made a little note inside the folder. 'When you are

ready, monsieur, your table is number eighteen. Just through that door on your right. Everything will be to your entire satisfaction.'

He went away smoothly as if he were being drawn along on wheels.

Feeling that he had at least one friend in the camp, Slug took up his position rather impatiently behind the palm again.

Rose came out of the ladies' room eventually, looking cool and beautiful. She seemed to fit in with the luxurious background.

Slug said, 'Gee, I thought you'd got lost.'

She shook her head. 'Have you arranged anything?' she asked, as if she quite expected that he had done no such thing.

More confident, Slug put a hot, heavy hand on her arm. 'Sure,' he said, 'I fixed all this up yesterday. We got number eighteen table. The eats are all ordered, so come on in an' get the nosebag on.'

She moved her arm, trying to escape his touch, but Slug was grimly determined that she should begin to realize that this wasn't going to be all her outing.

The splendour of the dining-room shook him considerably, but the head waiter was there to receive him, and under a battery of staring eyes Slug eventually sat down at a little table near the band.

Unfortunately, the dinner was quite beyond Slug's powers to appreciate. In fact, he hated nearly all of it. The champagne irritated the back of his nose and the various French dishes made him feel slightly sick. The problem of the mass of silver cutlery before him reduced him to limp, sweating embarrassment.

On the other hand, Rose thoroughly enjoyed herself. She did not appear to notice his silence, but talked gaily about the people, the band and the luxury of the place. She laughed heartily at the various cabaret turns and made Slug shuffle round the tiny dance-floor.

It seemed to go on for ever. New, clean plates kept appearing before him, dishes holding food he could not name were offered to him. His glass seemed to fill itself, and he became more and more sour as he realized how completely out of touch he was with this world.

In fact, when a tall, strikingly handsome man suddenly stopped at their table and asked Rose for a dance, he just sat there and watched them go away together. He was almost relieved to have a few minutes to himself.

The head waiter glided up to him and asked him if everything was satisfactory. Slug knew he had done his best for him, and he grinned ruefully.

'I guess this ain't quite my mark,' he said frankly, scratching his head. 'Maybe some guys get a kick out of this, but to me it's just one big pain.' He glanced at his watch and saw that it was nearly one o'clock. 'I guess we'll blow,' he said. 'Gimme the check before she comes back.'

The head waiter bowed and put a folded slip of paper on a plate and then handed it to Slug. He took it and glanced at it indifferently. He knew the evening was going to be an expensive one, and he was too far gone to worry about how much it was going to cost. When he saw the neat, pencilled figures he sat up. 'What the hell's this,' he asked – 'a hundred and twenty-five bucks?'

The head waiter bowed. 'That is correct,' he said gently. 'It is our usual charge.'

Slug went cold from head to foot. Any moment Rose might come back. He pushed back his chair hurriedly and was about to stand up.

'A moment, monsieur,' the head waiter said. 'I'm afraid the amount embarrasses monsieur?'

Slug blew out his cheeks. 'You got somethin' there, pal,' he said. 'I got a hundred bucks towards it. Hell! I didn't know this joint went in for daylight robbery.'

'Monsieur is mistaken. We have never had any trouble before with our bills. Perhaps monsieur shouldn't have come.'

Slug nodded miserably. 'I guess you're right,' he said. 'The dame wanted to come, so I just fell for it. What are you goin' to do – send for the cops?'

The head waiter glanced round quickly, then he slid a twenty-five dollar note on to the plate. 'Perhaps monsieur would accept a loan?' he suggested. 'I have been in similar situations myself when young.'

Slug gaped at him. 'Gee!' he said at last. 'Why, hell, that's white of you. You'll get it back, pal, you'll get it back all right.'

The head waiter lifted his shoulders. 'If monsieur will now settle his bill, I will call a taxi.'

Slug hurriedly dropped the hundred dollars on the plate and stood up. He had exactly two dollars left in his pocket. 'Sure,' he said, 'I guess I won't be around here any more.'

The head waiter bowed. 'Monsieur would be a lot happier somewhere else, no doubt,' he said, and went away, holding the plate before him.

The band had stopped playing and Rose was coming back to the table. The tall, handsome guy was laughing and talking with her. They looked very happy. However, as they approached he caught Slug's eye and decided that perhaps it would be wiser to retire, and with a few words to Rose he disappeared into the crowd that was surging back to their tables.

Rose sat down. 'I hope you didn't mind,' she said gaily; 'he could dance. Isn't this a lovely evening? Is there any more champagne left?'

Slug kept his temper under control with an effort. 'We're goin' home now, honey,' he said. 'Come on, let's scram.'

'Home?' she said. 'I don't want to go home. It's not late. Let's have another dance.'

Slug stepped round to her and drew her upright. 'I said we're beatin' it,' he said tensely; 'c'm on.'

As people were already glancing at them, Rose followed him out of the dining-room. Slug snatched up his hat from the check girl and hurried Rose into the street. A taxi was waiting for them.

As soon as they had settled down in the taxi, Rose rounded on him. 'What's the idea?' she asked. 'You've quite spoilt the evening. I was havin' such a good time. Why did you come away like that?'

Slug slid over to her corner. 'I just wanted to get you alone for a while, baby,' he said, feeling that, at all costs, he was not going to see his money spent for nothing.

'Oh, do get away,' she said irritably, 'you're crushing my dress,' and she tried to push him back.

He slid his arm behind her and pulled her to him. 'Never mind about your dress,' he said, trying to smile, 'you've had a good time, ain't you? How about givin' me a good time for a change?'

His thick lips pressed down on her mouth, holding her tightly to him. Her lips were hard and cold, but she did not struggle, and he finally drew away from her, feeling frustrated and suddenly hating her.

She drew her hand across her lips. 'You're rather coarse,' she said. 'Don't think that I allow men to kiss me after a few hours' acquaintanceship, because I don't. I am sure you would feel no respect for me if I gave in to you now. I would have no respect for myself. Please sit away from me.'

Slug drew further away. His mind was completely fuddled. His instincts told him to take this woman and break her as he had done others, but there was a barrier around her that he just could not break through. Her contempt held him at bay as effectively as if a bayonet were placed at his throat.

They sat in silence all the way to the barber's shop, and when they got out into the street she said: 'Thank you for the evening. I'm sorry it wasn't as nice for you as it was for me. Perhaps we had better not meet again.'

Slug was too angry and too bewildered to say anything. He suddenly felt horribly deflated. The realization that he had lost all his money in one worthless evening, committed himself to a debt of fifty dollars to his manager and to the head waiter, made the prospects of the next few weeks drab and colourless. His rules of life, though primitive, were simple enough. If you paid for anything, you got it. Well, he had given this dame a night out that ought to go down in history and she wasn't playing ball. All he had from her was a kiss that could not even be termed sisterly.

She said quite brightly: 'Well, good-bye, I live just across the way. You needn't bother further,' and with a casual wave of her hand she crossed the road and disappeared into a large apartment house.

Slug spat on the pavement. A little spark of rage was beginning to kindle in his brain, but so far he was still too dazed to do anything about it. He wanted a drink badly, so he walked with great slouching strides to an all-night bar on Forty-ninth Street.

Joe Renshaw, his manager, was sitting at the bar drinking neat Scotch. He looked at Slug in astonishment.

'For Gawd's sake,' he said, 'where did you get the outfit from?'

Slug suddenly realized that he had still to meet the hire charge for his clothes. He sat down on the stool close to Joe's and swore obscenely.

The barman and Joe regarded him with interest. They

saw that he was in a very ugly mood and they wisely refrained from interrupting him.

Slug abruptly stopped swearing and snarled for whisky. After he had had a few quick drinks Joe ventured to ask him what was wrong, and glad to have someone to unburden to, Slug told him all about it.

Joe said, when he had finished, 'You've had a bad break, pal,' and patted him on his knees. 'Why the hell didn't you tell me what you were going to do? I could have warned you. Rose Hanson is well known for that trick.'

Slug looked at him suspiciously. 'What the hell do you mean?' he demanded.

'The "Ambassadors" trick,' Joe said. 'That dame is bad, Slug, really bad. She married a guy two years ago and he found out what type of dame she was. Well, I guess she sort of sickened him, and he found some other dame he liked a lot better. He tried to get this Rose to divorce him, but she wouldn't do it. She liked to see this guy suffer, so she just wouldn't give it to him. He had her watched, hoping that she would slip up, but they never caught her with anything. She heard about it, so she took a boy-friend around to the "Ambassadors" every now and then to torture her husband. Just so that he'd spend more dough having her watched; but she made sure that the boy-friend didn't get anything out of it. That's why she took you there.'

Slug half closed his eyes. 'Why the hell should she want to go to the "Ambassadors"?' he asked.

'Why, her husband works there. He's head waiter or something.'

Slug stiffened. 'You mean the tall guy with the good manners?' he asked. 'The guy that slipped me twenty-five bucks?'

'Did he give you twenty-five bucks? That's like Johnnny. He knew the game she was playin' with you an' felt sorry for you, I expect.'

'This dame won't divorce him?'

'Yeah, that's right.'

Slug took another long pull from his glass. 'I see,' he said. 'I guess that guy was pretty good to me; I'd like to do him a good turn.'

Joe nodded. 'Yeah, he deserves the breaks for once,' he agreed, yawning. 'I'm goin' home. Gee! It's late. Comin'?'

Slug shook his head. 'I guess not,' he said. 'I wantta kill this bottle.'

Joe patted his arm. 'Don't worry about the dough I advanced you. You can pay that back easy from time to time. I ain't goin' to rush you.'

Slug nodded absently. He was thinking of other things.

'Well, I'll be blowin'. 'Night, pal,' and Joe went off with a slight roll in his walk.

Slug sat for some time drinking steadily, thinking about Rose and her husband. The fumes of the whisky mounted to his brain. The longer he sat there brooding the more convinced he became that he had to do something. At last he crawled off the stool and nodded to the barman.

'That's three bucks, pal,' the barman said hastily.

Slug squinted at him. Everybody seemed to want money out of him, he thought. 'Put it on the slate,' he said, 'I ain't got it now.'

The barman hesitated, then, knowing that he often saw Slug, nodded. He thought it would be wiser to tackle him when he was sober, as, right now, Slug looked very mean.

Slug went out into the street and began to walk back towards the barber's shop. 'I gotta see that dame, and fix this waiter guy up,' he told himself. 'He was pretty good to me, an' I don't like the way she's treated him. Yeah, I'll go right up an' see her, an' fix it.'

He arrived at the apartment block and let himself in. He had to go to the very top before he found Rose's name neatly printed on a card on the door. He tried the door very carefully, but found it locked. He went down the corridor to a window, pushed it up and glanced outside. A fire-escape ran past Rose's window, as he expected, and, pushing up the window, he got on to the escape and moved along the iron balcony until he came to the next window, which was partly open. Very softly he raised it and stepped into the room.

It was very dark, and he couldn't see anything. He struck a match, found the light-switch and turned it on.

Rose sat up in bed with a little scream. She stared at him as if she couldn't believe her eyes, then she swung back the bedclothes and slid out of bed. She whipped up a wrap and flung it round her.

'How dare you come here, you great oaf!' she said. 'Get out at once, before I call the police!'

The little red spark in Slug's brain began to blaze and he reached out his great hand and slapped her very hard across her face. She fell backwards over the bed with a little wail of terror.

All his lust for her rose in him and he ripped her nightdress from her with brutal violence. She tried to turn on her side, drawing her knees to her chin, but he hit her again, this time with an open hand on the side of her head. The blow stunned her and she went limp, breathing in short, gasping jerks.

He knelt over her and his hands outraged her. She struggled feebly, too breathless to scream, but his savage strength overwhelmed her. His hands on the softness of her body found no satisfaction, and when she began to scream faintly, his fingers shifted up to her throat.

He did not know exactly when she died, because he continued to maul and shake her body long after life had gone out of it, and when the red spark in his brain died to a dark, twisted ember, he drew away from her, swearing softly.

He knew then that he had meant to kill her. As he stood looking down at her carefully painted face, so horribly contorted in her death struggle, he felt a satisfaction far in excess of any sexual ecstasy he had ever experienced, and he knew also that he need not worry any more about paying the head waiter his twenty-five bucks. He had given him service instead.

He sat on the bed beside her and touched her breasts gently. The drink was dying on him and he felt very tired and a little sick of things. He sat there for a long time trying to keep the fading warmth in her body by putting his hands on her, but when her flesh became cold and hard to his touch he drew away from her.

He tried to reason things out, but his brain failed him. He just couldn't be bothered to make any plans and after some time he reached out for the 'phone and called the police. He didn't quite know how to tell them, but they were very helpful and in a surprisingly short time they came into the room and took him away.

THE END